TOO CLOSE FOR COMFORT

Tara was grateful when Hound wandered over and got her mind off the past. He stood far enough away that she couldn't touch him, but close enough to know he wanted her attention. "Hey," she said. "Good morning." He whined, then turned and trotted around the side of the mill. A few seconds later he poked his head out from the side of the building. Was he expecting her to follow?

She approached him, hoping to sneak in a pet. Instead, she smelled paint. She soon saw why. Across the building, in large sloppy black letters, was a painted message:

GO HOME YANKEE

She glanced at the hound. He was sitting up straight, tongue hanging out, happy to show her the writing on the wall.

She was beginning to wonder if she should add him to the suspect list . . .

Books by Carlene O'Connor

Irish Village Mysteries

MURDER IN AN IRISH VILLAGE

MURDER AT AN IRISH WEDDING

MURDER IN AN IRISH CHURCHYARD

MURDER IN AN IRISH PUB

MURDER IN AN IRISH COTTAGE

CHRISTMAS COCOA MURDER
(with Maddie Day and Alex Erickson)

A Home to Ireland Mystery

MURDER IN GALWAY

MURDER IN CONNEMARA

Published by Kensington Publishing Corporation

Murder in Galway

Carlene O'Connor

KENSINGTON BOOKS
www.kensingtonbooks.com

KENSINGTON BOOKS are published by

Kensington Publishing Corp.
119 West 40th Street
New York, NY 10018

All Kensington titles, imprints, and distributed lines are available at special quantity discounts for bulk purchases for sales promotion, premiums, fund-raising, educational, or institutional use.

Special book excerpts or customized printings can also be created to fit specific needs. For details, write or phone the office of the Kensington Sales Manager: Attn.: Sales Department. Kensington Publishing Corp., 119 West 40th Street, New York, NY 10018. Phone: 1-800-221-2647.

Kensington and the K logo Reg. U.S. Pat. & TM Off.

First Printing: May 2019
ISBN-13: 978-1-4967-2447-2
ISBN-10: 1-4967-2447-X

ISBN-13: 978-1-4967-1985-0 (ebook)
ISBN-10: 1-4967-1985-9 (ebook)

10 9 8 7 6 5 4 3

Printed in the United States of America

Acknowledgments

Thank you to my editor, John Scognamiglio, my agent, Evan Marshall, the entire staff at Kensington Publishing, and all my family and friends who are always willing to chime in on early drafts.

Chapter 1

Emmet Walsh never thought he'd find himself in the middle of a fairy tale, but if Johnny Meehan didn't answer his door and produce Emmet's prized pig, he was going to huff, and puff, and most definitely blow *something* down. He prayed with each plodding step on the way to the stone cottage, fists clenched at his sides, that it wouldn't come to actual blows. He just wanted what belonged to him. He'd paid Irish Revivals a fortune to source this collector's item, and he refused to put up with any more of Johnny Meehan's shenanigans. If Meehan was trying to hold out for more money, he was going to regret it. The agreed-upon sum was quite a dear one, it was done and dusted, and Johnny Meehan was going to hand it over. Today.

This rare gem, a cast-iron pig for the garden, was once owned by a Japanese princess. Imagine that, now. Emmet smiled as the photograph from the catalogue rose before him like a mirage in the desert, making his trek slightly less intolerable. The mud was thick here, something between a bog and a bother. The earthy scent of the Galway Bay was strong, effortlessly carried by the breeze that also succeeded in blowing stray hairs of his white beard into his mouth as he trudged onward. This hadn't been the plan when he woke up this morning. Johnny should have met him at the door to the salvage mill. How had it come to this, being forced to invade a man's home? Johnny Meehan had left him no choice. He had Emmet's money, didn't he? Why was he torturing Emmet?

He saw the pig in his mind's eye. It was photographed sitting in the garden next to that beautiful Asian princess. The cast-iron pig was about a foot high. Sitting on its bottom, the mouth open in a laugh, the hands (would you call them hands, like?) resting on its full belly, legs splayed out, mouth (snout?) open in a laugh. The patina of green around the ears. Gorgeous. And instead of hooves this little piggy had tiny fingers and toes. Eyes so open and real he could almost see the twinkle in them. And that was only from a photo. Emmet couldn't wait to feel the heft of the little piggy in his hands. Everything was made with plastic these days. Bollocks. Give him cast iron. Give him quality. Give him an item owned by royalty. He could not wait. Yet wait he had. He had waited, and waited, and waited. No more.

The sun was coming up over Galway. There wasn't a moment to waste. He picked up his pace, sweat breaking out on his brow.

He was already so in love. He would set the pig in front of his prize-winning rose bushes in the garden. It had taken Johnny Meehan an entire year to track the pig to a banker in Manchester, England, and another six months to convince him to sell. Emmet had paid dearly, both in desire and euro. Johnny Meehan was not going to get away with this.

The miscreant was hiding from him. *Meet me at the mill bright and early and we'll work it out.* What did that mean—*work it out?* The salvage mill was shuttered and locked tight. What kind of dirty trick was this? Irritation had morphed into rage. Emmet was Johnny Meehan's best client, his wealthiest client, and he would not tolerate this kind of disrespect. Maybe he would put Johnny Meehan out of business. Ben Kelly was mad to buy the mill, turn it into a boxing school. If Johnny's customers lost trust in him, he'd be forced to sell. Maybe Emmet would buy Irish Revivals. At least he'd have a place to store his treasures. Could all this have something to do with the shady folks Johnny surrounded himself with? Snakes, they were. Maybe it was time Emmet told Johnny everything he knew. Up until now, he'd kept the secrets to himself. *Leave well enough alone* was his motto. He was just the messenger and messengers never fared well. Neither did sneaks, and truth be told he had snooped around the mill a bit. Who could blame him? He had every intention of keeping his nose clean. But now Johnny's poor taste in people was affecting Emmet. *Someone* was messing with him. It would not stand. He was going to get to the bottom of this right here and now. If he had to point fingers then so be it, he would start pointing.

As Emmet rounded the bend, the tiny cottage came into view stone by stone. He couldn't imagine living in such a confining space. Emmet's mansion (some might call it a castle) was over three thousand square feet. Johnny's cottage was hardly bigger than one of Emmet's luxury bathrooms. He stopped to catch his breath and kick clod off his shoe. The only good thing he had to say about nature was that mostly it stayed outside where it belonged. Emmet had paved every bit of grass around his castle. More room for precious sculptures and a lot less dirt on his shoes. He should have brought his walking stick. A twig cracked behind him, and then another. He whirled around to see Johnny's dog—an Irish wolfhound—lurking behind him. The hound's tall body was on high alert, creamy fur blowing every which way, eyes wide and tracking, tail up in the air. Big as a small horse, he was in need of a good brushing. Emmet turned away. He much preferred items to animals.

His chest tightened, another reminder it was time to give up the smoking. It was hideous, getting old. What did he have to show for his time on earth? A wife and kids who wanted to be as far away from him as possible? Friends who took his money and left him empty-handed? Ungrateful. Everyone was so ungrateful. Except for his castle. And his items. Rare, architectural pieces that held real meaning. History. Stories. A pig owned by a Japanese princess!

The sun was fully up now, striking the surface of the Galway Bay and setting it on fire. From here, it stretched out to eternity. God's country. He'd like to see any man deny it. He turned back to the stone cottage and sized it up as if it were the enemy. The stones were rough and uneven, the blue door sported cracked paint, and the windows were smudged with grime. The last time he'd been up here, laughing with Johnny, having a whiskey to toast the regal iron gates Johnny had managed to source for his entry, the windows had been sparkling clean. His suspicions had just been confirmed. Something was seriously wrong with Johnny Meehan.

Emmet took the stone walkway at full speed, reached the house, and pounded on the door. Paint chipped off and fluttered to the ground like blue snowflakes. He waited and received only silence for his effort. "Johnny?" Emmet turned the knob and pushed. The old door swung open with an elongated creak, and seconds later a sour smell enveloped Emmet. What on earth was that odor? He stared into the dark. It smelled like mold and three-day bread, and something even worse. Like raw meat sitting on a counter for days. Emmet threw his sleeve over his mouth before he gagged. He could make out the sink in the wee kitchen to the left, piled with dirty dishes. He thought he saw something scamper across the mound and shivered. Had the dirty dishes been there so long they were attracting vermin?

"Hello?" Footsteps sounded on the path behind him, too human to be the hound. He turned. A figure lurked behind him, dressed in baggy dark clothing, face obscured by enormous dark sunglasses and an oversized hood. Some kind of costume. It looked like . . . the Grim Reaper. Fear rose in Emmet's throat. "Who are you?" The figure raised its right arm. Instead of a scythe, he or she was holding a cast-iron object. Was it the pig? Emmet threw his hand over his eyes. It was so hard to see with that blasted sun shining directly into his eyes, blinding him. He threw his hand up so he could see. "Is that my pig?"

His gut screamed that it did not matter. Death had come for him. The Reaper was real. His heart thumped, his voice quivered. He could not take his eye off whatever this thing was. And then the object was in the air. A blur flying directly at his head at warp speed. Try and catch it? Or duck? He tripped on the door frame and hit the ground, falling on his back, half in and half out of the house. He struggled to lift his head, muster a scream, but just as the thought struck, so did the object. It collided with his temple, sending a thundering pain through his poor head. The back of his skull slammed into Johnny's floor. He stared at the tilted beams in the ceiling as footsteps drew closer, and everything started to spin. The hood hovered over him.

He tried to speak but his mouth wouldn't move. *Why?*

The figure raised its arm and removed the hood. Emmet squinted. When his eyes adjusted, he could make out the eyes, nose, and mouth of his attacker, curled up in a cruel grin, eyes dancing with excitement. This was no Grim Reaper, this was all too human, and even more terrifying. For a second he forgot about the gash in his head as he pointed. "You," was all he managed to say. He stilled his body, held his breath. He heard a whoosh of air and pounding feet as his attacker fled. *Coward.* If only he'd listened to his wife and carried his mobile phone on him. He'd never warmed to technology. Did Johnny Meehan have a phone in the cottage? He could either spend his energy looking for it, or he could help the guards catch a killer. His poor head. There wasn't much life left in him and he knew it. He touched his fingertips to his wound, then used his dwindling energy to half crawl, half slide to the back wall. For once he saw the benefit of having a tiny home. He pushed onto his knees and began to write on the wall. He managed four letters before he fell back for the last time, and released his final breath with a moan. His last thought was of the princess and his pig.

Tara Meehan stood in the middle of the pedestrianized Shop Street, cradling the delicate tin box that held her mother's ashes, as she took in the pulsing city her mother called home. Galway, Ireland. The City of Tribes. Snippets of the song "Galway Girl" began to play in her head. *And I ask you friend, what's a fella to do? 'Cause her hair was black and her eyes were blue* . . . Having black hair and blue eyes herself, Tara had always been partial to the song.

"You're a lucky lass," her mother would say on those mornings when Tara was just a girl. Her mother was always gentle and patient while brushing Tara's thick black hair into something a little more manageable. "Black hair and blue eyes is a knock-out combination." Her mother always made her feel good. She was loved.

And now here she was. Not exactly a girl anymore at thirty-three, but that girl was still inside her, so excited to be here she was bursting at the seams.

Standing here, taking in the cobblestone streets, and pubs, and people, and music—there was live music playing from nearly every corner—her heart throbbed in her chest. It was love at first sight.

Shops splashed in bright colors cozied up on both sides of the street, and passersby crisscrossed from one side to the other as she stood still. Buskers staked out corners, filling the salty air with their songs, guitar cases flung open, crumpled euros and coins scattered inside. An Asian man in an orange jumpsuit

was on the sidewalk up ahead, bent over a large dog
he was sculpting out of sand, his thin hands knead-
ing as people gathered to watch him work. Next to
him a tall African man in traditional garb stood in
front of a table filled with beaded jewelry. Young
men lingered in front of pubs, cigarettes dangling
from their fingers, smoke curling into the air, as their
bright eyes followed the pretty girls in short skirts
laughing up the street. Galway was one of the youngest
cities in Europe, and for a second Tara felt ancient.
This was a college town, an art town, a music haven.
She could smell pints of ale, reminding her that Galway was sometimes called "the graveyard of ambi-
tion"—the numerous pubs and entertainment so
tempting that one could find him- or herself party-
ing seven nights a week and no one would blink an
eye—*right, he's drunk seven nights a week, it's up to himself to mind his own liver . . .*

Up ahead Tara saw a throng of people circled
around a street performer. The crowd hid him from
view, but whoever it was, he was generating excitement. Curiosity pulled her forward. It was a young
man riding a unicycle while juggling three large
knives. The wheel of his cycle jutted back and forth
as he pedaled, the large knives glittered as he twirled
them high in the air. Something made him turn his
head toward her, and stare. His eyes locked onto her
tin box. He jerked his head upward. "Toss it up
here," he said with a toothy grin. The crowd parted,
practically panting in anticipation.

"No." Before she could protest further, the box
was snatched out of her hands by a man in front of
her and tossed up to the performer, who caught it effortlessly and added it to his rotation with a wink and

a grin. The crowd cheered and clapped. The latch on the tin box remained clasped, but Tara knew it was only a matter of time. Was this really happening? "No," Tara said. "Please. Give it back."

"Don't worry, he's got it," a woman yelled out.

"It's going to come open," Tara yelled at the man. "Please." Panic eked out of her. The unicycling juggler ignored her as the box containing her mam's ashes tumbled helplessly in the air.

"Please," Tara begged. "Give it back."

"You heard the lady." A man appeared beside her, staring up at the juggler. He was tall, and Irish, and handsome, with tints of green in his hazel eyes and hair the color of sand, but all Tara cared about was the box. "Ronan," the handsome stranger said in a commanding voice. "Toss it here." The juggler—Ronan—nodded at the man, and with a flick of his wrist, the box was sailing back to her. Tara lunged to reach it, and although her hands caught it, her feet kept moving, until she tripped, and the box flew out of her hands, morphing into a projectile. There was the stranger again, standing right in its path. The box hit him squarely on the chest. The lid flew open and her mother's ashes exploded out, coating the stranger's face and chest in specks of gray. Tara could only stare. *Oh, no. Sorry, Mam.* He slowly gazed down at his body, then locked eyes with Tara. He blinked at the tin, which was lying at his feet, its tiny mouth open, contents expelled. His eyes met hers and locked on. "Tell me that's just a wee sandbox," he said in a low and easy voice.

Tara took a deep breath. Tried not to laugh. Tried not to cry. She forced a smile. "Is it too early to meet my mother?"

Chapter 2

❧❧❧

The man picked up the tin and tried to shake the ashes on his shirt back into the box, but the wind picked up and carried most of them away. Tara took a step forward. "I'm so sorry."

"You're joking me, right? This isn't your mother."

"It's my fault. I'm clumsy. She wanted me to bring her back to Ireland. She wanted her ashes spread near the Galway Bay."

He glanced down the street in the direction of the wind. "I'd say she's on her way."

Nervous laughter bubbled out of Tara. She grasped her mother's rosary that she'd tucked into the pocket of her jeans and silently said the prayer she'd prepared. She hadn't planned on spreading the ashes until she'd met her uncle Johnny, but on a whim she'd wanted her mother with her on her first exploration of the city, so she'd taken the tin out and carried it around for a bit of comfort. *Foolish lass.* She was sure they would have a different phrase for her: *Eeejit Yank.*

"Maybe she had a hand in this," Tara said. Her mother had had a wicked sense of humor. Some people hated it. Tara always loved it. It was just like Margaret Meehan to insist on doing her own thing.

"I'd best get this washed off me, I suppose," the man said, moving away. "No offense."

"Wait." Panic seized her, as if he were walking away with her mother. He stood still as she approached. She held her hands out, tears welling into her eyes. She did not want to cry. She held out her hands. "May I?"

He gazed at her intently, and nodded. She ran her hands over him lightly, his body strong and unflinching, until her palms and fingertips were soft and gray, and then she stepped back, feeling doubly foolish but somehow relieved. "Thank you."

He stood still as she picked up the tin from the ground and moved on, heading for the bay. She did not turn around, but she could feel him watching her. That was intense. She'd felt a flicker of something. That *thing* she hadn't felt since Gabriel. *And Thomas.* If held at gunpoint she would be forced to admit what it was: a spark.

Stop it. She was losing it. Jet lag and grief could do that to a girl. Tara took a deep breath and continued to the bay, where she prayed the waters would heal her heart, just a little, just for now.

The Galway Bay was spread before her, expansive and full of promise. Parked a few feet from the bay was a white caravan with a painting of a gypsy: long rainbow-colored hair blowing in the wind; big, knowing eyes; full red lips. *FORTUNES* sprawled across the side of the caravan in red paint, and underneath it: *READINGS HERE.* Paint cans were lined up along the base of the caravan, as if the job had just been completed.

As Tara took it all in, the door to the caravan was flung open, revealing a tiny woman with wavy black and gray-streaked hair down to her hips. She wore a long flowing yellow dress, her face was heavily made up, and a bright red rose was tucked in her hair over her left ear. A prickly sensation tickled the back of Tara's neck as the woman gazed at her openly. It was as if she had been expecting her. Tara laughed off the thought and lifted her hand in a wave. The woman lifted a crooked finger and beckoned Tara closer.

"Death is all around you," she said. "Why is that?" Tara started. Was the woman so observant that she'd already guessed the tin held her mother's ashes? But no. The tin was open and empty. "Go home," the woman said. "Before it's too late."

Anger surged through Tara. "I *am* home." In a way, it was true. Her mother had always referred to Ireland as home. *Their* home.

"Danger follows you."

So she was one of those. A con artist who used fear to draw in customers. Tara squared her shoulders. "Danger follows everyone."

The woman shook her head. Tara had to hand it to her, she'd certainly perfected an expression of alarm.

"This danger is coming straight for you."

"Let it," Tara said. "I'm a New Yorker."

The woman cocked her head and narrowed her

eyes. "You've been warned." The door to the caravan slammed closed, swallowing the fortune-teller with it.

That was strange. What an eccentric city with a cast of characters to match. Rocks crunched beneath Tara's feet as she moved past the caravan to the water's edge. She gazed out at the bay, and said the Irish blessing that was the closest thing to a prayer she had memorized. *May the wind always be at your back.* She wasn't going to cry, but when she reached the last verse: *May God always hold you in the palm of his hand* . . . tears flowed down her cheeks as she held out her palms where the remains of her mother rested. "You're here, Mam," she said out loud. "You're home."

She stared out at the sailboats bobbing on the water until the breeze dried her tears. Her mother's last words echoed in her ear. *Tell Johnny I'm sorry. So much time wasted. Take me home.*

Sharp metal bit into Tara's fingers. She cried out, only to see she was squeezing the tin so hard it was cutting into the fleshy part of her hand between her thumb and index finger. She'd forgotten she was even holding it. *Toss me.* Tara hurled the tin into the bay. It struck the water with a splash and began to playfully dance along the surface. The sound of a flute floated overhead, a soft lilting tune. Tara blew a kiss, and watched until it slowly took on water and submerged. "Until we meet again." She wished her mother was at peace, in a joyful place, where she would receive *céad míle fáilte*, a hundred thousand welcomes, a place, well—a place just like this.

The Bay Inn was situated in the middle of a quiet street just off the Quay Street. It looked more like a detached Victorian home, although it shared its right wall with a lively pub. Inside, it was like stepping back in time, with dark wood, muted flowered carpet, and a winding staircase up to the rooms. The floors creaked as Tara made her way to the check-in desk. Behind it stood an older woman with white hair pulled up in a neat bun. Beside her, a young blonde in her early twenties was polishing the counter with gusto, working the manufactured scent of lemon into the air. A light sheen of sweat had broken out on her forehead and her tongue hung out of the corner of her mouth. The older woman hovered behind her like a ghost refusing to leave its earthly home. "I won't tolerate your tardiness anymore."

"I told you when you hired me that class comes first," the girl answered. "You try making a soufflé." She continued to polish the counter as if it was of monumental importance.

"If you're late again I'm giving you the boot," the older woman barked. "And what self-respecting Irishwoman would make a soufflé? Meat, potato, and veg—now that's the way to a man's heart."

"I agree. If by that you mean heart *attack*."

"I won't stand for any more of your sass."

The rag stopped moving. The girl's chin shot up. "Go ahead. Give me the boot. Nobody else will work with you—you old crow."

"Hey," Tara said. Where she came from you didn't speak to your elders like that, and she had half a mind to grab the girl by her pixie haircut and toss her out the front door.

The two heads swiveled her way, conversation screeching to a halt as they stared at Tara.

"Welcome to the Bay Inn," the older woman said with a practiced smile.

"Thank you," Tara said, keeping her eyes pinned on the young girl, hoping that her stern look was getting through.

"American?" the young girl said. She made a face.

"Afraid so," Tara said.

"Do you have a reservation?" *So many reservations.* The older woman pulled a giant tome out from underneath the counter and began to leaf through it. Tara stared at it, expecting a cloud of dust to rise with the turn of each page. "I don't, actually. I was being spontaneous," Tara said. "Do you have a vacancy?"

The young girl snorted. "We always have a vacancy. Because *somebody* refuses to catch up to the times."

"Why don't you catch up to the times by showing up when you're supposed to?" the older woman said.

The young girl rolled her eyes. The old woman turned and removed a key from an actual cubbyhole behind her. Maybe it took age and experience to appreciate how quaint this throwback of an inn was. Tara wanted to tell her not to change a thing. Her excitement grew when soft papery hands slipped the key into hers. It was an old-fashioned iron key. It was exquisite and felt substantial in her hands.

"I love it," Tara said.

"You love what?" the young girl said.

"This key. This inn." Tara beamed. "It's perfect." Just as she said it she noted a splotch of red on the stem of the key. It looked like dried blood. She leaned in closer. It could have been paint. Or nail polish. Either way—too many germs. Still, it added a bit of character. If you liked your inns on the spooky side.

The young girl tilted her head and frowned. She had an athletic body and carved cheekbones. *Tomboy* was the word that came to mind, although Tara knew that was an outdated and misogynistic term.

"Room 301," the older woman said, nodding at the key. "Sixty euro a night."

"That's the room with the leak, remember?" the young girl said. She snatched the key out of Tara's hand and tossed it back in the cubby for room 301. "Here." She handed Tara the key to 305.

"I don't remember that." The older woman laid her hand over her head as if the answers were stuck inside.

"The plumber didn't have the part he needed. Remember? He's coming back next week."

Tara placed a credit card on the counter. The older woman wrung her hands as her eyes flicked away from the credit card. "We're euro only."

"I told you," the girl said, with a roll of her eyes. "Dinosaur age."

"I don't have euro yet," Tara said. "I'll need to go to an ATM."

"There's one next door in the pub," the girl said.

"I don't know how many nights I'm staying," Tara said. "Can I pay as I go?"

"You can," the older woman said. "We'll need at least one night up front plus a hundred-euro security deposit."

"The security deposit is more than the room?"

"Correct," the young girl said with a look that conveyed how utterly unreasonable the old woman was.

"It's fine," Tara said. Maybe they were playing her— the Irish version of good cop, bad cop. She wondered if she should find someplace else. But she liked this place, right down to the oddly matched women standing in front of her. "I'll be right back."

"You can leave your luggage," the older woman said. "We'll mind it."

It was an easy process slipping into the pub next door to use the cash machine. She hurried back to the inn and paid for two nights plus the deposit. The younger woman was no longer behind the desk. The older woman pointed to the staircase behind her. "There's no lift."

"I'm sorry?"

"You'll have to take the stairs."

Oh. Lift. Elevator. She loved the tiny differences in language. "Thank you." Tara was grateful she'd packed only one small suitcase, for by the time she reached the third floor, she was slightly out of breath. Room 305 was directly to the right. She turned the key in the lock and the door creaked open.

The room was tiny but neat. A four-poster bed was the dominating feature, flanked by mahogany side-tables. A black rotary phone rested on one table, a Bible on the other. Nestled on the wall across from the bed was a small desk with a tea kettle and cups. A simple cross made of wood hung above the bed. The room had two windows overlooking the street. Tara was thrilled. She could sit up here and people-watch all day if she wanted to. She went to the window and parted the heavy curtain. Sunshine streamed in, lighting up layers of dust on the side tables. Tara sneezed. So much for quaint. The young girl was right—it seemed as if no one had stayed in this room for a long time. She threw open both curtains and tried to open the windows. They wouldn't budge. She longed for just a little fresh air. She collapsed on the bed, too tired to lift the old phone to complain. Later she'd make sure they got the windows open, and maybe she'd ask for a vacuum and some of that lemon-scented polish.

Nobody was at the desk when Tara emerged just over an hour later. A shower and a change into a simple sundress had helped to revive her, and now she was off on her real mission of the day—to find out if her uncle was still alive and living in Galway. Johnny Meehan was her mother's only living relative in Ireland. Tara had never met the man. There had been some kind feud between brother and sister, but whatever it was, her mother took the details with her to the grave. Tara figured the best way to get information was to talk to some old-timey bartenders. Surely, they would be more reliable than a phone book.

It was nearing four in the afternoon, and the pubs were starting to swell with folks ready to take on the weekend. In the one next door to the inn, the bartenders were young and so were the patrons. Tara slipped in and out unnoticed and headed down the street. The next pub she entered had a middle-aged female bartender. Tara exited and kept walking, the energy of the city slipping into her, making her grin and pick up her pace. Finally, she saw it, a stone building with a sign that looked generations old: O'Doole's. She entered and immediately knew this was the place. It was like a cavern inside and smelled of beer and bleach. Fiddles and guitars squawked out from a jukebox. It was no-frills except for the older men in denim and boots, filling the stools. There didn't appear to be a single woman in the place. The bartender was a grandfatherly type with a head of thick gray hair and a protruding belly.

"How ya," he called brightly as she walked in. There were half a dozen old men seated in various states of repose, but all of them froze upon seeing Tara.

"Hello," she called. She knew she was a beautiful woman, but she could hardly take credit for her good looks. She smiled and pulled up a stool. "Guinness, please." Instantly her mind flashed to being in a New York City pub with her mother. *The Guinness here is okay. Wait until you try it at home. It's heavenly.* She imagined her mother perched on the stool next to her. The bartender took his time pouring her Guinness, waiting for it to settle before adding the head. All the while he watched her out of one eye; if she hadn't been tuned into it, she would have given him credit for being subtle. The rest of the men were watching her openly, some with mouths hanging open.

"I've never seen you in here before," one of the old men crowed.

"Just visiting?" the bartender said as he slid the pint of Guinness toward her.

"Yes," Tara said.

"Where would you be from?"

"America."

"Where in America?"

"New York City."

"New York City," an old man at the end of the counter exclaimed. "How many windows does the Empire State Building have?" He stared at her expectantly.

"I have no idea." He continued to stare. "A lot," Tara added, feeling like a fool. She had never even wondered how many.

The man lifted his pint. "It has 6,514 windows. Double-paned, which makes it 13,028 panels." He took a sip, then set his glass down with a satisfied smack of his lips.

"Wow," Tara said. "Sounds like a lot alright." The men laughed as the older man returned to staring into his pint.

"D'mind him," the bartender said with a wink. "He's old stock."

"Then what am I? Young stock?"————

"You're a mongrel."

Tara smiled. "I'm hoping to find another old stock."

"Ah, right. Who would that be now?"

"Johnny Meehan. He's probably in his late sixties."

"Doing a bit of shopping?" the bartender asked.

She frowned. Had he not heard her? "No," she said. "Not yet."

"He hasn't been open the past week," the bartender said.

"Pardon?"

"Johnny. There's been a closed sign on the shop for the past week."

"Danny quit, that's why," a beefy man rolling a cigarette on the bar said.

The bartender threw a look to the man and the inference was clear: *No gossip in front of the American.*

Shop? Danny? Tara felt as if she was losing control of the conversation. Tara leaned forward. "Johnny has a shop?"

The bartender raised an eyebrow. "Irish Revivals," he said. "Isn't that why you're here?"

"Irish Revivals," Tara repeated.

"They sell architectural wares. Is that not what you're looking for?"

Excitement trilled through her. She and her mother loved antiques. Was he talking about antiques? "Where is the shop?" Tara asked. Two could play the mystery game. She didn't have to reveal more information than necessary either. Besides, her head was spinning with the revelation. A huge bulk of her childhood had been spent digging through antique stores and flea markets with her mother. She blamed it for her career as an interior designer. Although all her rich clients in New York wanted everything new and modern, Tara much preferred the history of a lovingly used item. It had been so long since a client allowed her to decorate exactly how she wanted—with a mix of new and old. How long had he owned this shop? She couldn't wait to see it.

"As I said, it's been shuttered lately," the bartender said carefully.

"Do you know where he lives? Do you have his number? Do you know where he hangs out?" It was a mistake, she realized too late, to sound too eager and fire too many questions without waiting for a response. The bartender was on high alert now.

"If I see him, who should I say is calling?"

"Tara Meehan," she said. "I'm his niece. And it's urgent I find him. It's a family matter."

"Niece?" said the old man from a few stools down. "Well, I'll be. I didn't know the old wanker had any family left."

The bartender hushed him with a look. He edged closer to Tara as if trying to find the family resemblance in her face. "Are you sure you have the right Johnny Meehan, like?"

"My mother was Margaret Meehan," Tara said.

An immediate change came over the bartender's face. Delight, and then, just as quickly, he shut down, returning to a stern gaze. "My, my, my," he said. "How is Maggie?" Maggie. So he'd known her mother when she was young. The bartender leaned in. "My hearing isn't so good anymore. Did you say—*was*?"

"Yes. My mother passed away last week." Fresh grief stung her. Just last week. It still didn't feel real. She still expected to see her mam's smiling face before her.

Empathy filled the bartender's face. "I'm so sorry to hear that. I knew your mother when she was just a colleen."

Tara nodded, recognizing the Irish term for girl, and gave a soft smile. "I've come to find my uncle and let him know."

"She ended up in New York City?" the bartender asked.

"Yes."

The bartender whistled. "Was she happy?"

Tara tilted her head. "We had our moments."

The bartender took out a napkin and began to draw. "Here's the mill—the shop." He was a good mapmaker. "It's in the Claddagh."

"Claddagh? Like the ring?"

"The very same. Where it all started. But if it's thatched huts you're after, there aren't many left." The bartender winked. "Once you see the Spanish Arch, the village is just across the way. Johnny lives in a cottage up a wee hill, a short walk from the salvage mill."

"Irish Revivals," the trivia-man said. "Dats de one."

She smiled, hoping he wasn't going to ask her how many windows it had. "Thank you."

A middle-aged man burst into the bar, dressed in a red-and-white-striped tracksuit, his muscles bulging. He bounced rather than walked.

"Ben Kelly," the old man down the bar slurred. "Guess who this lass is?" He pointed at Tara. "That's Johnny Meehan's niece. Margaret Meehan's daughter. Can you believe dat?"

Ben Kelly turned to her, his brown eyes pinning her down. He reminded her of a dog tied in a yard, straining at the end of his leash. "Niece?" She stared at the vein bulging in his neck and nodded. "He never mentioned you, like."

Tara met his intense gaze. "He's never met me."

Ben Kelly squinted, then edged forward. "Now. Let me give you the best advice you're ever going to get in your life." She waited. He moved even closer until she could smell his whiskey breath. This wasn't his first pub stop. "*Don't.*"

Tara stared. "Don't . . . what?"

"Don't meet him. Go home. You'll be sorry if you invite that kind of trouble into your life." He turned and headed away from her before Tara could formulate a response. "But if you're too stubborn or too stupid to heed my advice, then you tell that bollocks he should sell the mill to me before I dig up too much dirt. Tick tock, tick tock."

"Dig up too much dirt?"

He winked, but it did little to take the venom out of his words.

"D'mind him," the bartender said.

"Let me guess—he's old stock too?"

The men in the pub laughed. Ben Kelly, face buried in the jukebox, didn't even turn around. "He is indeed," the bartender said.

Tara nodded and let it drop. She had no desire to get dragged into the local drama. She'd meet Johnny first and maybe he'd eventually tell her what this was all about. And maybe Johnny Meehan wasn't a nice man. There had to be a reason her mother left, never saw him again.

Tell Johnny I'm sorry. So much time wasted.

Tara would not let the locals color her opinion of her mother's brother. Her mother still had love for him or she wouldn't have asked Tara to apologize for her. Tara had the feeling the estrangement had been born out of pain, not anger. She digested Ben Kelly's anger with more curiosity than alarm. It dawned on her that in a country that claimed to have hospitality down to an irresistible charm, this was at least the second time in the few hours she'd been here that she'd been advised to go home. So much for a hundred thousand welcomes; she had yet to receive even one.

Chapter 3

Tara was given her first claddagh ring for her tenth birthday. She loved the clasped hands for friendship, the crown for loyalty, and the heart for love. Now here she was standing on the threshold of the community of Claddagh, the oldest part of Galway, whose history she knew well from her studies. Claddagh translated meant *stony shore*, and it was no surprise the community of Claddagh resided where the River Corrib met the Galway Bay. It was easy to find the community by first locating the Spanish Arch. Despite the name, the six-hundred-year-old stone arch, part of the old city walls, wasn't built by Spaniards. It was built by the Eyre family, but nicknamed for the Spanish sailors who used to dock at the edge of the city and trade at the Arch. Tara was thrilled to see the sights that previously she'd only known about from poring over guidebooks and videos on YouTube.

Claddagh didn't disappoint. The little fishing village dated back to the fifth century. Until the 1930s it was also dotted with thatched huts. Unfortunately, they were taken down as the community evolved. There was even a King of Claddagh, although it was in name only, and Tara couldn't for the life of her remember who it was or what exactly the king did. Semidetached houses awash in pastel colors dotted the landscape like a string of lights, and across the way sailboats and swans bobbed on the water. Here you could take the path—technically the Salthill Promenade or "the prom"—from Claddagh to the community of Salthill. Its Irish name was Bóthar na Trá, which means "sea road." It was a two-mile walk that Tara had every intention of taking when she got the chance. Across the bay, mountains completed the postcard-perfect view. Tara knew them to be the Burren, technically in County Clare, a gorgeous national park with a rocky landscape. Tara stood on the prom and followed the directions on the napkin until she spotted the old stone mill the bartender had marked with an X. From the front it looked like a normal stone building, but as she drew closer she could see that it extended for a long way behind it. A red sign above the massive doors read: IRISH REVIVALS. Next to the mill was a small creek and in the middle of the creek was a large wheel turning slowly. Did it pump the water? As the bartender warned, there was indeed a CLOSED sign on the door. Tara crept closer. Underneath the CLOSED sign someone had pinned a note:

You bollocks! Thief! I'm reporting you to
the guards!

Someone wasn't happy. Was it Ben Kelly who left this note? He'd used the term *bollocks* to refer to Johnny just minutes ago. Her uncle was certainly in a bit of conflict. She wondered why the shop was closed. Was he sick? Why was someone calling him a thief?

The mill was large, but the windows were situated too high to peer in, so she was left to wonder what was inside. She glanced at the map again to see the location of Johnny's cottage. She followed the map along the river until she reached the hill leading up to her uncle's stone cottage.

The air was fresh and smelled of limestone and the sea, the grass beneath her feet was soft and shining, and at the top of the hill the Irish blue skies domed what should have been a cheerful stone cottage. The sight before her was anything but. The cottage door yawned open, and an old man lay half in and half out of the doorway, the muddy bottoms of his shoes facing her. Was he hurt? Passed out from drink? "Hello?" She ran up to him, already reaching for her cell phone. What was the equivalent of 911 in Ireland? As she drew closer, she saw glassy brown eyes, open and staring straight up, covered by a milky-white film. His mouth was open too, as if frozen in horror. Only his beard moved, the wind whipping it against a face drained of all color. There was a nasty gash at his temple, and blood pooled down and around him and behind him like a macabre red carpet. There was no mistaking it; he was dead—viciously attacked.

She cried out and slapped her hand over her mouth. She whirled around and ran until she was a safe distance from the cottage, leaned over, and forced herself to breathe. When it came to meeting her uncle, she had imagined all possibilities, including that he might be dead—but she never once imagined this horrific scenario. She turned and ran, fear and adrenaline propelling her forward.

She ran down the hill to the first old man she saw, a skinny soul who was pushing a cart filled with fishing nets and gear down the cobblestone path with great concentration. "Help," she said. She had to say it again before he lifted his head and looked at her. She took out her phone and waved it. "I need to call the police. How do I call the police?"

She waited at the base of the hill for the guards. An ambulance arrived first, followed by two guard cars. They spilled out of their vehicles and huddled around her. She pointed to the top of the hill. "He's dead," she said. "Johnny Meehan."

A tall guard watched her carefully from his patrol car, cigarette smoke curling out the window. He stepped out, flicked his smoke to the ground, and motioned up the hill as he ground it out with his boot. The paramedics started to climb, the empty stretcher looming between them like a harbinger of doom. The officer approached Tara with weary eyes.

"How ya?" he said with a nod. "I'm Detective Sergeant Gable."

"Tara Meehan."

His eyebrows raised as he tucked his thumbs into the waist of his trousers. "You're related to Johnny?"

"He was my uncle."

"Are you sure he's passed?"

Tara swallowed as a shudder ran through her. "I'm sure."

"I've never seen you here before."

"It's my first time."

He shifted, glanced at her, then dug a notebook from his pocket. The breeze off the bay blew his salt-and-pepper hair from underneath his cap. "Your first time?"

"Yes."

"In Ireland?"

"Yes. And . . ." She glanced up the hill. "It would have been my first time meeting my uncle."

He let out a low whistle. "I'm sorry."

"Me too." Tara glanced at the hill. The group was only halfway up. There was no reason to hurry, but Tara found herself wishing they would. "I think he was murdered," she blurted out. "He has a gash on his head and there's a lot of blood."

"Murdered?" His face remained still, but she heard the incredulity in his voice. "We wouldn't be dealing with many murders out here, now."

"There's a terrible gash on his head. And . . ."

"And?" He took a step forward.

"I think his body was dragged to the doorway." She swallowed, remembering the carpet of blood behind him. "Or maybe he crawled to the door. Trying to get out and get help. But he didn't make it." A shudder ran through her.

He frowned. "Fancy yourself a detective, do you?"

"No. You asked. I'm answering."

"Let us do our job."

"I would expect nothing less. I can't believe this is happening."

"I'm sorry." He was still writing in a notebook. "Where are you staying?"

"The Bay Inn."

"Go there now. I'll call for you when we're done here."

"I'd like to stay."

"I can't stop you, but you're not to take a single step up that hill. If you're correct about the situation, this entire area may be a crime scene."

"I won't interfere. I just. I just want to stay here."

The detective sergeant tipped his cap to her, then turned his back and proceeded with the rest of the guards up the hill. "Don't leave town," he called out, just before he disappeared over the crest.

It was ridiculous standing here at the base of a hill, where she could see nothing, do nothing. The police and ambulance were drawing spectators. Men, women, and children dotted the path, assembled as if they had just been summoned to an emergency meeting. Gawpers, her mam would have called them. She missed her mother's colorful sayings more than she could have ever imagined. Everyone kept their distance from her, but she could hear their voices gather speed as they threw furtive glances her way, then up the hill. At least from down here you couldn't see the horrific site in the cabin. She needed some comfort—a cup of coffee would have to do. She walked down the cobblestone path until she could cross the street. She entered the first café she saw, with a sign boasting: THE SECOND BEST IRISH BREAKFAST IN GALWAY. "I don't know," a female voice said as a tiny bell announced her entry. "But there's two guard cars and an ambulance."

"I saw them going up the hill. Johnny Meehan's place," a male voice said.

"Maybe that's why the shop's been closed. Johnny could be sick. Has anyone checked on him lately?"

"He keeps his own company. You know yourself."

Tara pretended not to be listening for she wanted to glom on to every word. Tears stung her eyes, and she was surprised to know she felt grief for a man she'd never met, bar a few photographs in a dusty album. *My mother's brother.* She couldn't help but see the gash, the blood, his staring eyes.

"He's not sick," Tara heard herself say. "He's gone." *Hit over the head. Attacked.* She shouldn't have blurted out that he was dead, but there was no taking it back now.

Heads snapped her way, jaws dropped. People edged closer. The woman took out a rosary and started to pray.

"Gone?" a man said, rising. "Johnny Meehan has passed?"

"Yes. He's passed."

The female crossed herself.

"How is it you know?" a man asked, leaning so far forward she was afraid he'd keel over.

"I found him." Tara's voice was barely a whisper.

"Sit down, sit down, loveen," the man said, pulling out a seat. She was thankful and sunk into it.

"He's my uncle," Tara said as tears rolled down her cheek. "I went up there to meet him for the very first time."

"Oh, you poor pet," the woman behind the counter said. She was large and bosomy. "Now." She shoved something at the old man, who then placed it in front of Tara. It was a giant slice of lemon meringue pie. The kindness overwhelmed Tara. Her pent-up grief came pouring out. "Oh, petal," the woman said, her hand fixed to her heart. "I didn't know he had any family."

A lump rose in Tara's throat. "May I have a cup of coffee? To go?"

"Of course, of course," the woman said. "Coffee for takeaway coming right up." She set about pouring it.

"There, there." The old man patted her hand. These two were like the Irish grandparents she never knew. Other people were starting to shift to the windows, and she heard the word *dead* repeated several times.

"What do you t'ink?" the man said. "Would it be his heart, alright?"

"Ben Kelly will finally get his boxing ring," someone said.

"It's too soon for that talk, so," the woman scolded.

"Why didn't that gypsy know?" another called out. "Couldn't predict her own lover's death?"

Gypsy? *Lover?* Was he talking about the woman from the caravan? Her uncle was—*dating her?*

"Don't start rumors," the old woman cautioned. "His niece is sitting right here."

The man stole a guilty look at Tara. She gave a meek smile to show she wasn't offended. Somehow anything in an Irish accent sounded lovely.

"I told ye something wasn't right with Johnny Meehan a't'all," the old man said. "He wasn't right in the head, like."

"Hush," the older woman said again. The message was clear. Tara was a stranger. An American. No more insider talk. Tara paused at the door. She glanced at the sign.

"Who has the *best* breakfast in Galway?"

"Ah, there's a woman who owns a cookery school. Claims her students can all make the best Irish breakfast you've ever had in your life. It's a bit of a poke at her. And a nod to Shakespeare."

"Shakespeare?"

"To my wife, Anne, I leave my second best bed," the woman said in a theatrical voice. "Carrig Murray gave us that one." Tara simply stared. "He's part of some experimental theatre troop. They've rented the Nun's Island Theatre, so they have. They're about to do *Hamlet*. Some kind of twist on it; we've all been dying to see what he's concocted. If you're still here, you should definitely sort yourself out with a ticket, so."

"I see." At the moment her entire life seemed like a scene out of an experimental play. *To be or not to be.* Sadly, for Johnny Meehan, that question had already been answered.

Tara stood outside, clutching her cup of coffee, grateful for the unusual wind that had whipped up, dipping the temperatures considerably, and the gray clouds that had swallowed the sun. Somehow it felt appropriate, much more so than a warm, sunny day. She had thought about going back to the inn, but she was too keyed up. The crowd of curious onlookers had nearly doubled. If the craned necks were any indication, chiropractors were about to get an onslaught of new business. Tara thought about the note on the door of the mill. She needed to tell a guard to go check it out right away. What if the note had been written by the killer?

She found one guard still at the base of the hill

and hurried up to him. He listened to her, frowning the entire time. But when she was finished he radioed the message to someone—most likely the detective sergeant. At least now they could check it out. The note had been typed, but maybe there was some way to trace it. Or had she seen too many movies? And would a killer be so stupid as to leave a threatening note on the door of the man he planned to kill?

Perhaps it was an impulsive kill, and the shock of it made him forget all about the note. Her thoughts were interrupted by the paramedics who were walking down the hill, carrying the same stretcher, only it was empty.

"Excuse me," she said, running up to them. "Where is he?"

"Where is who?" one said, cocking his head.

"The deceased."

"We can't move the body until the state pathologist arrives and declares it a crime scene," one of the paramedics answered. They breezed past her, placed the empty stretcher in the ambulance, and took off. Tara sighed. She didn't know anything about the police procedures in Ireland. She would probably have to hold his funeral. If she had other relatives around here, it was news to her. She slipped past the crowd, listening to snippets of the gossip. "Murder," she heard more than once. And "American."

She wondered if there was any chance they *weren't* talking about her.

A male voice boomed out, rising over the din of the crowd. "Margaret Meehan's daughter here to meet him for the first time, like. Can you believe dat?"

Ask and it shall be answered.

Chapter 4

Tara was spent by the time she walked into the inn. *Knackered*, her mam used to say. Or *wrecked*. An image of her mother coming home, pulling her shoes off, and rubbing her delicate feet rose to mind. *I'm wrecked*. If she hadn't already, that was Tara's cue to put the kettle on. How mundane those moments were at the time, compared to how precious the memories were now. She'd give anything for one more cup of tea with her mam. All she wanted to do was fall into bed. She was halfway up the stairs when a voice called out.

"Come into the sitting room for tea and biscuits." It was the older innkeeper and it was an order. Tara headed down, and when she reached the landing she could see the parlor doors past the check-in desk were open, revealing an adorable sitting room with a fireplace, windows shaded by curtains, and red velvet high-back chairs. Teacups were already set up along with a tin of cookies. Tara sat. The woman smiled and handed her a cup of tea. "I never introduced myself properly. I'm Grace Quinn."

"Nice to meet you. I'm Tara Meehan." But Grace Quinn already seemed to know that.

"Now, luv," Grace said, "why didn't you tell me you were Margaret Meehan's flesh and blood?"

Tara almost choked on her tea and barely managed to set the cup down with a clink. "You knew my mother?"

"We were the dearest of friends," Grace said. Tara doubted that. It seemed her mother would have mentioned her dearest friend. Grace took out her rosary. "Is it true? Is Johnny Meehan gone?"

Tara nodded. "I found out where he lived and went to introduce myself. And tell him about my mother's passing."

"Oh, dear," Grace said, her hand to her heart. "I was afraid to ask. Oh! I so wanted to see her again. How did she pass?"

"Cancer," Tara said. There was no point in saying stomach cancer. It always made Tara worry that her mother's secrets had eaten her alive. Grace made a tsk-tsk sound. "Why did she leave?" Tara asked. "Why didn't she ever come back?"

A look came over Grace Quinn's face like a shop sign flipping from OPEN to CLOSED. "It was so long ago. Leave the past where it belongs."

But it wasn't the past. Not to Tara. It was the all-consuming present. Tara leaned forward. "At least tell me why she and my uncle didn't speak."

"What about you, luv? Are you married? Children?" Grace's tone was that of a detour sign, steering the conversation away from the past.

"Not anymore," Tara said quietly, as an image of her toddler son's smiling face rose before her. She pushed it away and was relieved when Grace Quinn didn't probe any further.

Grace pulled knitting needles out of a wicker basket at the foot of her chair; next came a thick ball of blue yarn. Her hands began to work the needles with the ease of a woman who had been doing it for a lifetime. "Johnny took a box to the head, is dat right?"

The calm rhythm of the knitting gave an unearned innocence to the question, nearly lulling Tara into answering right away. Tara hadn't said a thing in the coffee shop other than he had passed. How did Grace know he'd been hit over the head? Or was that just a turn of phrase? She was astounded at how fast gossip could spread. "He appeared to have been struck over the head. Yes." Grace nodded to show she was listening, although her eyes were trained on the yarn. "I ran into a man named Ben Kelly in the pub. He seemed very angry with my uncle."

Once again, Grace's eyes did not leave her knitting. "Oh, I'm sure the guards will want to talk to him. He and Johnny have been at each other's throats over the salvage mill."

"Johnny didn't own the mill?"

"I believe he does, alright. I wouldn't know the details, but Ben was insistent Johnny was in violation of city ordinances. He said if all the fines were called in, Johnny would be out of business. He suggested he'd be doing your uncle a favor, buying it from him before that happened."

At the same time threatening to be the one to make it happen?

"You won't find many places left in the city with so much space. Ben Kelly has that boxing school, don't you know. He is appalled the mill is being used to store junk instead. That's his word on it, mind you. I've no problem with Johnny as long as he keeps to himself. But every year Ben Kelly offers Johnny more money for it and every year Johnny says no."

"It sounds like he was being rather aggressive about it."

"Rumor has it he's been making a fuss with the city planners—"

Digging up dirt . . .

"—Imagine, doing all this while your daughter lives above the mill."

She had Tara's attention now. "His daughter?"

Grace nodded. "Alanna. The young girl who works for me. Always late, that one. I'd have let her go if it wasn't for her zealous attention to cleanliness."

An image of the young girl polishing the counter like it was some kind of penance rose to mind. Tara surmised it was more of a compulsion but she kept her opinions to herself. "She lives above the mill?"

"Yes. She's going to cookery school."

"The one with the best breakfast in Galway?"

This stopped Grace from knitting. She looked at Tara and frowned. "I wouldn't know about dat."

"Sorry. Just something I heard. So why is Alanna going to school to be a chef when she wants to box?"

"Because her da won't have it. He's the old-fashioned type. He thinks he knows what's best for his only daughter."

She didn't seem like the type of girl who would stand for being told what to do, but Tara was here to listen, not to add to the gossip.

When it came to Ben Kelly and Alanna, Grace didn't seem to mind chin-wagging a bit. "Johnny didn't like her living there," Grace was saying. "He accused her of mucking about the mill at night."

"Mucking about the mill?" Tara said.

Grace's voice dropped to a whisper. "Stealing." Her eyes twinkled with relief as if holding on to the secret had been a physical burden she'd been forced to bear.

"Was she? Stealing?"

"Heavens. I don't think so. Your uncle. He wasn't himself lately. Everyone saw it. He was going downhill before our eyes. He wasn't right in the head, I tell you." Her eyes widened as she realized what she'd said. "In a manner of speaking."

"Was Ben Kelly angry enough to kill him?"

Grace looked horrified. Her hand flew to her mouth. "How could a person ever be that angry? It's impossible."

"*Somebody* was that angry."

"Maybe he fell." Grace laid her knitting in her lap and stared into her cup of tea as if she were preparing to dive into it.

"He was lying faceup."

Grace covered her eyes. "I don't want to know."

"I'm sorry. I'm just saying. This was no accident." It felt good to say it out loud. It was the truth. Surely the guards knew by now they were dealing with a murder. "I take it you don't have a lot of murders in Galway?"

"No. T'anks be to God. We have robberies, and fisty-cuffs, and domestic situations, and lads who take to driving after too many pints, and poor souls who take their own lives, and property disputes, alright.

And ever since Carrig Murray started that experimental theatre on Nun's Island we have oddballs landing from all over the world with their piercings and tattoos, and purple-striped hair. The lungs on 'em! You can hear them all the way down the block when they finish their rehearsals and pour into the pubs. It's hideous, I tell you. But murder? No. We're not like America." Grace Quinn crossed herself and then began to rock back and forth slightly as if self-soothing. "If your poor uncle was murdered, it wasn't a local. A traveler or a foreigner, mark my words." Tara stared into the fireplace, imagining it crackling and popping in the cold winter months. Grace's bias was showing and it made Tara uncomfortable. "I suppose you own the mill now," Grace said with a trace of envy.

This jolted Tara out of her meanderings. "What?"

"You're his only family. Your mother owned half of it."

This was news. "Are you sure?"

"Yes. Your grandfather bequeathed it to the pair of them."

Her grandfather. Thomas Meehan. Another man she'd never met. She'd named her son after him. The thought of her little boy intruded again and made Tara's throat constrict. Thomas had died three years ago at three years of age. A terrible, terrible playground accident. Tara pushed the horrible memory away. She'd sworn an oath to herself that from now on when she thought about her son she would only think of the happy times. It was the only way she could think to honor him. She thought of Gabriel, his father. They didn't make it, not after such a loss.

She took a deep breath and trained her mind to focus on the present. "What can you tell me about my grandfather?"

"Johnny wasn't always difficult," Grace said, completely ignoring her question. "In fact, just recently he told me he found an item he thought I'd love." A smile spread across the older woman's face and suddenly Tara could see the young girl underneath.

"What was it?"

"I never saw it, mind you, but he said it was a cast-iron harp."

"Oh," Tara said.

"My mother played the harp. I told Johnny I'd love to have one but I don't have the room. I guess he found a wee one." She held her arms open about a foot high. "If you run across it in the mill . . . oh, you must think I'm a horrible, horrible woman! Thinking of myself and that harp at a time like this. Please, accept my apologies."

"Of course. It's okay. But I don't know how I would run across it. I don't have keys to the mill."

"Oh," Grace said, "you can get those from Johnny's employee. Danny O'Donnell."

Danny. The same one she'd heard mention of in the pub? "I heard he quit recently," Tara ventured.

Grace's eyes widened and a smile stole across her face. "You are your mother's daughter." Tara wasn't sure if she meant it as a compliment, so she held her tongue and waited. "She thought she knew everything, your mother."

Tara dug her fingernails into her palms. "She was extremely intelligent and highly intuitive, if that's what you mean," Tara said. Elderly or not, if Grace

Quinn didn't watch it, she would see the other ways in which daughter was like mother. Margaret Meehan had never suffered fools.

Grace waited a moment and then nodded. "Of course, luv. She was one of my dearest friends."

There it was again, that proclamation. *Liar.* Her mother would have loathed Grace Quinn. "Did Danny quit?" Tara prodded.

"He did. He and Johnny had a big row about a fortnight ago. The mill has been shuttered ever since. But he can give you the keys."

"Any idea where I can find him?"

"I'll fetch his digits for you. I'll have it at the desk."

His digits? Ah. His phone number. "Thank you."

"Just mind yourself around Danny. He's got too much of an eye for the ladies. He's not anyone you want to bat your eyelashes at. A *player* is what you Yankees call it." She jabbed the air with one of her knitting needles.

Tara almost choked on her tea. She suppressed a laugh, as Grace looked deadly serious. "I appreciate the heads-up." She didn't know what she found more absurd: the thought of falling for someone again, or Grace Quinn calling her a Yankee and a man a player. She thought of the note on the door of the mill. It wasn't necessarily left by the murderer, but whoever typed the note was certainly upset. Maybe it was from Danny. "There was a threatening note to my uncle on the door of the mill. Any idea who might have left it?" Someone who was afraid his or her handwriting would be recognized? Otherwise why go to the bother to type it? Where would you find a typewriter these days? Most likely at the home of an old-timer. Tara couldn't imagine anyone young recognizing a typewriter let alone using one. Grace interrupted her thoughts. "If it's suspects you're on about—the guards are going to have their work cut out for them."

"Oh?"

"Johnny Meehan didn't have many friends, so. None a't'all, I'd venture. But he had a lot of enemies, don't you know." Grace sighed, dropped her knitting back into the basket, then gathered up the tea and plate of biscuits and started for the parlor doors.

"Including you?" Tara said.

The tray rattled. Grace turned. "Pardon?"

"Which were you and my uncle? Friends or enemies?" Grace stared at Tara for a long time. There was a sharp edge to Grace Quinn, a Jekyll-and-Hyde switch that seemed to flip at random. *Tea and rage.* And not the first angry resident she'd encountered.

"I mind my own business around here," Grace Quinn said with a thrust of her chin.

"Do you know anything about the fortune-teller? The one who parks her caravan near the bay?"

"Rose?" Grace Quinn sounded startled. "She's a charlatan." The rebuke came without hesitation.

Rose. Tara thought of the bright red bud in the woman's hair. *Well, that makes sense.* "She told me death was all around me. *Before* I found my uncle's body."

Grace considered this. "Stay away from that woman."

"Is she new in town?"

"Heavens, no. She grew up here. *A traveler,*" Grace added with a flush. "Why do you ask?"

Ah, a traveler. Tara knew there was a divide between the travelers and the rest of the population in Ireland. There were prejudices and grievances in both camps—another class division between humans, mistrust and dislike that ran deep and strong. Tara had read that the suicide rate was rising in the traveler community. Besides being poor they were cut off from the same education and opportunities as the main population. Turned away at local pubs even. And she supposed the main population would argue that the travelers had *chosen* to be outsiders, refusing to obey the laws and norms of society. She'd heard they were dirty, and uneducated, and dishonest, and abusive to their animals, and would set up camp wherever they pleased, making their messes in plain sight. Tara was sure some of that was probably true. But it was always dangerous to paint everyone with the same brush. Judge them before you'd even met them. She loathed racism and prejudice in all forms. New York City was a melting pot, and Tara had grown up among diversity. So many cultures and colors. You could walk out your door one day and discover it was Pakistan Day and there was going to be a parade. Tara loved it, loved learning about others. It didn't mean everyone got along. Far from it. But Tara couldn't imagine a homogenous world, how boring would that be? It made her nuts whenever somebody said "I don't see color." *You don't? I do! And I love it. I celebrate it. It's beautiful and diverse.* But Tara couldn't change other people, and she wasn't here to challenge Grace's views.

She also knew that Rose must have had a very different life growing up in Galway than Grace Quinn did. Tara would have to navigate the conversation carefully. "It looks like the mural on her caravan was freshly painted."

Grace frowned. "It's the devil's work. Mixing in the black arts."

Ben Kelly wasn't the only old-fashioned one around here. She could see how Alanna Kelly had her work cut out for her, trying to convince her father to let her do as she pleased, not to mention getting Grace Quinn to catch up to the times. Her mind floated back to Gypsy Rose. "It's strange though. That she was so specific about death being all around me. Don't you think?"

Grace shook her head. "I'm glad your mother's not alive to see what became of her brother. It would have killed her." And with that, the conversation was over.

Chapter 5

By the time the sun was sinking into the Galway Bay, Tara still hadn't heard from Detective Sergeant Gable. She distracted herself with a hearty seafood chowder that tasted like the shrimp, scallops, and crab had leapt directly from the bay into her bowl, a hearty slice of brown bread with butter, and a pint of heavenly Guinness. After, she resisted the urge to fall into a happy food-coma, and took a stroll toward the bay just as the last shards of sunlight were hitting the gypsy caravan, setting the painted colors aglow. Tara stopped to drink in the beauty. Ever since dedicating herself to a few minutes of meditation every morning with a trusty phone app, Tara was noticing the little things more. She loved the marriage of colors on the caravan, the vibrant green eyes and long black lashes of the gypsy, her long hair streaked with rainbow colors. The artist had done an amazing job. Life was magical, yet so few stopped to observe these tiny miracles. There had been a time in her life when she let these slip by, when she ran herself ragged, and went from one problem to the next with hardly a breath in between. She vowed never to do that again. It was easier to practice in Ireland because here nature ran raw and wild, insisting with each lash of water against the rocky shore that one stop and pay attention.

Rose was hurrying toward the front door of the caravan as if she was being pursued. Tara had to run to catch her before she disappeared inside.

"Wait," she called out from a few feet away. Rose's hand had just touched the handle. She whirled around. This time she was wearing a black dress and mascara-tears streamed down her face. Tara took a few steps back. "Are you alright?"

Rose lifted a hand and pointed at her. "You," she said. "I warned you!"

Tara took another step forward. "You're talking about my uncle?"

Rose was shaking now, practically vibrating. "Go home!" She entered and slammed the door shut. Tara could have sworn she saw the caravan shake. Well, that was odd. What in the world was she being blamed for, and why?

Had the man in the coffee shop been on to something? Had Rose and her uncle been lovers? But if so—why in the world wouldn't she talk to Tara?

"I can't go home," Tara said to the caravan. "The detective sergeant ordered me to stay." *Because he thinks I could be a killer.* Her cell phone rang. It was one of the guards. Detective Sergeant Gable wanted to see her right away at her uncle's cottage. Tara replied she was on her way and set off for Claddagh.

* * *

When Tara arrived at the base of the hill, Sergeant Gable led her to a stone wall near the bay, handed her something in a takeaway cup, and gazed out at the few boats that were making their way to shore. There were enough streetlights to give everything a glow, except for the bay, which had morphed into a mysterious blackness. She wondered what was going on beneath the surface, with all of them unaware. Tara peeled the lid off her cup, and the sweet, sweet aroma of coffee filled the air. "It's not tea!" Tara exclaimed.

Gable nodded. "I took a chance, even though the sun is down. You're from the city that never sleeps, are you not?"

"I could drink three shots right before bed and still fall into a deep slumber," Tara said. It was also true that she'd barely slept since finding her uncle murdered.

She heard the detective laugh, a sound that surprised and then warmed her, but when she grinned back, his smile disappeared.

"Grace Quinn said you didn't finish the mug of tea she served you." *Didn't I?* Panic struck Tara for a moment, until she heard the detective laugh again. "I'm partial to sludge as well," he said, lifting his coffee cup. "Who needs sleep?"

"Hear, hear." The detective had already talked to Grace Quinn about her? Why? She was going to have to watch herself in this city. Tara breathed in the sea air and held the cup of hot coffee in her hand, while a warm breeze caressed her cheeks.

"You say you'd never met your uncle?" His tone

was friendly, but Tara sensed a bite lurking beneath the words.

"My mother never said why," Tara said. "They were estranged. You probably know more than me." She studied him carefully to see if he would confirm this. His face remained still and he continued to gaze out to sea.

"I'm only going to ask you this once." He turned to her and stared into her eyes. "Do you know where I can find your uncle?"

"What?" Was he trying to trick her? Her head jerked to the hill in the distance. "Is his body missing?" When she took a step forward, he stopped her with his hand.

"The victim's name is Emmet Walsh," he said. "Ever heard of him?"

She shook her head, trying to absorb what he was saying. The image of the man's body lying in the doorway accosted her. "That wasn't Johnny Meehan?"

"No. It was not."

"My God. No. I've never heard of him." *Emmet Walsh.* Her uncle had not been murdered. She thought of how she'd raced down the hill and told everyone Johnny Meehan was dead. Announced it in the café even. What would they think of her now? *Stop it, Tara. This isn't about you.* A man was still dead. She shuddered. "Why would I have heard of him?"

"He's one of the wealthiest men in Galway. He was a client of Irish Revivals. A very unhappy client."

Even more unhappy now. Tara's world tilted. "My uncle's still alive?" She whispered it. Gable shook his head. "When I find him, and charge him with murder, he's going to wish he wasn't."

"Murder? You think my uncle murdered Emmet Walsh?" It was impossible to take this in.

"It's the simplest case I've ever seen. An angry client storms up the hill, confronts him. He bashes him over the head. Then panics and runs away."

Tara's mind was spinning, trying to catch all the revelations. She wondered if this was how the unicyclist felt when tossing his sharp knives into the sky. "You found the murder weapon?"

Gable's eyes flicked back to the bay. "He must have took it with him."

"You don't know that my uncle did this."

"You don't know that he didn't. You don't even know *him*."

"You're right. But . . ." *But my uncle couldn't be a murderer. He just couldn't.* She knew this was not a logical statement to make, so she clamped her mouth shut.

"Do you know what this murder is going to do to this city? Emmet Walsh was a connected man. This is going to cause an uproar. Not a single guard is going to be allowed to rest until his killer is found."

He sounded as if he was blaming Tara now. Just like Gypsy Rose. For all she knew, Grace Quinn was spreading horrible lies about her as well. *Just like her mother* . . . She'd made a terrible mistake coming here. But she wasn't going to let them bully her. "You weren't as upset when you thought it was my uncle who was murdered," Tara said. "I find that reprehensible."

His eyes slid over to her. "Do you now?"

"I do."

"Johnny brought this on himself."

"Why was Emmet angry with my uncle?"

"Emmet paid him dearly for a cast-iron pig. Apparently, it had royal provenance."

"What?" Tara had no idea what he was talking about.

"The pig. It belonged to an Asian princess."

"Okay." She was getting a very bad headache. She suddenly wished her coffee were of the Irish variety.

"Johnny sourced it, then claimed it vanished—after taking Emmet's money. Emmet was on the warpath. Ever since he bought that fancy mansion outside of town Emmet has single-handedly been keeping Johnny in business."

I bet Ben Kelly doesn't like that.

A missing cast-iron pig. Just like the cast-iron harp Grace said she never received. Was that relevant? "If my uncle disappeared with the pig and the money," Tara said, trying to piece it together, "then he may not have even been around when Emmet was murdered."

"Or. He ran away with the pig and the money *because* he accidentally killed Emmet." Gable looked smug.

"So you think this was an accident? Not a murder?"

Gable frowned. Then glared out to sea. "It's early days yet."

"I wonder if it was Emmet who left that threatening note on the door of the mill."

Gable's head snapped toward her. "What threatening note?"

"I told your guard about it. There was a note on the door to the mill. Someone threatening to file a police report."

"Let's go." The detective took off at a jog down the cobblestone path and Tara was forced to abandon her coffee and follow. She wasn't really a runner, had never felt the urge to run unless she was being chased, and if she were going to take up the sport, it wouldn't be in sandals. The *slap slap slap* of them annoyed her, but she pressed on. She was out of breath before they reached the front door of the mill. Gable stood in front of it, steam practically rising off him. There was no longer a note pinned to the door.

He turned as she approached, doing her best not to be too obvious as she sucked in air. That's it. She was going to have to start working out again. He just looked at her. She pointed at the door. "It was right there."

"You should have called us immediately."

"It was before I discovered the body. Sorry, but that jolted everything else out of my head, and when I did remember I *told* one of the guards."

"Which one?"

"I don't know. He was dressed like you, but a lot younger." Tara didn't mean for it to come out that way, but it was too late to take the words back.

Gable absentmindedly patted his graying hair and then glared at her again. "What exactly did the note say?"

"It said—'You bollocks! I'm going to report you to the guards.' "

"Was it signed?"

"Who signs a threatening note?"

"What was the threat?"

"Reporting him to the guards."

"Not much of a threat."

"I'm just telling you what the note said." She stared at the spot where the note had been, as if willing it to reappear. "It was typed."

"Yes?"

"Don't you think that's odd?"

"What? That we still have typewriters in Ireland?" He nodded at the mill. "I'm sure you could find a number of them in there, alright."

"Even so. The person who left the note couldn't get inside. That's why they left a note on the outside door."

"Would you be getting to the point anytime soon?"

Tara sighed. "Whoever left the note had to leave, return home, or to work—type it up—come back."

"Perhaps he or she brought the note with him or her."

Who brings a typewritten note with them? "I suppose. But only if they expected to find the mill still closed." She threw her arms up. "And why not just leave a handwritten note?"

"Some people have terrible handwriting."

"Or they didn't want the handwriting to be recognized."

If Gable agreed, it was odd he wasn't going to let on. She made a mental note never to play poker with him. "Do you have a key to the mill?" Gable rattled the door. It was locked.

"No. Grace Quinn told me to contact a Danny O'Donnell."

A shadow fell over Gable's face, but he just nodded.

A thought occurred to Tara. "What if someone intended to kill my uncle, and this Emmet Walsh was just in the wrong place at the wrong time?"

"It's more likely that the note was left by Emmet, then after writing it, he went to confront Johnny at the cottage."

"In that case, Johnny may have killed him in self-defense."

"How do you figure that?"

"Because Emmet was inside Johnny's house. How do we know he was invited? Maybe he broke in. Maybe he was planning on killing my uncle. You said he was enraged."

Gable pointed at her. "I will arrest you if any of these wild theories start floating around."

"I didn't know it was illegal to explore possibilities."

"Keep your nose clean and your gob shut. Do you understand?"

"I'll keep my nose clean and my gob shut as long as you keep your mind open."

He jabbed a finger at her. "You're the one who didn't know what Johnny Meehan looked like. And I suppose you thought with Johnny Meehan out of the picture—you'd inherit the cottage and the mill."

Tara bit her lip. Was this what Grace Quinn was gossiping about? The nerve. She should check out of the Bay Inn immediately. "I understand you have to look at *all* the possibilities," Tara said. "Even if I were the dumbest criminal ever, to go around town asking everyone where I could find Johnny Meehan, then murder him—the man I thought was him—then run to town to figure out how to call the guards. Without a trace of blood, not to mention a murder weapon

on me. But I'm glad you're thinking. I really am."
She shouldn't be yelling at a detective like this, but
she couldn't help it. This was ludicrous.

"Now I see the Irish in you," Gable said, with a
tone somewhere between agitation and admiration.
He took a step toward her. "Did you step foot inside
the cottage?"

"No."

"Are you sure?"

"There was a dead body lying in the doorway. I'm
sure."

"Did you have any kind of contact with Johnny
Meehan about your visit? A letter? A phone call?"

There was a sense of urgency in his voice that she
did not understand. "No."

"Are you sure?"

"I didn't have his address or phone number. I didn't
even know if he was alive." She winced.

"Did anyone else contact him on your behalf?" His
eyes were like balls of steel. He was asking for a reason. What was it?

"How could they?"

"That's what I'm trying to find out."

"Why are you asking me these questions?"

He glanced around. "There's something you need
to see."

Fear rippled down Tara's spine. "What?"

Detective Gable held up a finger, then radioed
one of his guards. "Has the body been removed?"

The radio crackled and a voice sang out. "The
state pathologist just finished. They're taking him
down now. A crowd is starting to form. Everyone still
thinks it's Johnny."

"Let them keep thinking it. The longer we delay the riot, the better." He clicked off and turned to her. "Let's go."

Outside the cottage, the detective handed her booties and gloves, and a paper apron like they give you in hospitals. They put them on, then the two of them stepped over the crime-scene tape that marked the entrance. It was eerie, entering a cottage where a murder had taken place. She made sure to avoid the blood on the floor, the trail that ran down the middle of the cottage from the front door to the back wall. Once she stepped clear of it, she looked around, desperate to focus on anything else, get the horror of what had occurred here out of her mind. Whoever Emmet Walsh had been, old or young, nice or mean, rich or poor—he didn't deserve to die like this. She barely had time to take in the wood-burning stove, the sitting area, the small yet functional kitchen, the windows looking out onto the hill and the Galway Bay—for the detective was making a beeline to a back wall, where he directed his flashlight.

"Here," he said. "Can you tell me why he spent his last breath to write this?"

Tara followed his beam to the back wall, which was covered in crude splotches of red—God in heaven, was that blood? Yes. There was blood splatter on the wall. Only it had been used to paint a sprawling word. The T was nearly a foot high, three times as high as the rest of the letters, for the second A was capitalized but smaller than the T, the R looked to be on a lower line altogether, as if trying to run away from the word, and the last A was not capitalized, the small A seeming to shrink from the rest of the letters, but none of them had escaped, for when you put them all together there was no mistaking the writing on the wall:

TARA.

"Odd, isn't it?" Sergeant Gable said. "Ever hear the expression 'the writing is on the wall'?"

She couldn't answer. She felt icy cold. This wasn't possible. She didn't know Emmet Walsh, and he didn't know her. Her uncle was a total stranger. Why on earth was her name on the wall, written in blood? She followed the trail of blood across the floor to the doorway. "Did Emmet Walsh write that?" *It wasn't possible.*

"I don't know. We'll wait for the state pathologist to come to a conclusion."

"I didn't know him. He didn't know me."

"So you say," Sergeant Gable said. "Yet there's your name. The only question is . . . is someone warning you . . . or was he naming his killer?"

""I didn't kill him. I could never kill anyone."

He stared at her for a long time, then gestured for the door. She was only too happy to leave. When they were ready to part, Sergeant Gable stopped her. "Would you be willing to hand over your passport?'

He didn't trust her. Why should he. She was a stranger. "Is that a command? Do you have the authority?"

"It's a request. A very strong one. This is a murder probe and you're a suspect."

"It's in my room at the inn. Do you want to follow me back now?"

He sighed. "Do I have your word you have no intention of leaving town?"

"You have my word."

"I'll arrange to get it another time."

"Understood." She didn't like it, and she suspected he had no legal right to ask for it. But given that her name was written on a wall in blood she wanted to be as cooperative as possible. She had been called many things in life, she just never imagined "murder suspect" would be one of them.

Chapter 6

The next morning, Tara was at Irish Revivals before the sun came up. Danny O'Donnell had agreed to meet her at seven thirty, or half seven as they said here. Ever since she'd seen her name written in blood on the cottage wall, her mind had been racing. She couldn't even get through her morning meditation. Being near the sea helped. The gentle lap of the water, the cry of the gulls, the green, green grass, the lilting voices of the people, her mother's people—Galway was indeed a bustling destination that seamlessly integrated a unique country feel to the bohemian city. She absolutely loved it. Even though they hated her. Suspected her of murder even. She wasn't welcome here, yet she'd been told several times not to leave. She'd never felt so conflicted.

A young lad was approaching, holding a set of keys in his outstretched hand. He couldn't have been more than eighteen. Was this the *player*?

"Danny?" she said.

The lad shook his head. "He's not feeling well. Asked me to meet you here." He tossed her the keys and started to walk away.

"And who are you?" she called after him.

"See ya," he said in reply.

She sighed. One of these days she was going to get someone here to like her. She unlocked the door and stepped into the cavernous space. Her hands fumbled along the wall until she found a light switch. At least three thousand square feet of treasures sprawled before her. This was no small business. This was massive.

Stone statues, old fireplaces, stained-glass windows, iron gates, claw-foot bathtubs, boxes of fancy knobs, cast-iron figures for the gardens. Row after row of architecture and decor. A sense of awe thrummed in Tara as she took it all in. The space was organized. This did not look like a business that misplaced or lost items. Why, she could spend all day in here. Half of this business had belonged to her mother? Why had she run away from it?

Maybe if she found the cast-iron harp Grace Quinn had been promised, she could get some answers. Grace knew something about the past, Tara was sure of it. Now that she saw what good order the place was in, she could start a thorough search. Johnny also had to have an office in here. If only Danny had bothered to show up. *Not feeling well.* What did that mean? Hungover? Bedding a new addition to his harem?

She caught herself—gossiping mentally about a man she'd never even met—just like others were doing to her. Just because a few locals had hinted that he was a womanizer didn't mean he was. She should be ashamed of herself.

She came to a row of fire pokers lined up in wooden containers like a platoon of soldiers. There must have been a hundred of them. She picked one up, marveling at the weight and heft of it. It could double as a weapon. She set it back and moved to the next row. She hadn't realized how much she'd been looking forward to meeting Danny until he didn't show up. He seemed to know her uncle better than anyone else in this town. Wouldn't he want to meet her? Was he worried about her uncle? Or . . . was he the killer?

Stop it. What was she thinking? This was the name of this murder game—wasn't it? Trust no one? She hated it.

Innocent or guilty—it was just bad manners for Danny O'Donnell not to show up. At least he'd sent a lad to give her the keys and let her in. She picked up a porcelain bowl. It was so smooth and substantial. An old sink? Just as she set it down she heard the floorboards creak behind her. Emmet Walsh's dead face flashed before her—milky eyes staring at the ceiling, the gash on his temple, the blood pooling around him.

The creak sounded again. It was coming from the doorway. She crouched down, moved to the next row, grabbed a fire poker, and whirled around.

A man stood before her. He put his hands up. "Easy." There was something familiar about him. Tall. Handsome. Around her age. Something about his green eyes? Oh, God. He wasn't covered in ashes but it was *him.* He seemed to recognize her at the same time. "You," he said. He glanced at the fire poker. "Don't tell me. I'm about to meet your father?"

The joke took her off guard. She put the fire-place poker down as she laughed. "I'm sorry. You startled me."

"Apologies are all on me. I didn't mean to sneak up on you."

"Who are you?"

An easy grin spread over his handsome face. He stuck his hand out. "Danny O'Donnell."

She shook his hand, taken aback. *Of course you are.* He was attractive. And charming. Grace was right. A player. No wonder she felt something with him. She'd always been drawn to the bad boys. Until Gabriel. He was a decent man. One look at him and the word *trustworthy* rose and formed a bubble around his head. And look how that turned out. She realized with a start that they were still holding hands. She pulled hers back. "Thought you weren't feeling well?"

"I just needed a bit more of a lie-in. But I had a feeling you would be punctual, so I didn't want to keep you waiting."

Had he been out late the night before? Drinking at a pub? Dancing with a pretty girl? She wondered what his life was like here. His easygoing grin would be out of place amongst hectic New Yorkers. "Thank you." She gestured around. "This place is amazing."

A look of pride crossed over his face. And then something else. Sadness? "It used to be."

"Used to be?"

"When Johnny was himself."

Good. He was willing to talk. She just couldn't

look too eager. She glanced around. "It looks very organized."

"He had good help." He winked.

"Did you do this?" Tara gestured around the tidy space.

Danny frowned. "Actually, no. But this is part of what I mean about Johnny's head lately. When I walked out, this place was in a heap. He must have worked day and night since to organize it."

Tara nodded. That was for sure. "There's so much I want to ask you."

Danny nodded. "Why don't we start with a tour?"

Danny O'Donnell was no slouch. He had an impressive understanding of the items in the mill and the history associated with each. He rattled off the year something was made, its worth, the demand, and even where they found some of the items. Old churches, castles, mansions, even mortuaries. Every object was a vessel of history, a holder of stories. By the time they were finished, she was almost dizzy. The inventory was vast.

"It's wonderful," Tara said.

"We had our moments," Danny said with a smile that seemed forced. They ended the tour in a cramped office. Unlike the main floor, the office was cluttered. Papers were stacked on the desk, which loomed large in the small space, and the shades were drawn, giving it a cave-like feel. "Does Johnny have a computer? Or a typewriter?"

Danny laughed. "We tried. He refused. Did everything by hand, even the books."

"I see." The note had been typed somewhere else.

"Do you need a computer?"

"No," Tara said. "I was just curious." She had her laptop, couldn't imagine getting work done without it. Although she still did her initial planning using blank canvases to create vision boards. She'd first started doing them in college. Creating a collage of her design. Most designers had switched to computer renderings, or used their iPads. She supposed she was old-fashioned in that sense. She loved creating the boards, fixing materials and colors, and photos, and textures to them. Some of her clients preferred it too. That way they could touch the materials, see what it would be like to live with them day in and day out. There were probably a few people who whispered about her behind her back for still doing it this way. Perhaps being old-fashioned and stubborn were inherited traits.

Danny was watching her intensely. She felt heat rise to her cheeks.

"We have a back garden," Danny said. "A bit more cheerful. I can make some tea. If you fancy a chat?"

"That's so lovely. And yes. I do." She took a deep breath, hoping he wasn't going to hate her. "But I am not a tea person. I'm a coffee person. Like a really big coffee person."

Danny laughed. "I'll give the café a bell. We can get coffee and if you like—scones with butter and jam. Does that suit?"

"Yes. Thank you. Cream and sugar."

"The door to the garden is down that way and to the left." He pointed down the length of the warehouse.

"Great." She assumed he meant he'd meet her there, so she followed his directions, reminding herself on the way back through that she needed to ask him about Grace Quinn's harp, and the cast-iron pig that had belonged to a princess.

The garden was a gray stone patio with shrubs of heather lining the back, their gorgeous purple flowers spilling over a low stone wall, and several planters interspersed between a wrought-iron table-and-chair set with large, soft cushions. It felt good to sit for a moment. She took a few deep breaths and closed her eyes.

The sound of a door opening jolted her awake. She hadn't realized she'd dozed off. Danny, his hands full with coffee and scones, smiled. "Oh," she said. "Sorry." She sprung out of her seat.

"What for?" He cocked his head.

"I fell asleep."

"You've been through a lot." He gestured to her chair and she sank into it again.

"These are way too comfortable."

"Thank you. I had to beg Johnny to let me put them out here." He set the coffee and the scones in front of her. The scent of the freshly brewed java and the sweet blueberries from the scones perked her right up. This was the business. Scones and butter and blueberries and jam. With a nice cup of coffee. She didn't want to think another thought all day. After spending several minutes focusing on nothing but the coffee and scone, she looked up to find Danny watching her. They held eye contact too long; it caused a pulse in her neck to start throbbing, and she glanced away.

"You must have been shocked to hear the news," she said, while looking at the heather.

"Which time?" he asked. Her eyes darted to his.

"First I heard that Johnny Meehan was dead. Then I heard that Johnny was alive. Then I heard that Emmet Walsh had been murdered. I was shocked all three times."

"Oh, no." She felt the heat rush to her cheeks. "That's because of me."

He scrambled forward, almost falling out of his chair. "Oh, no. I didn't mean it was your fault. How could you know?"

"I should have just said—a man is dead. But you're right. He was lying in the doorway of my uncle's cottage. I've never met him. I think anyone would have made the same assumption."

"'Course they would."

"The town seems to hate me now."

"Oh, that's just their way. A bit guarded about outsiders. Especially Americans. No offense."

"Right." She sighed. *How could I take offense at that?* "Do you think my uncle killed Emmet Walsh?" Tara was hoping for an immediate no, maybe even expected it, but as the seconds dragged on, she knew it wasn't coming.

"A few months past I would have said *no way*."

"But now?"

Danny shook his head. "He wasn't himself. Seemed startled when anyone came into a room. As if he was surprised to even see other people around him. Prone to absolute fits of anger. And paranoid. I'll tell you. In the past few months, Johnny Meehan was one paranoid Irishman."

"And you have no idea why?"

"It started with Emmet Walsh."

"The cast-iron pig."

"So you've heard."

"News does travel fast here."

"That it does. Yes. I believe it did start with the pig. Emmet Walsh was determined to possess it. Saw it in some magazine. Rumored it belonged once to a Japanese princess. Ended up with some banker out of Manchester. Johnny was on it. He went to a good deal of trouble to source it."

"Does that mean he got it?"

Danny nodded. "Traveled to Manchester after some old-fashioned bargaining with yer man."

"Yer man?"

Danny nodded. "The owner of the pig. A banker."

"You're sure Johnny got it?"

"I saw it myself. He brought it into the shop." He shook his head. "I didn't see why Emmet would want the thing, let alone a princess, but who am I to get in the way of a sale?"

"And then?"

Danny shifted in his chair and for a moment looked as if he were debating whether or not to tell her. "Then one day he came in and said it wasn't where he put it. He got really worked up. I helped him look. We touched every object in the warehouse. He went home and searched his cottage. By the time he came back down, he was accusing everyone he knew of being a thief. Including me."

Everyone. That was a lot of suspects. "So that was the start of the anger and paranoia?"

"That was the start."

"He never found the pig?" Danny shook his head. "And then one day Emmet came looking?"

"Oh, Emmet came looking many days. Johnny at first offered his money back. But it wasn't about money—for either of them. And to make matters worse—when

Emmet finally did come around to wanting the money back, Johnny had already spent it."

"How much?"

"It was just shy of ten thousand euro."

Tara was grateful she'd already swallowed her coffee for she would have spit it out like a cartoon character. "For a pig?"

"A pig owned by a princess." Danny winked, and then grinned. Tara felt an unexpected flush of pleasure.

"Are you saying the business doesn't even have ten thousand euro on the books?"

"We do, but it took a bite. Johnny didn't like to reach into his pocket. The theft had him bonkers. The morning they were to meet, I believe Johnny intended on giving Emmet his money back."

"You believe?"

Danny nodded. "I did my best to convince him. I told him we'd figure out a way to make up for the loss. I assumed he was going to take my advice but . . ."

"But?"

"Emmet Walsh was one of our best customers. He was threatening to ruin our reputation if he didn't get his pig. He didn't want the money back, he wanted his precious item."

Her uncle would have been stressed. Desperate even. What happened that morning? "There was a note on the door to the mill that morning. Someone very upset with my uncle. I told the guards, but by the time they came to check it out it was gone." She quoted the note and waited to see how he would react.

Danny looked thoughtful. "Sounds like it could have been Emmet, alright."

"Did Emmet live close to the mill?"

"Not too far of a drive."

"How long?"

Danny raised an eyebrow. "Forty minutes, I'd say."

That was way too long for Emmet to have gone home to type the note. Was Sergeant Gable right? Had Emmet anticipated trouble and typed the note ahead of time? She filled Danny in on her thoughts.

"Ah. That's why you were asking after a typewriter."

Tara nodded. "It doesn't seem believable that Emmet would drive home to type that note." Either way, note or no note, Johnny had been expecting Emmet. So much for Emmet taking Johnny by surprise, and Johnny killing him in self-defense. A thought suddenly occurred to Tara. She turned to Danny. "If you had quit already—how do you know Johnny and Emmet planned to meet that morning?"

Chapter 7

Danny's head snapped up. He looked as if she'd caught him doing something untoward. "I came to see him the day before. I was supposed to pick up my last check."

"I thought he didn't write checks."

"It's a turn of phrase. I stopped to pick up my earnings." The friendly tone was guarded now.

Tara wondered if Johnny had paid Emmet. Would the guards find ten thousand euro in the dead man's pockets? "Did you tell any of this to the police?"

"Tell any of what?"

"That Johnny had been expecting Emmet that morning? And he was going to give him his money back instead of the pig?"

Danny shook his head. "Do you think it's important?"

"I'm sure it will be. Until the murder is solved, everything will be important."

Danny exhaled. "They haven't come knocking yet."

That's because they were too busy blaming Johnny for the murder. Or her. And Danny's story didn't help her uncle's case. He'd known Emmet was coming. If he'd wanted to attack him he had time to plan it out. There were plenty of items in the warehouse that could have been used to bash someone in the head. She shuddered just thinking about it.

"Is that why you quit?" Tara asked. "Because he accused you of stealing?"

Danny stared at her for a long time. Was he angry? Should she not have asked? He stood abruptly. The chair scraped the patio. "I have to walk Johnny's dog."

"His dog?"

"I guess he's your dog now." Tara stood as Danny let out a loud whistle.

"I can't take a dog. I'm only visiting. I'm staying at an inn. I can't take a dog." Just then a small horse-like animal trotted onto the patio. He had creamy white fur that was sticking out in every direction, wide-eyes, and perked-up ears. "This?" Tara said, pointing at the beast before her. "That's not a dog. That's a hairy pony."

"A *sexy*, hairy pony," Danny said to the dog as he scratched him behind the ears. "He's an Irish wolfhound."

"Hey, Wolf," Tara said. The dog cocked his head and kept his distance. Yep. Even the Irish animals hated her. "Definitely no room at the inn for you." Danny laughed. She felt herself relax a smidge. She tried to get close enough to pet it, but it skittered away, stopping after a few feet to give her a dirty look.

In New York City she was a sought-out interior designer. Here, she was a Yankee Doodle minus the Dandy. "What's his name?"

Danny looked startled. "I don't know," he said. "Johnny just always called him Hound."

"Oh," Tara said.

"He wasn't exactly the type to name things." He looked at Tara. "Do you want to join us for that walk?"

She glanced at the plate where a scone as big as her head used to sit. Now crumbs were the only hard evidence. "Yes, please."

They rounded the building with Hound trotting behind, just in time to see Alanna approaching, her blonde hair gleaming in the sun, a backpack slung over her shoulder. Now that she knew the girl was a boxer, or wanted to be a boxer, Tara could see it in Alanna's compact, bouncy gait, just like her father's. Tara smiled, but it was as if the world had distilled to a single focus and Alanna could only see Danny.

Danny made the introductions. "This is Alanna. She lives above the warehouse."

"We've met," Tara said. "She also works at the inn." Tara smiled. Alanna blinked back.

"Where are you going?" she asked Danny, apparently saving her lip-muscles for him.

"We're taking Hound for a walk," Danny said.

"Grand. I'll just drop my bag upstairs and be with you in two shakes."

Tara tried to squelch the negative feelings bubbling in her for the girl. She could feel the jealousy radiating off her. "Sorry," Danny said quickly. "We have to discuss business."

"Business?" Alanna's voice rose. "What business

would you have with her?" This time her eyes flicked over Tara. "Buying a gnome for your garden back home?"

"I live in NYC," Tara said. "I have a fire escape, but plants tend to shrivel and die on it."

Alanna blinked again. "This is Johnny's niece," Danny said.

Tara almost flinched. Instinct told her that the less this girl knew about her, the better.

"Is she now?" Alanna said. "Then how is it she couldn't even identify his body?" A look that could only be described as hatred came into her eyes. Even Hound whined. The wind seemed to pick up. Tara wanted to move.

"It was a horrible mistake," Tara said. "I'm sorry if it personally caused *you* any trouble."

Alanna stared. She was probably picturing herself pummeling Tara in a boxing ring. Tara clenched her fists, wondering if she would be able to get in any counterpunches of her own. Probably not. Danny placed his hand on Tara's waist and gently pushed her forward.

They followed the promenade even though it wasn't always a straight line. Hound trotted way ahead, in his happy place, aware it seemed of every spot to stop and sniff, the places on the stone wall where sea gulls would gather, and the location of rubbish bins where maybe a scrap or two may have missed the mark. In the distance, she could see the hill leading up to Johnny's cottage. A line of people snaked up it. She halted. "Oh, my God," she said, pointing.

"They're leaving flowers and crosses," Danny said. "Paying their respects."

"They're ogling a crime scene."

"That too."

"Why are they allowed up there?"

"I'm sure the guards have it organized."

Tara wasn't so sure they did. She stopped along the stone wall. Hound settled a few feet away. He refused to get too close, but Tara could tell that he was also tracking her. It was kind of sweet. "Do you have any idea where my uncle would have gone?"

"It's been wrecking my head," Danny said. "Except for business runs, he never went anywhere. He was literally born in that cottage and—again, except for business trips—has never wandered outside this city."

That was sad on its own, but in this case added to her growing worry that he was out there—hurt. Or worse. Another victim. "Friends? Other family?"

"Not outside Galway. That I am aware." He looked Tara over. "We didn't even know about you."

A slight sense of shame washed over her, although she was hardly to blame for her mother and uncle's feud. Whatever it was.

"There's a rumor he might have been dating the gypsy who lives in the caravan by the bay."

Danny folded his arms. "I'm not in the rumor business."

Tara felt a flush of shame. She was just trying to figure out where he might have gone. "Did he keep a record of all of the places where he bought items?"

"If he did—it should be in the office. But if you're thinking of checking every one of them out—it would take you years."

"Maybe I could check out his most recent clients."

"You?"

"Why not me?" Tara took a deep breath and took in the people passing by, and the occasional restaurant by the sea. She wondered what she would have for lunch.

"Besides the fact that you've never met him?"

Tara bit her lip. "Yes. Besides that."

"The guards are looking for him. Don't you think you should leave it to them?"

"Detective Sergeant Gable seems most interested in nailing my uncle as a murderer. And he didn't raise the alarm until he discovered the victim was Emmet Walsh."

Danny nodded. "He's a very wealthy man." He flinched. "*Was* a very wealthy man."

"That's my point. Does that mean his life was worth more than a poor man's?"

"Of course not," Danny said. "But there will be more media coverage because of it, which puts more pressure on the guards to solve it quickly. I didn't make the world the way it is."

Her uncle was in deep trouble. No wonder he was in hiding. Maybe he didn't trust the guards to find the real killer. Or maybe he was guilty . . . "It seems odd that a very wealthy man was this upset over a cast-iron pig."

"Before working at Irish Revivals I would have agreed with you."

"And after?"

"These collectors get insane. I told you. Emmet was obsessed with this Japanese princess that supposedly once owned the pig. Bit of a tall tale, if you ask me."

The scent of curry wafted in the air, and Tara clocked the restaurant, storing it away as a possibility for later. "What else can you tell me about Emmet?"

"He's a local character. Made his money off insurance, and then some tech investments. He lived in a limestone mansion just outside the city. He was known to call it a castle, although it's a relatively new build, so he was exaggerating there."

"Is he married?"

"His family lives in England, I believe. The castle in Ireland seems to be his bachelor pad. That's how he played it. I can only assume he was having marital difficulties."

"You said his house is about forty minutes from here?" Most likely Emmet had driven here for his meeting with Johnny. Had the guards located his car?

Danny's eyes slid over to her and, in step, they started walking again. "I'm sure the police are going to have it covered," he said. "I wouldn't get too involved." His tone was gentle but also carried a warning.

"I know it's crazy. I've never met him. I may not even like him. My mother must have had her reasons for not speaking to him. But he's still the only family I have left. And I don't think he's going to be treated fairly by the guards."

"So your plan is to make it worse by trespassing on the murder victim's property?"

It sounded bad when he put it that way. "I'm just thinking through my options."

"Maybe stick to the weather, music, and the *craic*."

Craic. Tara smiled at the Irish word for fun. "Got it." They reached a natural end to the cobblestone, where land took over and in the distance a row of houses framed the view. They turned and headed back in the direction of the warehouse. Hound followed without a fuss. "What do you know about Rose?"

"Rose?"

"The fortune-teller." Danny stopped abruptly, and Tara had to swerve so that she wouldn't plow into him. "I'm not asking you to engage in idle gossip. Just the facts."

"I might have underestimated you."

"How so?"

"You've learned a great deal in a short amount of time. Johnny was obsessed with that woman."

"Obsessed?"

"I got the feeling he was sweet on her. I don't know if they were romantically involved or not. I worry she was taking advantage of him."

"Taking advantage how?"

"He was spending a ton of money on her predictions. And they were all terrible. Doomsday stuff." He stopped and put his hand on Tara's arm. "She's a charlatan. I'm not joking. Stay away from her especially."

"Although—" Tara said. She left it hanging.

"Yes?"

"Isn't what happened at the cottage . . . kind of in the doomsday territory?"

"Are you saying she *predicted* it?"

"Either that—or she caused it."

"She's either a psychic or a murderer. Is that what you're saying?"

"I must sound like another gossip. That's not my intention. She had a few doomsday predictions for me too."

They were within a few feet of the salvage mill.

Hound took off. Tara watched him go, then turned to Danny. "I'll mind him for now," he said. "He wanders from the cottage to the mill. I'll make sure he has his food and water."

"Thank you."

"What would you like to do now? Go back to the inn or go through Johnny's office?"

"Have the guards been through it?"

"Not yet."

Tara sighed. Danny had a point about her not getting in the way of an official investigation. Besides, what were addresses of past employees going to do anyway? She didn't have a car here, and even if she did she wasn't an avid driver. She grew up in New York City where she didn't get much practice driving. There was no way she was going to learn to drive on the other side of the road. And didn't they all drive a stick here? She only knew how to drive an automatic and even then she feared for everyone else on the road. "I think I need to go back to the inn and lie down."

Danny winked. "Those scones will do that to you. Come on, I'll walk with you." They fell into a comfortable silence as they headed for the heart of the city. Morning workers were out, going to and from their jobs, mothers pushed baby strollers, shoppers handled bulging bags, a few young people were still out from the night before, leaning against buildings smoking cigarettes, staggering down the path, or sleeping it off on the sidewalk. Music filtered through the air, along with the smell of baked goods and ale, all mixed with the sea air. Galway was a drug, and Tara was addicted. When they reached the inn, Danny put his hand on her arm, stopping her before she went inside.

"I think we should keep Irish Revivals open," Danny said. "I'm happy to run it until Johnny is back."

"That's very nice of you," Tara said.

"It's not just nice. I wanted to be more involved with the business. I have ideas for expanding. I even told Johnny he should open a smaller shop in town—sell to tourists."

"That sounds like a great idea." She meant it too. The mill was so large it was overwhelming. But in a smaller space, she could imagine picking and choosing the items, and staging them for optimal viewing. Her hands suddenly itched to work. It had been weeks since she created a vision board. In her head she was already creating one for this retail shop.

"If only Johnny had seen it that way," Danny said, his voice filled with regret.

"He didn't like the idea of a shop?"

"You'll find the older generation in Ireland is averse to change."

"Yet you're stepping up to help him now."

"We might have had our disagreements, but if we don't keep it open, he's going to have nothing when he returns."

"Meaning Ben Kelly might swoop in and try to take it over?"

"Jaysus," Danny said. "You know everything."

"Only a few things. What do you think of Ben Kelly?"

"He's not someone I'd mess with. Was a boxer in his day. Still fierce." He put his hands in his pockets. "It gets a little more dramatic."

"Go on."

"Alanna accused Johnny of leering at her."

"Leering?" Now her uncle was a pervert. "Was he?"

"I never saw it. And I told her da that. But Johnny was erratic lately. I'm not calling her a liar either."

"Why is she living above the mill?"

Danny shrugged. "She's an adult now, wanted her independence I suppose. She's going to cookery school in Galway. That pleases her father."

"You think that's the real reason?" Tara asked. She had a feeling she was *looking* at the real reason. Alanna definitely had a crush on Danny.

Danny frowned. "What are you on about?"

"Sorry. Nothing. Just curious." She had to watch herself. For all she knew Danny had a crush on Alanna as well.

Danny laughed softly. "Johnny thought that Ben Kelly wanted her to live up there so that she could torture Johnny. Make him think he was going crazy. Drive him out."

"That's why he accused her of mucking about in the mill."

"Supposedly Ben Kelly has been cozying up with the city planners. It isn't out of the realm of possibility that Alanna was doing a bit of spying."

"Then why let her stay?"

Danny shrugged. "Keep your enemies close, I suppose. And Johnny didn't want to live in the flat, so there's no use leaving it empty."

"Where do you live?"

"In town."

She waited for more, but he didn't provide any additional details. For a second she found herself wondering what his place looked like. "Do you think

Johnny could have been telling the truth? Could Alanna be a thief?"

"What would a young girl want with rusty old items?"

He sounded defensive. Once again she wondered if the crush was mutual. Tara decided to drop it for now. "How can I help?"

"When are you going home?"

Tara sighed, her agitation bubbling to the surface. "Maybe I'm not."

"Pardon?"

"Everyone keeps asking me that. I'm starting to feel I'm not welcome."

"I didn't mean that a't'all. I didn't know what you have at home. A family? A job?"

What could she say? Her mother was dead, she never met her father, and she divorced shortly after her only son died falling from a jungle gym? She wasn't going to be an open book. Not around here. "I work freelance. I can afford to take a long break."

His eyes were pinned on her as if he knew she was holding back, but then he relaxed and flashed her a smile. "Grand."

"I want to help at the mill."

His smile evaporated. "That's not necessary."

"It's not a request."

"And what experience do you have in sourcing, selling, or organizing architectural items?" A clip of disdain was obvious in his voice.

"I'm an interior designer."

"Okay."

"I went to Parsons School of Design. I've been buying items and staging apartments and businesses in New York City for the past ten years."

"Look, you don't need to impress me."

"Ditto." It came out harsh. Danny flinched. "You asked if I had any experience." She tried to sound calmer, but the damage was done.

"That I did." He held his hand out for a shake. "It's your business. I'm just the employee."

"I didn't mean it like that." Tara played along with the handshake. He held her hand for a moment, then let it go. She offered a genuine smile. "I'll be there bright and early tomorrow morning."

Danny started to walk away. "Not too bright," he said over his shoulder. "And definitely not too early." She watched him until he was out of sight. She felt eyes on her, and looked up to find Grace Quinn leaning out of the top window, watching her. She suddenly had a very good idea why her mother left and had never come back. Forget smiling, around here *Irish eyes were prying.*

Chapter 8

In the morning, Tara discovered Danny had dropped keys off to her at the inn, solidifying her theory that he didn't like to roll out of bed until the sun had been up a good while. Years of working for the corporate world in New York had made a morning person out of her. She opened the mill, then closed and locked the door behind her. She'd let Danny deal with potential customers; she wasn't in a position to help any of them just yet. She headed straight for the tiny office. There was a desk and chair, a file cabinet, and stacked cardboard boxes. In the center drawer, she found a black notebook with notations about customers and sales. Perfect. Maybe there was a clue in here somewhere as to where her uncle was hiding.

But if he was innocent—why was he hiding? That was the one thought she couldn't get out of her head. Maybe he'd witnessed the murder. Why not go to the guards? Maybe he was getting senile. Or maybe he too had been a victim. And the last option was the worst: *He may not be hiding. He may be dead.*

She didn't want to work in the cramped office, so she took his appointment book and a notepad out to the patio. It was cool in the mornings and she wrapped her cardigan around her. A boat horn sounded in the distance, and the fresh air made it easier to think. What would her life have been like had she grown up here? Who would she have become? They could have at least spent their holidays in Ireland. Christmas and summer. She could have brought Thomas here. She did that too often, carved new memories of her son out of the blank spaces. What might have been. She had already imagined him here with her, and had even advanced his age. He would have been six. What did six-year-olds act like? He probably would have loved Hound, and the boats rocking on the bay, and the lively street performers. Pancakes with faces for breakfast. The park after, his hands sticky with syrup . . .

She couldn't have changed it, could she? Her fate. It wasn't Gabriel's fault for taking their son to the park. The jungle gym was too high, his little hand was too sweaty—the drop too sudden—

If she'd been there, would she have thought to dry his hands off? Would she have been standing just below him, just in case, instead of five feet away chatting with Judy Bell? *Stop it.* Gabriel had tortured himself enough, she had tortured herself enough, and the vicious replays did *nothing* but threaten to swallow her whole.

She was grateful when Hound wandered over and got her mind off the past. He stood far enough away that she couldn't touch him, but close enough for her to know he wanted her attention. "Hey," she said. "Good morning." He whined, then turned and trotted around the side of the mill. A few seconds later he poked his head out from the side of the building. Was he expecting her to follow?

She approached him, hoping to sneak in a pet. Instead, she smelled paint. She soon saw why. Across the building, in large sloppy black letters, was a painted message:

GO HOME YANKEE

She glanced at the hound. He was sitting up straight, tongue hanging out, happy to show her the writing on the wall. She was beginning to wonder if she should add him to the suspect list.

Tara called the guards from Johnny's office. No one was available to speak with her, so she left a message. She found Hound wandering near an empty food bowl on the patio. A quick search turned up dog food in a closet near the patio. She fed him, and he even let her sneak a pet. She wondered if he missed Johnny. Or had he been a witness? If only Hound could speak.

She should take a picture of the side of the building. She retrieved her phone from her purse and took several shots. The smell of paint hung in the air. *At least it isn't blood.*

She didn't know what to do with herself and she was keyed up now, so she went inside Johnny's office. For a second she just sat in his chair in front of his desk and wondered what the man was like. She finally opened his appointment book and flipped to the latest entry. It was dated a week before she ar-

rived—which meant approximately a week before
Johnny disappeared.

Wait. Everyone was just assuming Johnny disappeared at the exact same time that Emmet was murdered. But what if he'd been long gone? What if his
disappearance was unrelated to Emmet's murder?
No, that couldn't be. Danny said he came by recently
to pick up his earnings. Unless he was lying . . . She
focused on the entries:

> Nun's Island Experimental Theatre—
> Carrig Murray
> Cookery—Talk to A's instructor
> Tattoo Shop—Rose
> Inis Mór—Talk to D

Several folks had already mentioned Carrig and his
experimental theatre. He must be popular around
here. She glanced at the second item. Didn't Grace
and Danny say that Alanna was going to cookery
school? It stuck in Tara's mind because of the phrasing. Americans would have said she was studying to
be a chef or going to cooking classes. Cookery was
the Irish way of phrasing it. Did the A stand for
Alanna? Why on earth would Johnny Meehan want
to speak with her instructor? Had he spoken with the
instructor? Did Alanna know about it?

Tattoo shop. Rose. Did this have something to do
with the fortune-teller? Or was Johnny going to get a
tattoo of a rose?

From her studies of Ireland, Tara knew Inis Mór
was one of the Aran Islands. She'd planned on taking
a sightseeing trip there before going home. Who was
D? Did it stand for Danny?

Tara headed back outside and made her way around to the side of the building. Did Alanna paint this message? Or her father? Tara glanced at the second floor. All she could see of Alanna's flat was a window, but the shade was pulled down tight. Alanna could have slipped down in the middle of the night, or the crack of dawn, to paint the message. This side of the building was up against a small wooded area and the bay. The only witnesses would be the gulls circling overhead, or the swans gliding on the bay.

And if it wasn't Alanna, then Johnny was at least right about one thing. *Someone* was mucking about the mill at night. Alanna shouldn't be living up there alone. Tara was going to have to make sure a security system was installed right away.

Tara entered the mill and took the stairs going up to the second floor, where there was nothing but a single door. She knocked. No sound came from within. Her hand hovered over the knob. She couldn't just open it. She knocked again. "Alanna?" She was probably at school. Tara wished she had the key and a good excuse to enter.

Tara jogged back down the steps and stood, wondering what her next moves should be.

She was going to have to pay Gypsy Rose another visit. Ask the sorceress if she knew where they could find Johnny Meehan. See how good her psychic powers really were. She turned the corner to go back to Johnny's office when there came a rap on the front door. She opened it to find Detective Sergeant Gable and a female guard waiting.

"That was fast," Tara said. She wasn't even sure if they were going to get her message.

Detective Sergeant Gable handed her a key. "We were just finishing with the cottage."

Tara stared at the key. "What's this?"

"The key to your uncle's cottage. You're going to need to hire someone." He handed her a business card. It was for a crime-scene cleanup company. She shuddered. "Show me."

She led the guards to the side of the building. There was a moment of silence as they all took it in. Gable folded his arms across his chest. "Making friends already."

"Do you recognize the handwriting?" Tara joked. She was treated with puzzled looks. Didn't they get it? She thought the Irish invented sarcasm. It went so well with Guinness.

"It's not bad advice," Gable said, flashing a smile.

"You told me not to leave town," Tara replied.

"So I did." He instructed the other guard to photograph the side of the building. "Have you found any cans of paint, brushes, the like?"

"No," Tara said. "But I didn't think to look."

"I'll give a quick search with your permission."

"By all means." She followed him as he began to walk around the building. "What about the cottage? Did you find the murder weapon? Fingerprints? Signs of a struggle?" She slammed into him. Darn it. She hadn't realized he'd come to a stop. He was a solid man.

"Who are you?" he said. "Feckin' Nancy Drew?"

"I just want to find my uncle. And whoever did *this*."

"Are you saying that you think the murderer is threatening you now?"

"I'm just asking you to consider the possibility that

my uncle might be innocent. What if he's a victim too?"

"I'll keep that in mind."

She sighed and stopped following him. She waited by the front door until they were finished, so that she could lock up.

He told her he didn't find any paint cans or brushes. "Do you want me to look inside?"

"I've been through the mill several times," she said. "But I'll let you know if I find anything."

He suggested she get a security system. She nodded her agreement. "If your uncle tries to contact you in any way—you need to call us. Tell me you understand."

"Of course," Tara said. He eyed her. She kept silent. He told her she could pick up a copy of the report from the Garda office. She thanked them politely, knowing it was too late to sway them. If her uncle was innocent, he had no one to fight for him but her. If he was guilty, she would turn him in herself.

Hound followed her to the cottage. This time the door was closed. Footprints trampled the ground, and remnants of crime-scene tape hung from the door like tinsel left long after the Christmas tree has been dragged out. Would Johnny even want to live in this cottage when he returned? Such a small cottage, she couldn't imagine staying inside after someone had been murdered. She could barely bring herself to enter. She opened the door but didn't step inside right away. It couldn't hurt to let fresh air in. Maybe she could redecorate it, breathe some peace and new life into it. She could start with a vision board. It would help her focus; she was jittery when she wasn't designing. She made a mental note to look for an art shop in town so she could buy some canvases and materials, imagining a cottage makeover. Of course she wouldn't make any major changes while her uncle was still missing, but the activity alone would be relaxing. She heard a whine and turned to see Hound standing a few feet away. He wouldn't come any closer. She got the feeling he was on edge. "You were here," she said. "Poor thing."

She entered the cottage, stepping over the blood in the entry, then scanned the interior. What was she doing here? Gable was right, she needed to hire the crime-scene cleanup crew. She didn't have it in her to do this. She stared at her name on the wall. Had Emmet Walsh done that? How was that possible? Somehow, someone knew she was coming. Tara couldn't imagine who—or how—but the writing was literally on the wall. And why were all the letters at different heights? It was probably the designer in her—imagine picking on the writings of a dying man. Still . . . it *was* odd. Just like the typed note. She glanced at the sofa and coffee table, the small kitchen table. The cottage was tidy. Dishes were neatly stacked in the drying rack. It looked like a lot of dishes for a single man. Had he recently had a guest over? Perhaps Rose? If there had been any clues, the guards would already have them as evidence. She took a photo of her name on the wall, and hurried out. Hound was waiting for her down the path. He followed her back to the warehouse.

She found Danny on the side of the building, power-spraying the graffiti off the stone façade with a hose he must have rented for the occasion. "You don't have to do that," she said.

"I checked with the station," Danny yelled over the water. "They've documented it. No need for it to stay a second longer."

"Thank you."

"This isn't the spirit of Galway. I'm sorry."

"I didn't even realize it was about me at first."

Danny laughed. "Did you not?"

"I don't think of myself as a Yankee," Tara said. He tilted his head in confusion. This was one cultural chasm she would have to leave yawning open for now. She had bigger things to worry about than the fact that one silly song hundreds of years ago forever cemented Americans as Yankee Doodle Dandies. "I just came from the cottage."

"And?" He shut off the spray and stepped back. She handed him the business card for the cleaning crew. Her look must have conveyed it all, for Danny nodded and tucked the card in the pocket of his jeans. "I'll take care of it."

"Are you sure?"

"Absolutely."

"I was thinking of giving it a makeover," Tara said. "When Johnny returns it will need everything, including new floors."

"I happen to be handy," Danny said. "If you pick out the materials I can lay the floor."

"I'll pay you."

"Consider me hired."

"The detective also suggested we get a security system for the mill."

Danny nodded. "I've been saying that to Johnny for ages."

"Can you set it up?"

A look of worry crossed his face. "Johnny won't be happy about it if he returns." He caught himself. *"When* he returns."

"I'll take responsibility," Tara said. "Grace said the business also belonged to my mother."

Danny took this in stride. "I'll see to it."

He was a good employee. But *someone* had been mucking about the mill. And *someone* had killed one of their wealthiest clients. Was there any connection? "Did my uncle ever mention my name to you?"

Danny frowned. "No. Why?"

She hesitated. Besides her, only the guards new about the message in the cottage. Although soon the cleanup crew would know. "I just wondered." She thought of the appointment book. "When you're finished, I'd like to take you to lunch, ask you about a few items in Johnny's appointment book."

"Well then," Danny said, flashing a smile. "I'll try not to be too flattered."

They went to one of Danny's favorite restaurants by the bay. The outside was made of stone and wood, the window trim and door painted a vibrant green. The interior resembled a sparse beach house: white walls with blue trim at the top, rustic wooden floors and matching tables, and aside from a few potted trees and seafaring photographs on the wall, the main attraction was out the large windows—a front-row seat to the bay.

Once they were served, they fell into a comfortable silence. Tara was too in love with her fish and chips to speak. He watched her with an amused smile.

"So," she said when there wasn't a crumb left on her plate, "I heard you're a ladies' man." A surprised look flashed across his handsome face. It was fun to see.

"Now who would say a t'ing like that?" His tone was playful, but she could see a pinch of concern behind his attentive eyes.

"Oh, just everyone I've met who knows you."

"Bachelors aren't trusted in Ireland. If we don't settle down, have a wife, two young ones, then we must be trouble. I would think a single, independent American woman like you would get me."

"I'm not saying you have to be married with kids," Tara said.

"As long as I'm looking for one, is that it?"

There was a bite lurking underneath his smile. She felt as if she'd lost control of this conversation. "I was just teasing."

"You were passing on what you've heard. Don't be so quick to believe everything you hear."

"Noted."

"What about you? Where are your husband and kids?" She should have thought this through. The pain of losing Thomas sliced through her, condensing three years into three minutes. Before she could stop them, tears were pooling in her eyes. She loathed crying in public. Danny registered it all quickly. "Don't mind me," he said. "I'm only messin'. What did you find in Johnny's office?"

She welcomed the change of subject and slid the appointment book over to him. She wiped her eyes while he buried his face in the appointment book and pretended not to notice. "Look at the last entry. What can you tell me?"

Danny took his time. He tapped the first item. "Nun's Island Experimental Theatre."

"Nun's Island," Tara said. "That's a neighborhood?"

"Yes. Just like Salthill. All in this area."

"Fun name. Why is it called that?"

"It's just a bad habit." It took her a moment to realize it was a joke. Then she laughed, and so did Danny. She liked the wrinkles around his eyes when he did. "Ah, back in the day there were nuns alright. The order of Poor Clare nuns. They took refuge here during troubling times."

"Do you know why this theatre is on the list?"

"I think Carrig was looking for a prop for his current play. You'll have to ask him whether he got it or not."

Tara made a note. "And the next one?"

Danny frowned at the Cookery Instructor entry. "I have no idea."

"Do you think he's talking about Alanna?"

"Why in the world would he want to talk to her cookery instructor?"

"Do you know the name of her school?"

Danny stared at her. "The Galway Cookery School."

Tara laughed. "Okay. I will look them up."

"What do you care?" Danny asked. His tone had shifted, just like the Irish winds across the bay.

"Excuse me?"

"You never even visited the man. Not once."

Tara set her jaw. *That wasn't her. That was her mother.* But that was private family business. She wasn't going to say anything negative about her mother to this man. He didn't know her. He didn't know a single thing about her. She stood and reached for her purse. "I need some air." She started to fumble for her money when Danny's hand shot out, stopping her.

"It's on me."

Tara shook her head. "I asked you to lunch. It's on me."

Danny looked horrified. "You're the guest here. She sighed. "Go on. Get some air. I'll be out in two shakes," he said.

Tara was standing on the footpath soothing herself, watching boats bobbing on the water, when Danny came up behind her. "I'm sorry."

She took a deep breath, then let it out. "I'm sorry too."

"You've nothing to be sorry for."

"You're not wrong though." She wished he was. She wished her mother and Johnny had remained close, she wished she knew the man who was her mother's brother. She wished her son was alive, and human beings couldn't kill each other. That was the problem with wishing: Once one started, it was impossible to stop. "I should probably just go home."

"Sure, lookit. I didn't mean to suggest you were responsible for your mother and Johnny's falling out."

Danny was staring at her again, an intense focus she hadn't experienced in a long time. She didn't know she would ever feel anything like this again. She didn't know if she wanted to. Grace's warning floated in front of her. *A player.* Watch yourself . . .

"Did he ever say why he and my mother fell out?" She made a point of not looking at him.

"I know Johnny was a man in a lot of pain. I don't know for sure if it had anything to do with you and your mother."

She knew the pain. She'd seen it on her mother's face nearly every day of her life. Not constant. Her mother could put on a mask and keep it there longer than anyone she knew. But once in a while it would slip. And for a second not even her mother could hide the emotion carved into her face—*grief*.

Danny edged closer. "You've never mentioned your father. Is he an Irishman too?"

"I don't know," Tara said. "My mother said she wanted to write 'virgin birth' on my birth certificate. She would never tell me his name." Tara always assumed the identity of her father was another reason her pregnant, unwed mother had fled prying Irish eyes.

"Ah, the Irish," Danny said, as if reading her mind. "They do like their secrets."

Indeed. And some of them could kill.

Chapter 9

Everyone, especially Danny, warned Tara not to pay a visit to Ben Kelly, so Tara moved him to the top of her list. She wanted to know more about this boxing ring of his and why he had been harassing her uncle over the mill. When she'd met Ben Kelly at O'Doole's, he'd warned her to stay away from Johnny and his cottage. Was that because he knew exactly what—or who—she would find there?

She headed for the pub in the afternoon. She needed the break anyway. She had gone through all the inventory in the warehouse, but she could find neither a cast-iron pig nor a harp. She had even popped upstairs to see if Alanna would let her in so she could scope out her flat, and at the same time see if Alanna had been stealing from the shop. But once again there was no answer, and her repeated knocks were met with dead air.

At least she could sit and have a pint, if nothing else.

The same grandfatherly bartender was wiping down the counter at the old men's bar, and for all she knew it was the same old men sitting on the same old leather stools. But this time, they were all talking when she walked in, and she lingered by the doorway listening. The lilts and cadences of their voices were like a melody she wanted to lose herself in, until she started to comprehend what they were actually saying. "He done it, of course he did," one of the men said. "I told you he wasn't right in the head."

"But why would he just kill a rich man and get nothing out of it?" the bartender said.

"Maybe he did. Maybe dat's why he ran off," a voice replied.

The bartender wasn't buying it. "Johnny wasn't easily rattled. He might not have been right in the head, but did we ever see him lose his temper? He was more likely to take a nap than deliver a box to anyone's head."

Tara clenched her fists. Everyone knew Emmet Walsh had been hit over the head. The guards were being too careless with the details of the case. She stepped in farther and the men noticed her at the same time. It fell silent at once and all eyes were on her.

"Guinness, please," she said to the bartender.

He pointed at her. "It's you."

Men scooched their stools in closer. "You found Emmet, did you now?" another called out.

"You shouldn't have said you found Johnny—you should have just said you found a man," yet another reprimanded.

"Ah, leave her be," the bartender said, as he prepared her Guinness. He nodded to her. "Sorry, but it's been a right old shock."

"I'm sorry too. I've never met my uncle. I had no idea it wasn't him."

"It's not your fault, pet," the bartender said, sliding her the pint.

She glanced around, but the muscular, angry boxer was not among the customers. Asking about him by name would bring a world of scrutiny. She would finish her pint, see what she could learn, and then head to the address she'd googled for Ben Kelly. He already had a location where lads took boxing lessons. She would just show up.

It took the men a while, but they finally relaxed around her. One pint turned into three. She kept trying to pay for rounds, which was apparently how it worked here, but someone always beat her to it. She had pints lined up, more than she could drink. She begged the bartender to stop, and insisted she pay for a round for the others. He finally got the message and she felt some relief when he accepted her money.

Tara decided it was now or never. "I was hoping to find Ben Kelly here."

"He's probably at his ring," the bartender said. "Will you be needing another napkin, will you?"

At first she had no idea why the bartender was asking that, but then she realized he was offering to draw her another map. "Yes, please." She watched as he sketched. "What's your name?"

"I'm Paul, luv."

"Tara. Nice to meet you."

He slid the napkin over to her. *The Ring of Kelly.*

Cute. A play on the Ring of Kerry—situated on the southeast coast of Ireland, another place she hoped to visit one day. The address of Ben Kelly's boxing ring wasn't familiar to her, but the map was clear.

Paul gestured to the napkin. "Do you have a car, luv?"

"No," she said.

"Do you want me to call you a joe maxi?"

"What?"

He winked. "Sorry. A taxi cab."

"Yes, please."

He nodded and dialed. "One will be here in about twenty minutes. Do you fancy another pint?"

"No, thank you. But buy the lads a round on me." She handed over payment. She wondered how many pints until they stopped gossiping about her. *Bottomless* was probably the answer. She thanked him, hopped off her stool, and headed outside to wait for her joe maxi.

He drove like he just got his license the day before, and he might have, given his youthful glow. He seemed to know every dip in the road, but instead of avoiding them he was accelerating, and by the third time the taxi bounced and she almost hit her head, she was forced to yell at him to slow down. He did, but not without a sunglasses-stare through the rearview mirror. "I'm in no hurry," Tara said as cheerfully as she could. "I'd rather live." Instead of answering, he turned the music on, a loud, thumping beat.

They were outside the city and she'd been dizzied by at least three roundabouts, but finally he was pulling up at a storefront. On one side of the building there were cows grazing, and on the other side of the building there were cows grazing. Tara couldn't see around the back, but she had a feeling she'd find cows grazing. The squat cement building was half the size of the mill. She was starting to see why Ben Kelly wanted a new location. THE RING OF KELLY sign flashed neon green.

The taxi driver screeched to a halt and the aspiring race-car driver immediately lit a cigarette. His head bobbed to the pounding noise torturing her from the stereo. She sighed, paid him, and nearly hurled herself out of the car. He screeched away, leaving behind a cloud of dust.

It was only then that she realized the parking lot was devoid of cars, and the windows were shuttered and dark. A rusty red bicycle leaned against the building like it just couldn't keep going. She knew how it felt. Maybe she should have listened to Danny. Or the men in the pub. Or the guards. Maybe she should just start listening to everyone. Being stubborn was not always an admirable trait.

Maybe she'd walk back. No. She'd never be able to figure out how to get there on foot. For all she knew, the cheeky driver had gone around the same roundabout each time. The skies were gray and hanging low. Just as she was about to call for another taxi, she heard a soft *whup-whup-whup* from inside the ring. She tried the door. It swung open.

The stench of sweat and gym socks mixed with strong cleaning fluid hit her as she entered. A large ring took up most of the space, and a few punching bags hung from the ceiling, dropped low enough to hit. Alanna was at one of the punching bags, laying into it as if it were her mortal enemy. Tara wasn't surprised to see she was good. Despite her father's objections, she'd obviously been training right alongside all the men. Step, step, punch, punch, punch. Bounce, bounce, bounce. Tara immediately wanted to join in. Hitting something would feel extremely good. The door slammed shut behind her. Alanna stopped. "What are you doing here?" So much for pleasantries.

"I was hoping to find your father in," Tara said. She kept her voice bright.

"You haven't." She resumed punching.

"Sorry. I haven't . . . what?"

"Found him in," Alanna said without missing a step or a punch.

Tara reached in her purse and grabbed her small notepad and pen. "Do you know when he'll be back?"

"Nope."

"I've knocked on the door to your flat several times," Tara said.

"Why?" Alanna asked.

"Someone spray-painted the side of the mill."

"It wasn't me."

"Did you hear me knocking on your door?"

Alanna finally stopped bouncing and punching. Sweat dripped down her face. She quickly dabbed at it with a small towel draped around her neck. "I've been staying with my da."

"So you haven't been to the mill in a few days?"

"Given that a murderer is running loose, he doesn't want me there."

"Then he'll be happy to know I'm having a security system installed. I will need to get into your flat.

Can you give me a key—or do you know where Johnny kept a key?"

Alanna stopped moving. "Why do you need to get in my flat?"

"In case the security team needs access."

"You intend on spying on me in my own home, like?"

Tara shook her head. "No, no. But they might need access for wiring and such." Tara felt a bit of heat rush to her cheeks. It was true that she would love to get a look at the flat. But she didn't intend to use the key to break in. *Do I?*

"Tell me when they're coming. I'll let them in myself."

Tara nodded, for she didn't have much ground to argue with that. "Danny is handling it, you can speak with him."

"Grand. Anything else?" She put a boxing glove to her hip.

"I heard your father was keen to buy the mill. Move this establishment." Tara looked around. It was kind of small for a boxing ring.

"The mill would be a perfect location. Johnny was getting too old anyway. He didn't even like the job anymore. Anyone could see it."

"When's the last time you spoke to Johnny?"

Alanna ripped off the gloves and began stretching. "What's it to you?"

Tara sighed and stared at her handwritten note to Ben Kelly. Where was she supposed to put it? To her left was a closed door. The word OFFICE was written on a piece of paper that had been tacked to the door. She didn't bring tape. Should she just slip it under the door? Give it to Alanna? Had Alanna driven here? Tara stood with her note, not sure what to do. "Any chance you're headed back to the mill?" she said finally.

"No," Alanna said through a stretch. "But if you need some wheels, the red bike out front is looking for a home."

"Oh," Tara said. The bike looked as if it had spontaneously retired, but as long as it still worked it would be safer than another speedy taxi driver mad to kill her. "Thanks."

"Not a bother."

"Where can I leave this note for your father?"

"On his door."

"I don't have tape."

"Slip it under."

Tara went to the door. Thick carpet prevented the note from going under. She tried resting it on top of the knob. It slid off. She dug in her purse. Found a stick of gum left over from the flight. Desperate times called for desperate measures. She chewed the gum, stuck it on the back of the letter, and pressed it to the door.

"You don't know anything about the graffiti on the side of the mill?" Tara called out.

"Hearing or your head?" Alanna said.

"What?"

"I already gave you me answer, so I'm wondering what your problem is. Is it your hearing or your head?"

As Tara fumed and tried to think of a good retort, a smirk emerged on Alanna's face and she pummeled the bag even harder. The door opened and a group of women filed in wearing long black robes and carrying swords. Alanna barely glanced at them. They soon spread out all over the small space, paired up, and began fencing drills. "What's this?" Tara smiled so they'd know it was a friendly question.

"They're with the experimental theatre," Alanna said. "Da is letting them train here. It would be so much nicer if we had the room." She stopped beating the bag to look into Tara's eyes, making sure she got her point across. She was obviously supporting her father in his quest to take over the property. Tara suddenly wished she could throw her out on her ear.

"Come to my office tomorrow morning," Tara said.

Alanna's nostrils flared as she breathed heavily. "What?"

"I would like to see you in my office at the mill in the morning."

"*Your* office?" The scorn in her voice was unmistakable.

"For now. Until we find my uncle. I'm running the business."

"I have cookery school."

"What time?"

"Not that it's any of your business, but it starts at half six."

Now that was early. "What time can you meet me then?"

"What's this about?"

"Your safety, for one."

Alanna held up her gloves. "I can take care of myself."

"When can you meet?"

"I finish class at half three tomorrow."

"I'll see you in my office at—six p.m.?"

"I suppose." Alanna threw her boxing gloves into a bin. Tara watched the women fence for several minutes before she realized what was puzzling her about the actors. These were all women—there were no men. Was that Carrig's experimental angle on *Hamlet*? She was looking forward to meeting this man. She went outside and was about to call another cab when she remembered the bike. She stood it up and squeezed the tires, then rolled it forward and back and tested the brakes. Only when she was convinced it wasn't a death trap did she hop on and ride off. At least by now she had her bearings and as long as she could see the bay, she knew she was headed in the right direction. This visit had been a waste. Alanna hadn't told her anything new. Tara would've had better luck getting the cows to talk.

When Tara arrived at the mill to find another note tacked to the door, she hesitated, her mind flashing back to that first threatening note. She opened it, relieved to see handwriting as opposed to typing.

> *The cottage has been cleaned. I'll start on the floors as soon as you let me know the material. Invoice is on Johnny's desk. Security firm coming in a few days to install cameras. Any idea why your name was written on his wall? Danny*

Why on earth were so many details of the crime scene leaking out? The cleaning crew must have told Danny about her name splotched on the wall. At least the cottage had been cleaned, and soon they would have security at the mill. She would go online

and look at flooring. The old floors had been wood—
but nothing fancy. She would stick with wood—
maybe something dark like chestnut. With a small
space you could afford to splurge a little. And when
Johnny returned, she'd share her design plans, and
if he approved, it would be one less thing he'd have
to deal with. Unless of course he was guilty, and he
wouldn't be seeing the inside of his cottage for a
long time.

Tara left a voicemail for Danny, informing him
that she liked dark wood, like chestnut, for the floor,
and mentioned she'd need to talk to him about ac-
cessing Johnny's finances. Danny had said Johnny
wasn't a check-writer, so he must get cash from his
bank. Or maybe he was the type to hide it under his
mattress—

Was anything missing from Johnny's cottage? Maybe
Emmet had disturbed a burglary in progress. Hard to
say when *the one person who could answer that question for
sure was missing . . .*

Hound was pacing in front of the office door. She
got the feeling he missed Johnny. Or was worried
about him. It was heartbreaking. He'd been fed, so
she let him outside. But instead of taking off, he took
a few steps, and then looked back. Apparently, she
was now part of his routine. "You're right. A walk is
just what I need." The morning mist had turned into
a gentle rain, so she donned a baseball cap and rain
jacket she found in a nearby closet, along with rub-
ber boots, and then she locked up before following
Hound. The dog immediately trotted in the direction of Johnny's cottage, down the cobblestone path
along the bay, and Tara followed. Fishermen were
still out, their little boats rocking in the rain. Hound

kept a good clip, but constantly swiveled his head back to make sure she was following. By the time she reached the base of Johnny's hill, she was having second thoughts.

The rain lashed out like sharp spikes, chilling her to the bone. Hound was waiting at the top of the hill, ears back and tail tucked. Tara pushed on, her feet slipping in her oversized boots, making the slog all the more cumbersome. By the time she reached the top, the dog was out of sight.

"Hound?" she called out once, then twice. After a third time, she saw Hound move toward her, a blur of wet fur. She wished she'd brought a flashlight; it was difficult to see. Hound stopped a few feet from her and whined. "Now what?"

He turned and headed to the back of the cottage. She followed. On the other side of the hill, a patch of grass was visible, surrounded by a collection of large stones. Hound bounded for it as if the stones were alive and had just whistled for him.

Before she could follow him, Hound came racing back, a piece of dark fabric clenched in his mouth. Tara bent down and coaxed him closer. When she tried to reach for it, Hound growled and skittered away. The object appeared to be a man's cap. Did it belong to Johnny? That would explain why the dog didn't want to let it go. He missed his master. Tara felt a pang of sorrow for the poor horse-dog.

She hurried over to the spot marked by the stones. She had to see if there was anything else to find. It was so dark. She took out her phone, grateful for the flashlight app. Near the largest stone, she found evidence of a disturbance, dirt flung, leaves parted. The cap had probably been lying right there. She contin-

ued a little farther on, just to make sure there wasn't
another dead body. Grass, and dirt, and stones. There
was nothing more to see. She hurried away with
Hound at her heels, cap clenched in his mouth.

She and Hound stood in front of the Mill Street
Garda Station, a stone building with a blue door and
ornate iron sign hanging above. They were dripping
wet, probably looking like they'd been washed up from
the bay and spit out onto the rocky beach. Hound had
refused to give up the cap, and it took considerable
coaxing to get him to come inside the station. She
approached a long counter, dripping water as she
went, and asked for Detective Sergeant Gable. The
woman behind the counter was carrying extra weight
but she had a beautiful, friendly face, and a cute
brunette bob. A bag of potato chips and a can of
Coke sat next to her.

"No dogs," the woman said, sticking a chip in her
mouth and flicking a look to Hound. She leaned
over the counter and smiled. "Even cuties like you,"
she crooned. Hound wagged his tail.

"This is my uncle's dog," Tara said.

"No," the woman said, plucking a chip from the
bag and pointing it at Hound before plopping it into
her mouth. "That's Johnny Meehan's dog."

"Correct." The woman tilted her head. "And he
found this." Tara pointed to the cap. I haven't touched
it. It was found near the crime scene."

The young clerk put on gloves, came around the
counter, and knelt by the dog. She tried to remove
the cap from Hound's mouth. He pulled back, ready
to engage in a game of tug-of-war. It was clear he in-

tended on being the winner. The girl sighed and stood up.

"I have cats," she said. "They're easier."

"Maybe he'd give it up for one of your chips," Tara said.

"I don't have chips."

Tara pointed at the bag of potato chips.

"Oh. My *crisps*. Are you mental? This is my supper. You'd have to pry them out of me dead hands."

Tara laughed and the woman winked. "Will you ring Detective Gable, let him know I'm here?" Tara asked.

The clerk smiled as if letting Tara in on a secret. "You're American."

Tara waited to see if there was more. There wasn't. "Yes."

"And you say you're Johnny Meehan's niece?"

"Yes."

"You live in New York?" Her eyes radiated excitement. Tara understood the feeling. Cities like Galway and New York got under your skin, worked their magic on you.

"I do."

She gave a wistful sigh. "I've always wanted to go to New York."

"You should. It's a great city. Although it's not too shabby around here either."

"Galway is the best city in all of Ireland. At least we t'ink so." She laughed. "I loved Irish Revivals. I bought me mam a stained-glass window for her birthday."

"That's nice." Tara suddenly realized that this woman was being friendly. "I'm Tara Meehan."

"Breanna Cunningham," she said, beaming. "Nice to meet you."

"You as well. I'm glad you like the salvage mill. I intend to keep it going."

"Aye. It's lovely. Took me ages to find what I wanted though, like rooting through a jungle." She looked down at Hound, still gripping the cap in his teeth. She reached around the counter and grabbed a potato chip. She held it out in front of her. "Okay, luv. I suppose one wouldn't kill either of us. Crisp for your cap."

Hound dropped it immediately and snapped up the chip. The guard was quick. She had the cap in her gloved hand before he had even swallowed. She brought the cap closer, then shrugged as she looked at it. "It's not a crime to find a cap."

"I'm not asking you to arrest the dog."

Breanna turned the cap over as if she hadn't heard Tara. "Almost every Irishman around here owns a cap like this. And woman. I'd say I have one lying around somewhere m'self." She reached behind the counter again, and this time came up with a plastic bag. She dropped the cap into it, then tried to reach for Hound. He backed away. "Shy one, is he?"

Was she not going to call Detective Gable? "The cap was found in a patch of grass near Johnny's cottage. I need to speak with Detective Gable."

The woman nodded. "Take the dog outside before he kills me. Humans are the only animals allowed in here. I'll send the detective sergeant out to you."

Outside, Detective Gable showed more interest in Tara's discovery than the young woman had. His gaze shifted in the direction of Johnny's cottage. "You'll show us where he found the cap?"

Tara shivered. "Of course."

Detective Sergeant Gable gazed out at the dark

and the rain. "I wish you would have waited until the morning."

There was no good reply. She nodded. He radioed in for help, and a few minutes later they were off. As they headed for the cottage, Gable used the opportunity to grill Tara. "What time did you discover Emmet that day?"

"I headed out around four p.m. to find him. It must have been five or so in the evening."

"What time did you arrive in Galway?"

"My bus from Shannon got in around eleven in the morning."

"And you can verify that?"

"I should still have the bus ticket."

"Who else did you see when you arrived?"

She wasn't sure why he was going into all of this right now, but it was a welcome distraction from the rain. "I ran into Danny O'Donnell." She didn't mention that she'd also covered him in her mother's ashes. "I saw Rose the fortune-teller." Should she mention the woman's ominous words? "And then Grace Quinn and Alanna Kelly at the Inn. That's all before I went to O'Doole's. I ran into Ben Kelly there."

Detective Sergeant Gable nodded. "I'd say you're in the clear."

"How is that?" She didn't want to sound like she was arguing about that, but it was obvious he had some information.

"The medical examiner says he was killed at sunrise. If we can verify you were on a bus, then you're in the clear."

An early morning killer. Johnny Meehan struck her as a morning person, but she wasn't about to say that out loud. Did that cross Danny off her list? He definitely wasn't a morning person.

"Why don't you take cover in the cottage?" Gable said once they arrived. It sounded like a polite suggestion, but Tara knew it was an order. She was more than happy to let the four guards go hunting around for themselves. She made her way to the cottage, grateful she had the key in her purse and that the cottage had just been professionally cleaned.

Once inside, she was relieved to see the results of the cleaning crew. The place was immaculate, and smelled like lavender. The cleaning crew surpassed her expectations. She glanced at the wall where her name had been, and the floor where she'd found Emmet. They were pristine. Of course she could still *feel* it. Every time she glanced at the back wall, ghost-letters spelled out her name in blood.

Some people believed that negative energy remained in a space long after a traumatic event. She wondered if it was true. She hoped not. The jungle gym her son had fallen from had been taken down, and a Winnie-the-Pooh statue had been erected in his honor. Thomas had loved Winnie-the-Pooh. He would have outgrown that by now.

She immediately stripped off her wet clothes in the tiny bathroom and found a large shirt and a robe in the back bedroom. Unlike the front room, the bedroom had not been touched and it was a mess. The bed was unmade, clothes were strewn on the floor and piled on the single chair in the corner. The dresser was cluttered with objects: loose change, empty beer bottles, even potato-chip wrappers. Why was he Felix in the kitchen and Oscar in the bedroom? Maybe he always needed one space that was

cluttered, like his office in the mill. He would probably hate that she was here, silently judging his mess
when she was the trespasser. She left the room as
quickly as possible.

Wow, this was weird, borrowing clothes from an
uncle she'd never met, never mind one on the lam
and suspected of being a killer, but it seemed a better
alternative than walking around in her birthday suit
and getting sick. Besides, if he did return he'd have
bigger things to worry about than his wardrobe. She
hung her wet clothes on the racks in the bathroom,
and pulled the robe tight. Kindling and cut firewood
were tossed into a large tin bucket near the wood-
burning stove. Matchbooks were stacked in a jar on
the mantel. She thumbed through them, for no
other reason than in the movies, clues were always
planted in matchbooks, but she learned nothing
other than Ireland had a lot of pubs and Johnny
Meehan seemed to pick up a matchbook or two from
each one.

Minutes later Tara had a roaring fire. She entered
the kitchen and put the kettle on. She found a mug
and a tea bag. For once, she didn't care what the sub-
stance was, she was just looking for a bit of comfort.
Rain and wind pounded the windows. The poor
guards, out in these conditions. She found a pitcher
of milk in the refrigerator and a bowl of sugar next to
the sink. She fixed her tea, curled up on the sofa,
and stared out the front window. She had the porch
light on now, so she would see the guards pass by the
front of the cottage when they were done, and if they
needed to speak with her, they would know she was
inside. For now, she was surprisingly cozy, one might
even say at home.

Chapter 10

After drinking her mug of tea, gazing into the crackling fire and daydreaming about the ways she'd redecorate, Tara fell into a deep sleep on the sofa. It wasn't until she felt the sun on her face, shining directly in through the windows, that she realized she'd spent the entire night. She bolted upright, thinking how foolish it was to spend the night where a man had just been murdered, given the murderer was on the loose.

Too late for that. It was morning, and she was alive. Her sundress was dry, and she quickly slipped it back on and made herself another cup of tea. She took her mug outside and gazed down at the bay. Light bounced over the surface like dancing diamonds. Tara had once seen a photography exhibit in which a woman photographed the same deli in New York City nearly every day for twenty years. The deli stayed the same as the people and seasons changed around it. Tara imagined doing the same with the Galway Bay. Every time she gazed at it, there was something new and exciting about it. It had been here long before her time on earth and would remain long after. She was the visitor on the planet, and for her the thought was a pleasant one. The morning air smelled crisp with just a pinch of salt.

She had an urge to get to the mill and start planning her day. As she was locking the door to the cottage, she looked down to see something odd resting on the ground. A rose stem lay on the ground, stripped of the rosebud. Just the thorns. Had this been here last night? It had been too dark to see.

Tara bent down and picked it up. It was deliberately left here, she was sure of it. Was it *from* Rose? Some kind of bizarre calling card or warning? Or was this place getting to her, sowing seeds of paranoia? *Was she in danger of becoming like her uncle?* She let the thorny stem lie where she found it and headed off for the mill.

There was a light breeze blowing across the bay. Tara stopped for coffee and scones, and besides folks offering their polite hellos, nobody bothered her. She wondered if Grace had noticed her absence last night. What did it matter? Tara was a grown woman. She'd slept much better at the cottage than she had at the Bay Inn. Could she move into the cottage? Should she? She had no idea how long she was going to be here and it would be nice to save the money.

As she was putting the key to the mill into the lock, she thought of the key from the inn, room 301, and how there had been a splotch of dark red at the base. She'd made a mental joke of it looking like dried blood—but what if it *was*? Who had stayed in that room last? Should she tell the police, or was she being completely ridiculous?

Grace Quinn would have a fit if Tara turned in one of her keys as evidence. That was a woman you did not want to cross. But Tara had to tell them—didn't she? She certainly didn't want to be accused of holding back evidence. Then again, who knows how long ago it happened?

"Hello?"

Tara whirled around to find an older woman in a tailored navy suit, clutching a white designer bag and blinking fake lashes. She had gray hair in a stylish bob—the kind some young girls now sported for fashion. It looked striking on this woman, who had light blue eyes like Tara, but that's where the resemblance ended; everything else about her screamed money.

"Hello," Tara said with a cautious smile. "Have you come to have a look around?" She wasn't sure how common drop-ins were, but she wasn't against letting in a potential buyer, even if it was a tad early.

The woman placed her hand over her heart as if the very thought was appalling. "I've come to have a look, alright. A look at where my husband wasted all his money. A look at the type of business a murderer owns."

This was Emmet's widow standing before her. Had the guards told her Johnny was the murderer, or was she making assumptions like everyone else? "Mrs. Walsh," Tara said, keeping her voice measured, "I don't think my uncle murdered your husband. But I hope to prove that, and regardless, I am very, very sorry for your loss."

"Your uncle?" she said, her eyes blinking faster. "You sound American."

"My mother moved to New York before I was born," Tara recited. She felt as if her nationality was a handicap she constantly had to explain.

"I was hoping they had caught him by now." Emmet's wife looked around, as if Johnny might be hiding, waiting to ambush her.

"Would you like to come in?"

She shook her head. "No. I would not."

Tara nodded. The woman turned and started to head off. "If you wish to sell back any of the items Emmet purchased, we'd be happy to take a look." The minute it came out of her mouth Tara prayed the woman wouldn't take it the wrong way.

Her eyes flicked over Tara as if trying to ascertain *her* worth. "Will you pay the purchase price?"

"If I can find the records, then yes, of course." Was that bad business? She was glad Danny wasn't around to chide her. She wouldn't mind having a look around this castle that belonged now to the widow.

"I have no use for junk," she said. "I'll let you know."

"Anytime," Tara said. Her instinct was to defend the salvage mill, insist that the items were valuable, not junk. But the woman was grieving and it wasn't Tara's place to start an argument. A thought occurred to her. "May I ask . . . did you find a typewriter in your husband's home?"

Mrs. Walsh squinted. "Are you joking me? He loved technology. Owned every gadget there ever was. He didn't have a typewriter. He used laptops, and iPads, and smartphones."

"Maybe he kept one around for decoration."

"I've been through every square inch. He collected a lot of odd things. Typewriters weren't one of them. Why do you ask?"

"Someone left a typewritten note on the door a while back. I wondered if it might be him."

"Not a chance."

"Thank you. That's helpful."

Mrs. Walsh frowned as if helpful were the last thing she wanted to be. "When they find your uncle, he'd better be dead. Or I'll make him wish he were." She strode away, heels tottering on the rough terrain, backside swaying, handbag thumping against her hip.

After her encounter with Emmet's wife, Tara didn't feel like conducting any more business. If she believed Mrs. Walsh, as she was inclined to, then Emmet didn't write that note. Who did? And where did it go? With everything else going on, she forgot to ask Sergeant Gable if the younger guard found it and bagged it as possible evidence. She bought her second scone of the day and found herself strolling into town, and when she realized she was near the Bay Inn she decided it couldn't hurt to pop in and maybe, somehow, get another look at the key to room 301 and check on the red smudge. The check-in desk was unstaffed. Tara hurried up to her room and threw her belongings into her bag. She was grateful she'd packed light. She locked the door, then hurried down to the check-in desk. She was startled to see Grace at the bottom of the steps as if she was waiting for her.

"You didn't come home last night." It sounded

like an accusation, as if Tara were a child, and Grace the stern headmaster.

Tara wanted to tell her she was a grown woman and she didn't have to answer to her, but Grace was an elderly Irish woman and it just wasn't in Tara's nature to do that. "I had to help the guards."

"Oh?" Grace's face blossomed. "What's the story?"

"I can't say." She didn't know whether she could or not, but she wasn't going to take the chance.

Grace's gaze fell to Tara's suitcase. "Going somewhere?"

"Yes. I'm going to stay at the cottage."

"What cottage?"

"Johnny's."

Grace gasped. "It's a crime scene."

"The guards are finished with it and a professional cleanup crew has already come through. Danny will eventually replace the floors and I'm thinking of redecorating it. It will be as good as new." *Except—you know—there's possibly traumatic energy hovering around and maybe Emmet Walsh's ghost . . .*

Grace shook her head and took out her rosary. Her lips started to move in a silent prayer.

"I'll need the key back," Grace said, going behind the check-in desk.

"Right." Tara set her room key on the desk. "Speaking of keys . . ."

"Yes?"

"Can I see the room key for 301?"

Grace raised an eyebrow. "Whatever for?"

"There's blood on the key."

"There most certainly is not."

"I noticed it when I first checked in. Remember you almost gave me room 301?"

Grace frowned, then turned to the cubbyholes. She removed the key to 301 and just stared at it. Tara could tell from her expression that the red stain was still there.

Tara leaned in. "I think we should look up who stayed in room 301 recently. What if they had something to do with the murder?"

Grace's head snapped up. "You're my first guest in ages. This is nonsense."

Tara sighed. "Then why not tell the guards, let them figure out if it's blood and whose blood, and then we'll know for sure."

"Know what for sure?"

"If the blood on that key has anything to do with the murder."

"For all I know—you could be the killer."

Was that what she really thought? Why was she this defensive over the key? "Then you'll be relieved to know the guards have cleared me of the murder."

Grace didn't look convinced. "Why do you think that?"

"I wasn't anywhere near the cottage when Emmet was murdered. I hadn't even arrived yet."

Grace pursed her lips. "What time would that be?"

"You'll have to ask Detective Sergeant Gable." She wasn't going to leak information about the murder like the rest of the folks here. "Was anyone working the desk that morning?"

"Yes," Grace said. "Myself and Alanna."

"You're sure?"

"Why wouldn't I be?"

"You said before me you hadn't had a guest in ages. So why would the two of you be behind the desk bright and early?" *Is Grace lying? Giving both her-*

self and Alanna an alibi? After all, Alanna had told her she'd been at cookery school. Tara stepped forward. "Are you sure Alanna was here?"

"Yes. I'm sure."

"That's very strange."

Grace paled. "What?"

"Alanna said she was in cookery school that morning."

Grace morphed into a child who had been caught red-handed. She began to stroke her left hand with her right. "Morning. Yes. You're right. I must have forgotten. She came to me after school. In the afternoon."

"Yes. I know. I was here. But you just said—very specifically—that you and Alanna were here bright and early, standing at this desk."

"And I corrected my mistake. I'm old. It's not easy." Like an award-winning actress she managed to paint a pitiful picture. Her shoulders drooped, as if each word she uttered was causing her to shrink.

"I just thought—maybe you were telling the truth, and Alanna was lying." *Or maybe you're both lying.* But why?

"Why are you asking questions?" Grace said. "Why don't you go do touristy things? Take a ferry to the Aran Islands. Ride the Ferris wheel at Salthill."

"I can't," Tara said. "I'm afraid of heights." Thomas must have felt as if he were up so high.

"Off with you then," Grace said. She used her hand to shoo her away.

Tara felt as if she'd been slapped. "You'll call the guards about the key?"

"I most certainly will not."

"I just want to find my uncle."

"I can't help you." Grace turned away and avoided eye contact.

"Who's the plumber you called to fix the leak?"

"Come again?" She focused on a spot on the counter as if hypnotized by it.

"Was there even a leak?"

"I believe you're leaking right now."

Grace didn't know a thing about the leak. Either her memory was giving her problems or she was covering for Alanna.

"I'm just trying to find my uncle," Tara said again, speaking softly, hoping to appeal to her sympathies.

"Be careful what you wish for." Grace's eyes remained hard. Tara nodded, and turned away.

After depositing her belongings in the cottage and having a spot of lunch, Tara made her way back to Rose's caravan. The door was closed. Tara wanted to knock, but then thought better of it. If Rose was telling some poor soul his or her fortune, it wouldn't help their mojo if she interrupted. Once she was back to the mill she decided to hop on the rusty red bicycle and go to Nun's Island Experimental Theatre. Maybe Carrig Murray would be friendly and helpful. He could tell Tara what item he had asked Irish Revivals to find for the theatre, and whether or not he received it.

Nun's Island did not look like an island. The Nun's Island Experimental Theatre, a stone building with a fire-engine-red door, was set behind iron gates, also painted red. Between the gates and the front door, a patch of grass lay, flanked by a low stone wall. Hooded figures were fencing on the grass. In the middle of them reigned a tall, heavyset man dressed in a black suit with a red bow tie. He shouted encouragement as the women sparred.

"Hello?"

His head snapped up. The women kept fencing. "Oh. Hello," he said in a booming voice. He followed it with a big smile, then immediately came to the stone wall to greet her. He extended his hand well before he reached her. "Carrig Murray, director."

"Tara Meehan . . . tourist." His grip was strong yet welcoming.

"Meehan?" he said. She saw the light dawn in his eyes.

"Johnny Meehan is my uncle."

"Well, well." He glanced at the actors. "Carry on. Or have a break. Practice your iambic pentameter. Whatever you'd like." He hopped over the stone wall, surprisingly graceful for a man of his size. "Why don't we go inside the theatre. They're allowing us use of it for this very special production."

"Wonderful."

They rounded to the front of the theatre and passed through the red iron gates. Soon they were in the simple yet functional theatre. The seats were the typical folding type on an incline, but instead of red they were blue. As a designer, Tara would have liked the seats to match the door and the gates, but she wasn't here for work. She sat in an aisle seat and Carrig took the one on the aisle across from her.

He clasped his hands. "I've heard it's been quite a trying visit for you. I'm so sorry."

"Thank you."

He shook his head. "I've known Johnny Meehan a long time. I'm sure he didn't do it."

"Really?"

"You sound surprised."

"Everyone else thinks it's possible."

"What do you think?"

"I couldn't say. I've never met him."

Carrig nodded. "He wasn't a perfect man. Who is?" He threw his hands up in the air. "As a man of the theatre, I know the complexities we all hide inside. No man is a total saint, nor a total sinner. But a murderer? There's not a chance." He crossed one leg over the other and folded his hands on top of his knees. He looked the part of a giant stuffed in a child's seat.

"I'm so relieved you think he's innocent," Tara said.

"Well, I suppose there's a chance. It's always the one you least suspect, isn't it? I would have never suspected him. It's quite confounding. In my line of work, I have become an excellent judge of character. A connoisseur of human nature, if you will. Johnny Meehan—a murderer? I just don't see it. Although it's always good to go against typecasting. Now that I think of it—he could very well be our killer." A light shone in his eyes and for a second it was as if he'd forgotten Tara was even there. "How can I help?"

"I found a note my uncle scribbled on one of his to-do lists. Your name is mentioned. Danny thought maybe my uncle was trying to find a particular item for your theatre?"

He nodded. Then stood. "Follow me." He led her out of the theatre and to the grounds in the back. Here she could see the remnants of an old church.

"The order of the Poor Clare nuns," he said. "Two are buried there."

"I've heard a bit about them."

They walked past the remains of the church. In a small clearing near it was a stone slab. The face of a man was carved into it. "Isn't it remarkable?" Carrig said.

Tara didn't know what to say. "It's quirky."

"It's from the fifteenth century."

"Wow."

Carrig grinned. "And there's a female slab just like this."

"Ah." She knew where he was going. "And you asked Johnny to find it for you?"

"In a manner of speaking."

"I don't understand."

"A friend of mine would love the female mate to this granite slab. In exchange, he was going to do a swap with me. I did ask Johnny to keep his eyes and ears open." He nodded to the stone slab. "About a week ago he called me and said he had a lead. I was so excited. And then . . . well . . . you know yourself. I don't suppose you know anything about it?"

"No," Tara said. "I'll check the warehouse for you." *This makes three missing items.* What was going on? Although this time Johnny didn't say he had the item, he said he had a lead on the item. This was all so frustrating. Carrig glanced at the actors, huddled in the yard. "I know you're busy," Tara said. "Thank you for your time. I'll keep an eye out for the slab."

"I doubt I've been much help." Carrig began to walk her back to the gate. On the wall next to it, a theatrical poster hung by the door. HAMLET screamed across the top in red. Below it was a hooded figure with just the eyes peering out. WITH A TWIST was written in red below. Carrig noticed her reading it.

"You should come. The twist will blow you away."

"In addition to the all-female cast?"

Carrig's face fell. "Well. I guess the twist will only blow *some* folks away."

"Sorry. I noticed them rehearsing in the Ring of Kelly and now here. Your secret is safe with me."

"A *female* Hamlet," he said, as if she were still in the dark.

"Wonderful." He stared at her as if he were still not pleased with her reaction. She mustered up some enthusiasm. " 'To be or not to be,' " she said.

"Exactly. Exactly." He grinned. "To be or not to be *a woman.*"

"Ah," Tara said. "Plenty of drama."

"Correct! Estrogen will be the undercurrent that will run through the entire play, making it sing electric!"

Tara's jaw was getting sore from smiling, not to mention her neck from nodding. "What was the item you wanted to swap for the stone slab?"

Carrig stared into the distance as if the object had just materialized over the River Corrib. "A rare theatre light. An enormous globe held up by ornate wrought iron. I acquired it ages ago but was forced to sell it when times were lean. I sold it to a friend of mine on the condition that I would buy it back some day—with interest, of course. He knew it was temporary. It seems he's grown fond of it. Refuses to give it back. Or . . . he's not really much of a friend."

Tara took notes. "What's his name?"

"I'm afraid I don't give out private information about my friends. That would be a sure way to lose them."

"I'm just wondering if Johnny paid him a visit."

"Perhaps the guards will figure it out."

Her uncle had written *Inis Mór* in his notebook. Is that where this friend lived? Did his name start with a D? "Did you ask your friend if Johnny came to see him?"

"No." He gestured to the actors, who upon seeing him had resumed their fencing practice. Every once in a while a grunt rang out as they parried, and sparred, and thrusted, or whatever the fencing lingo was. "I've been very busy."

"When did Johnny come to see you?"

"I'd have to check my calendar. But it was over a month ago."

"Do you know what this D might stand for?" Tara held out her notes. Carrig squinted, then patted his pockets.

"I don't have my glasses. I'm afraid without them I have blindness of bat." He smiled at his turn of phrase.

"It says Inis Mór, but then he wrote the letter D."

"Perhaps it's a G."

Does his friend's name start with a G? "You think it's a G?"

His eyes darted around. "I have no idea."

Now that he knew his play was no longer the focus of her visit, he was starting to tire of her. "Is there anything else you can tell me?" she asked.

"Like what?"

"How did my uncle seem?"

"Grand." Carrig's eyes darted away from her.

Was he avoiding her gaze? Maybe Johnny wasn't grand, but for some reason Carrig didn't want to admit it. "Was he acting—I don't know—paranoid, or angry?"

Carrig tugged at his bow tie as if it was cutting off his oxygen. He removed a handkerchief from his pocket and patted his brow. "No." A pained smile broke over his face. For a connoisseur of human behavior, he wasn't a very good liar.

She waited to see if there was more. There wasn't. "I'm just trying to find out what really happened."

Carrig Murray smiled, but it didn't reach his eyes. "I'd be happy to comp you a seat for our production. Unless you're going home soon?"

The last bit sounded hopeful. She was never going to be wanted around here. Especially if she continued to go around interrogating everyone. But how else was she supposed to find her uncle? "I'll have to see."

"Well, if you're here for opening night, do let me know what you think." He gave her a little bow, and headed back through the iron gates. She was halfway down the path when she realized she'd left her purse inside the theatre, on the floor near her seat. She hurried back in. As she entered and headed for the seat, she could hear Carrig's voice, somewhere backstage, raised in anger.

"What do you think I told her? Nothing, George. Absolutely nothing. Exactly what *you're* going to tell her if she comes to see you." Tara froze. He had to be talking about her.

Was George the mysterious friend? *Perhaps it's a G.* Well, that was one mystery solved. And he was calling him literally the second she left. Why?

She was debating what to do when suddenly he bolted onstage, and then stopped when he spotted her. His face was scarlet. He looked at her, then his phone. "Were you eavesdropping?"

"No. No. I left my purse." Tara pointed at it, like an idiot.

He held up his phone. "That wasn't about you. It was a personal matter."

Tara snatched her purse and slung it over her shoulder. "I didn't hear a thing." She turned to go.

"You shouldn't go sneaking up on people."

"I told you. I was getting my purse."

"This is a welcoming place," he said. "Until it's not."

"Yes," she said. "I'm beginning to realize that." She let door slam behind her.

Chapter 11

The fishing trawler bobbed out in the water, and whenever Danny cast his line, the boat tipped and Tara thought for sure she was going to be thrown overboard. Each time, she screamed and he laughed. She'd already read that Aran jumpers—or sweaters, as she called them—used to be stitched with the colors and patterns of specific families, and that was so they could identify fishermen's bodies when they died at sea. Maybe coming out here hadn't been such a great idea.

She had found Danny at the dock, preparing to go out, when she started badgering him with questions about Carrig. He'd insisted she tag along. Every time she tried to talk, he shushed her. "This is fishing. Fishing is like meditation. There's no jibber-jabber." Finally, he forced her to take a fishing rod and told her he'd only answer her questions if she caught a fish. Ridiculous.

Now here she was, in this rickety little boat, willing herself to catch a fish. She had to admit, the rocking, and the silence, and the waiting, were somewhat calming. Danny had caught three fish already, silver floppy things that thrashed in the bottom of the boat until he tossed them in the cooler resting in the middle and shut the lid.

"Salmon," Danny said with delight. "This will be grand for supper."

Tara winced.

Danny gave her a side glance. "You're a sensitive one."

"It's hard to watch anything die," she said. *If only everyone in this city felt the same.*

"It's easier when they're on your plate with a pint of Guinness." He winked.

"I'm sure it is."

"You'll see, tonight." She raised her eyebrow. He nodded to the cooler. "As I said. This is supper."

"Are you really not going to answer my questions until I catch a fish?" He'd already told her he had no idea who this George might be. After that he laid down the no-talking-until-she-caught-a-fish rule. She was having a hard time playing by it.

He put his finger to his lips. She laughed, then gazed back out at the water. "Thatta girl," she heard him say. A warmth flooded through her. *Ladies' man.* She would have to watch herself.

She was nearly falling asleep when she felt a tug on her line. She jolted, and pulled on the rod. "Something's there."

"Easy now." Suddenly he was behind her, his arms around her, holding on to the rod with her. "Give it a tug." She tugged. "Reel him in." She started to rotate the crank. Danny fell back. "That's it. Keep going."

This was kind of exciting. The closer it got, the harder it was to reel in. Her tongue was hanging out the corner of her mouth as she turned the handle, her breath labored. "Come on, little fish," she said.

"I think it's a big 'un," Danny said.

The line jerked, nearly knocking Tara over. She thrashed, refusing to let go, and put all her strength into reeling it in. Finally, she could see its head cresting out of the water, the sun bouncing off its shiny gills making it look like it was showered in glitter.

"That's one good-looking salmon," Danny said. Tara had an urge to throw it back, save its life. But then she imagined it on her plate, a pint of Guinness next to it, along with a heap of potatoes. When would she ever get the chance to catch another one like it?

"It is big, isn't it?" Tara said. Danny whooped and high-fived her.

A nearby fisherman heard their excitement. He rowed close enough to reveal a gap between his teeth.

"Looks like you had better luck than me." He stared longingly at their cooler.

"No catches?" Danny asked.

"I didn't say dat." The man reached into the boat and hauled something up. "Tell me. What am I going to do with this?" His catch sat in the palm of his hand. It was a cast-iron animal head. The body was missing. Green patina was visible around the ears. Its snout was open in laughter. The fisherman laughed. "Not every day you catch a little piggy, now is it?"

* * *

Danny called the guards, and by the time he'd finished mooring and securing the boat, Detective Sergeant Gable was waiting onshore with an evidence bag.

"Do you think it's the murder weapon?" Danny asked.

"I think there must be a reason someone rowed out to sea and tossed it in," Detective Gable said. "We'll send a team in to search for the rest of it." He gazed out at the bay. Had Johnny escaped by boat?

"Did Johnny own a boat?" Tara wondered out loud.

Danny and Detective Gable both snapped to attention. She was happy for a moment that she'd thought of something they hadn't.

Detective Gable looked at Danny. "Do you know where he kept it?"

Danny nodded and started down the dock. "This way." They followed him past ten slips with boats snugged into them, where he stood looking at the only empty space on the dock.

"It's gone." Detective Sergeant Gable was the first to state the obvious.

"It is indeed," Danny said. The two of them lifted their faces to the bay. Tara could see what they were imagining. Johnny Meehan hitting Emmet over the head with the cast-iron pig. Fleeing down to his boat. Rowing the murder weapon out to sea, and tossing it in. And then what? Did he keep going? Or were he and his little boat out there somewhere, lost, or worse—buried at sea?

* * *

Danny was right about one thing. There was nothing like fresh-caught salmon and a good pint of Guinness. He had prepared the entire meal at his place, which also included potatoes and veg, but instead of inviting her over, he brought it all over to the cottage. Tara set up the tiny kitchen table, already thinking if she had her way she would replace it with something new—maybe a built-in breakfast bar. But this wasn't her cottage, so she would only go as far as imagining and pricing the possible renovations until her uncle returned and could be consulted. Tara had just taken her last bite of salmon when something sharp poked the side of her mouth. It felt like a knife. She cried out and spit the offending object into her hand. In her palm sat a jagged shard of broken glass. If she had accidentally swallowed it, she could have choked to death on it.

"Oh my God," Danny said. He jumped up from the table and stared at the shard in her hand. He shook his head. "I don't know where that came from."

"It came from the piece of fish you cooked," she said slowly.

A red flush crept up his face. "I didn't cook it."

Tara shot out of her chair. "Who did?" But she knew. From the shade of scarlet his face turned. "Alanna."

"She's studying cookery. She offered." *I bet she did.* "I wanted it to be special. Your first catch and all."

Tara could only imagine how Alanna felt about that. Or maybe she didn't have to. She held up the piece of glass. "What do you think happened here?"

Danny shook his head. "I'm sure it was an accident."

Tara glanced at the pan Danny had brought the

fish in. He'd only brought two large pieces. "Did she ask you which piece you intended on giving to me?"

His face remained still as he mulled over the implication of her question. He shook his head. "You can't think she did it on purpose. I probably put her under the gun." He snapped his fingers. "She was drinking a glass of wine while she cooked. Maybe it broke. I'll ask her. But *please.* Don't go around accusing her of trying to murder you with a piece of salmon."

"Did she cook it at your place, or her dad's—"

"No. No. Her flat at the mill."

"Were you there?"

Danny sighed. "I was downstairs."

"Then how did you know she was drinking a glass of wine?"

"I brought the salmon up to her flat, and when she opened the door she was holding a glass of wine."

"I bet she was."

"What's that supposed to mean?"

It was now or never. "You know she's in love with you."

"What are you trying to say?"

She noted he was no longer denying it. "You don't ask a woman who's in love with you for favors—especially if that favor is cooking dinner for another woman." Tara set the piece of glass on the table. "Did she know she was making this for me?" Danny dropped his head. Did this give Tara a reason to search Alanna's room? Probably not.

Danny stood, and began to pace. "It was an *accident.*"

"Or she tried to kill me."

"She couldn't have known you were going to eat that piece. It could have been me. And according to you, she's in love with me—"

"You know she is—"

"Which means it was an *accident*."

Tara sighed. "I hope you're right."

"I am. I'll talk to her. If I think there's anything fishy about this—I'll tell you."

Tara laughed despite the uneasy feeling gnawing at her. "Very funny."

He reached for a bottle of whiskey on the counter. "How about a nip?"

Tara accepted. They took their nips of whiskey over to the sofa near the fire. Once again Tara brought up her meeting with Carrig Murray.

This time he listened intently. "You're saying two other items are missing?"

"Yes—we've located the pig now, but there's also a cast-iron harp he promised Grace Quinn, and a stone slab with the face of a woman, that whoever this D or G is—maybe George—" She sighed. "Do you think he threw those out to sea as well?"

Danny frowned. "Why is Carrig being so secretive?"

"Nobody here likes me."

"He said this friend—presumably George—owned something that once belonged to him?"

Tara nodded. "An old theatre light. Does that ring any bells?"

"It neither rings any bells nor lights any bulbs," Danny said. "But people were always asking Johnny for things. I'd say he's bought something for nearly every local in Galway at one point or the other. I'm not sure how any of it will help us find Johnny."

"Could Johnny have rowed all the way out to Inis Mór?"

Danny contemplated this. "It's not just the bay you're crossing, but the ocean. It can be rough enough in the commuter ferries. Johnny liked to fish like the lot of us around here. But he wasn't one of the professionals. If Johnny tried to row his boat to the Aran Islands—" He let the sentence hang.

"But we know Johnny was thinking of going there before he disappeared. That's something at least." She thought of Alanna's room above the mill. "Does Johnny have a key for the upstairs flat?"

"Alanna's flat?"

Technically it wasn't hers. It was Johnny's. "Yes."

"Why?"

She sighed. Danny seemed protective of Alanna. "Grace Quinn said that Johnny thought Alanna might have been stealing from him."

"And you want to break into her room and find out?"

"It's not breaking in if you have a key."

"It's trespassing."

"It wasn't a sliver of glass. It was a shard."

"An accident," Danny repeated. "I'd bet me life on it."

"It's not just that. She seems pretty hostile." *Like her father.*

"She can be a bit moody alright. She's a woman, isn't she?" He flashed a grin.

"Hell hath no fury like a woman scorned."

"Are you saying I scorned her?"

Tara simply stared at him.

"Listen. You've got the wrong end of the stick." He ran his fingers through his hair.

"Then give me the right end."

He groaned. "I hate to talk out of school."

Whatever he had to say, he didn't relish spilling secrets. Tara liked that about him. "It won't leave this room," Tara said. *Unless I feel someone is in danger.*

"Alanna wasn't cooking alone. I believe she was on a date."

This was news. "With who?"

"Hamlet."

"Hamlet?"

"Correct. As in the *actress* who plays Hamlet."

"Oh."

"Yes," Danny said with a wink. "I'm back to being unloved." His grin was back.

Tara could have sworn that Alanna was in love with Danny. "Why are you assuming it was a date?"

"Just a feeling. Besides. Why on earth would she want to steal architectural items from the place where she lives?"

"What if she was trying to drive Johnny out?"

"By stealing?"

"Driving him mad . . ."

"You think she'd be cheeky enough to hide the stolen items in her room?"

"It couldn't hurt to look." Some people stole just for the thrill.

"It could hurt. It could hurt *her.*" They were at an impasse. Tara fell silent. Danny looked around the cottage. "It's strange to be in here."

"Do you think he'd mind that I'm staying here?"

"He must have known you were coming." At first Tara didn't know why he said that. She caught him staring at the space on the wall where her name had been scrawled. He caught her staring at him. "The cleaning crew sent me a photo." He stood and went over to the spot. "Here?"

"Yes," Tara said. "In blood."

"Emmet's blood?"

Tara nodded again. "I assume so." It was horrific.

"Why?" Danny wondered out loud. "What was he trying to tell you?"

"Warn me? To get away?"

"Emmet was already dead. Who was he worried about?"

"The killer," Tara said. "Assuming it wasn't Johnny."

"But how does writing your name do anything to warn you?"

"I don't know. I didn't even come into the cabin. But *had* I come into the cabin and seen my name—I think it would have made me run."

Danny continued to stare at the wall. "He knew you were coming."

Tara went to the window. She didn't want to look at that wall. "I didn't tell him I was coming. And as far as I know, my mother hadn't spoken to him in years." *And yet somehow, he—or someone—knew.* "I wish I knew what really happened here. What he'd been trying to tell me."

Danny sighed and glanced at the floor. "This would only take a few days. We could wait for a spell of nice weather and move all the furniture onto the lawn."

"Go ahead and order the flooring," Tara said. "I'll use my credit card. I don't have access to Johnny's accounts."

"I'll get you a good deal." He moved in closer. They stared at each other. She wondered if he was thinking about kissing her. She wanted him to, but something told her it was a bad idea. They were working together. He was the only person here who seemed to like her. She didn't want to mess that up. She made a point of yawning. Danny took the cue right away.

"I'd better go." He started to put the dishes in the sink.

"I can get those," Tara said.

"It will only take a minute and I'll be out of your hair." He began to do the dishes. Now she really wanted to kiss him. "I could never come in here when Johnny was around."

"Why is that?"

"The mess. The pile of dishes always in the sink. I told him to hire someone to do his washing, but he was too prideful."

Tara tried to remember her first entrance into the cottage. She didn't remember a pile of dirty dishes. Then again, her eyes were glued to her name splashed across the back wall. Even so. She had an eye for spaces. She would have noticed an inordinate amount of dirty dishes. Had Johnny recently gone from being a slob to being neat? If so—why the change? "I think the kitchen was tidy when I went in."

Danny cocked his head. "That's a first."

"Do you think the crime scene cleanup crew would have washed dirty dishes?" The minute it came out of her mouth she heard how ridiculous it sounded.

Danny stopped and looked at her. "No. I don't."

"Me neither."

Danny shrugged. "Maybe he hired someone after all. Or finally got around to washing them."

It was a bit puzzling, but there was no use wasting time on it. If he had hired a person to clean, they hadn't come forward. She'd keep her eyes and ears open. Danny finished the dishes, and soon Tara was holding open the door for him. "Thank you." She reached for him and gave him a hug. He held on to her for a beat too long. She pulled back.

He smiled down at her. "For what?"

"The fishing. The meal."

"You almost choked to death on a piece of glass."

"I can still be polite."

Danny threw his head back and laughed. "Are you free on Friday? All day?"

Was he asking her on a date? "Why?"

"I'm getting a group together to go to Leisure-land."

"Leisureland?"

"It's in Salthill. Rides, and games, and burgers, and the sea."

"What's the occasion?"

"It's summer, Miss America. Remember summer?"

She laughed. "Barely."

"See? This murder has our customers on edge. It would be a nice way to keep them loyal. And it wouldn't hurt to have a bit of *craic*."

Not a date, but Tara liked the sound of it. Maybe she could also learn more about what was going on around here. "Could I invite some people?"

"Like who?"

She shrugged like she hadn't given it any thought at all. "Rose, Alanna, Ben Kelly, Carrig Murray, and Grace Quinn?"

Danny's eyes narrowed. "In other words, you want to round up the suspects." He really was sharp. She blinked and tried to look innocent. "Do you really think Grace Quinn could be a killer?"

"She knew my mother," Tara said. "She might have *other* answers I'm looking for."

Danny registered that but stayed silent. "And you think you'll get them by inviting her to the fair?"

"I'm just trying to be a good neighbor."

"Good luck getting Grace to leave the inn. I've only seen her do that for bingo night."

Danny was already gone when Tara realized she forgot to tell him about the stem without a rose that someone left by the door. It was a good thing she hadn't. When she went back out to have a second look at it, it was gone.

Chapter 12

Leisureland, in the seaside town of Salthill, was abuzz with sugar and grease, and laughter and screams, and colorful blinking lights and rides that twirled and jerked, all encapsulated by a single word: summer. All the folks on Tara's list had agreed to the day out, including Rose, who had sat at the back of the small bus they had chartered and hadn't engaged in any conversation. Tara was determined to change that by the day's end.

Alanna was dressed in a short skirt and tank top, and Tara had a pretty good idea why. Her eyes were a heat-seeking device and the target was Danny. If she was dating another woman, she was doing a good job of pretending to be infatuated with Danny O'Donnell.

And if Alanna had *accidentally* cooked a piece of salmon with a shard of glass in it, she was certainly waiting a long time to apologize. Maybe Danny hadn't mentioned it to her. Otherwise, shouldn't she be receiving something along the sorry-I-almost-killed-you lines? Tara made a mental note to never turn her back to the girl.

Ben Kelly went straight for a carnival dart game, followed by muscular young men from his boxing ring. They were all such compact athletes, so much bounce. Tara wanted to take a nap just looking at them. She noted how they excluded Alanna, who could probably outpunch all of them.

Tara slipped in behind Ben Kelly when Danny was preoccupied. She wanted to observe the suspects without anyone's watchful gaze.

Ben Kelly threw dart after dart, hitting the bulls-eye. His crowd of aspiring boxers whooped, and the kid manning the booth grew more petrified with each cheap stuffed animal he was forced to turn over.

"You're really good at that," Tara said, stepping up.

His eyes flicked over her. "T'anks. You wouldn't be wantin' one, would you?"

She stared at the hideous blue gorilla. "I'm good."

A group of young women strolled by and Ben Kelly tossed the stuffed animals to them. They screeched and giggled, and Ben grinned and nodded, his eyes trailing them as they swished away, all hips and hair. Tara wondered what Alanna would think of her father, not only *not* saving one for her, but shamelessly flirting with women young enough to be his daughters. And he was accusing Johnny Meehan of being a letch? *Hello, pot, kettle here . . .*

"I stopped by your boxing ring the other day," Tara said. "I left you a note."

Ben Kelly didn't make eye contact with her. "I'm going to get a burger. If you want to follow me and have a chat, I won't stop you."

Her stomach growled at the mention of a burger, and she followed, silently reprimanding herself for reacting like one of Pavlov's dogs. Then again she hadn't eaten all day, unless coffee could be counted as a food group. She had decided to pace herself with the blueberry scones that were as big as a baby's head. She only had one set of clothes with her, and she wasn't keen to size up.

The line was sufficiently long to allow Tara to chat up Ben Kelly. Tara was trying to figure out how to get his alibi without the cliché *Where were you on the morning of . . .*

Maybe she'd start with the question he didn't seem to want to answer. "Did you get my note the other day?"

This time Ben Kelly did make eye contact, and his look was so searing Tara took a step back. "You're actually going to cop to it?"

"Excuse me?"

"You think sticking gum to a man's door is a polite thing to do?"

"I'm so sorry." Darn. She'd forgotten about that. Ben Kelly certainly held a grudge. "I didn't want the note to get lost."

He shook his head. "What do you want?"

"I've heard from a lot of people that you weren't happy with my uncle. And that you've been trying to get him to sell the mill."

He stared straight ahead at the men flipping burgers inside the truck, his fists clenched at his sides. "It's the perfect spot for a boxing school. I offered him good money."

"Were you angry that he wouldn't sell?"

"Angry enough to kill him, is that what you're getting at?"

"Why would you say that? My uncle is a missing person, not a murder victim." *Unless you know something we don't?* A shiver ran through Tara despite the midday heat.

Ben Kelly wiped his brow with his hand, then wiped his hand on his shorts. "Yes, I was angry. He was a stubborn old man."

Tara started. "*Was?*"

Ben sighed. "Don't go reading into that. *Is.* He is a stubborn old man."

Had it been an innocent error, or did he know something sinister had happened to Johnny? "How are you any different?"

He registered the dig with a calm blink. "He could move that warehouse of junk anywhere. With the money I was offering he could have retired."

"It doesn't sound like he wanted to retire."

"He was just doing it to spite me."

"Was he now?" Ben Kelly was one of those people who thought everything was about him. "Have you been to the warehouse? You might be surprised that it's well organized and vibrant."

"Are you joking me? It's a junk heap."

"It's hardly a junk heap."

"That's the American point of view, is it?"

He was getting under her skin. "Who do you think you are to demand someone else move their established business?"

"Now just a minute—"

"One my family has owned for a very long time." Tara didn't know where it came from, this passion, this family connection, but it bubbled up in her as real as anything she'd ever known. Perhaps that was the power of family, a connection forged by blood and DNA, a bond that held even if you'd never met face-to-face.

"Who do you think *you* are? You show up out of nowhere, Miss America, and think you have a right to speak to me like that?" He shook his head. "Bugger off."

Lovely. Tara was starting to feel sorry for Alanna.

"Where were you the morning Emmet was killed?" Sometimes a cliché developed for a reason. He didn't seem in the mood to give much up.

He laughed, then stopped when he saw she was serious. "I was at the ring. If you want, I can give you the names of ten lads I was training." He stepped forward into her personal space. "I have a sweaty, unshakable alibi."

"Were all your students in attendance that morning?"

"What is it you do for a living, Ms. Meehan?"

Tara took a deep breath. "I'm an interior designer."

"I'm afraid I have no need for your services. But if you keep questioning me like you're a detective sergeant, we're going to have a problem."

"I'm trying to find my uncle. He could be hurt, or not in his right mind."

"Oh, rest assured he is not in his right mind."

"What if it were a member of your family who was missing?"

His cold eyes flicked over her. "When this business is all over, I'll extend the same offer to you. It's a solid price."

"I hope you're not actually suggesting I sell the mill right out from under my missing uncle?"

"Your uncle is a murderer. He's not going to come back. If he does, it will be in handcuffs."

"Why are you so sure he did it?"

"Because, unlike you, I know the man. He was losing his mind. And Emmet Walsh was furious. He stormed up the hill that morning and Johnny must have panicked."

They were next in line. Tara paid for Ben Kelly's three cheeseburgers and curried chips, plus one of her own. Instead of thanking her, he glowered. "Why are you doing that?"

"To make up for the gum."

He barely grunted, then shoved a cheeseburger into his mouth. Tara watched in horror as he finished it in two bites before starting on the next one. He laughed. "Start boxing and you too can have this metabolism." He started to walk away.

"Why is Alanna living above the mill?" she asked.

He turned, and from his scowl he wasn't happy about it. "I told her to stay away from that man."

"Was she keeping an eye on him for you?"

"You heard me, did you not? I wouldn't be wanting her anywhere near him, now."

"Because she told you he was leering at her?"

"If you know so much, why are you talking to me?"

"I'm just trying to get my facts straight."

"I guess you didn't bring us here to get to know us."

That one hit its mark. "I did," she said. "I'm sorry. Enjoy the fair." She could feel his eyes on her as she walked away. She took a bite of the cheeseburger. It was perfect. Maybe she should just relax and enjoy the fair too.

While her uncle was out there somewhere. Alone, and probably afraid. Without a family member left in the world but her. After that, the burger lost most of its taste.

* * *

Carrig Murray was tossing coins into the mouths of tiny bottles. His aim was spot-on. Didn't he claim to have problems with his sight? He wasn't wearing glasses. Had that been a lie?

"Great aim." He whirled around and stared at Tara. It took him a moment to place her. "Ms. Meehan." He grinned. "This was a wonderful idea. T'ank you."

"You're welcome. I thought you were nearsighted."

"Pardon?" He began to blink rapidly.

"You couldn't read the print in the notebook I tried to show you—the D, or G, next to my uncle's note about going to Inis Mór? But here you are successfully tossing coins into the tiny mouths of bottles from several feet away."

He squinted but this time out of confusion. "I've been to the eye doctor since," he said. "They sorted me out."

"What's the name of the eye doctor?"

"Why?"

"I could use a checkup."

"I'm terrible with names. I'll be wanting to get back to you on dat."

"You're not wearing glasses."

"Contact lenses. Little miracles they are."

"It's odd that for a director, who I assume needs to read scripts all day, you only recently sorted out your eyesight."

"What does my eyesight have to do with the price of tea in China?"

"Can you please answer my question about why Johnny wrote the letter D, or as you suggested, G, in his notebook after Inis Mór?"

"I suggested, did I? Probably just trying to be polite. Why on earth would I have any idea what your uncle was trying to write?" His blinking continued. Drops of sweat beaded on his broad forehead.

Tara closed the step between them. "Who were you talking to that day on the phone?"

He retrieved a handkerchief from his pocket and wiped his brow. "I don't remember. Why?"

She shrugged. "I was just curious. It sounded like a heated argument. I believe you said his name was George." She was taking a risk, pushing him, but he was hiding something, and she was curious.

He glared at her. "Previously you stated you hadn't heard a word of it."

Shoot. He had her there. "I didn't want you to think I was purposefully eavesdropping. It's not my fault if you have a booming voice." She shrugged. "Can't help that I'm curious."

He suddenly straightened up, his face hardening. The fear was gone, and now he was going to act tough. Which man was the real Carrig Murray? The nervous one with bad eyesight, or the seething director? Why did she get the feeling there was more than one production he was directing?

"Don't get too curious," he said with a wink. "Just remember what it did to the cat." With that he strode away from her without so much as a backward glance. One thing was clear. The mysterious friend he had been speaking to on the phone could most likely be found on Inis Mór.

Tara was cutting through the crowd, trying to spot Rose when she felt a hand on her waist and a male voice in her ear. "There you are." Danny.

God, that Irish accent. She could see why it was named Sexiest Accent in the World, like every year in a row. It was hard not to melt. Even as a young girl she was furious she didn't have her mother's beautiful lilting accent. *I don't sound like you!* Many a night she literally threw a fit over it. *Ah, pet, you don't want to sound like me. You sound like you. Feisty, wonderful, you. Now put the kettle on and leave me to a bit of peace, will you, pet?* The memory made her smile.

She turned to see Danny, dimple flashing in the sun. "Why do I get the feeling you're not really here to have a good time?"

"I am," she said. "I ate a cheeseburger."

He laughed. "You had a cheeseburger with Ben Kelly, and then had a heated chat with Carrig Murray."

"Heated?"

"I could see the steam comin' off him from over here."

"Just being neighborly."

"What did you learn about our suspects?"

"I don't know what you mean."

"Am I a suspect?"

She made the mistake of maintaining eye contact with him. There was a twinkle there, and a bit of a challenge. And then there was that other thing—that *current*. She found herself looking at his mouth, still sporting an easygoing smile. God, that zing, that tug of desire reflected in his eyes. It could get a girl in trouble. She took a physical step back and looked away.

"Why don't we go on a ride?" he said.

Was that meant to have a double meaning? Or was she losing her mind over his handsome face and cute

Irish accent? *A player. Oh my God. I'm losing it.* Thank God Grace Quinn wasn't here to witness it. Tara turned red as she remembered Grace Quinn actually *was* here. Her head whipped around to see if she could spot her. Was she hiding behind a puff of cotton candy, spying on her?

Oh, no. Was I smiling? Every time she was around Danny her mouth spontaneously stretched open. It was embarrassing. But it wasn't her fault. It was his. That charm of his was a deadly weapon. "That's okay. I just ate."

He grabbed her hand and started pulling her along. "The dodge-ems."

"The dodge-ems?" She looked ahead where colorful cars were slamming into each other. "Oh. Bumper cars."

"Bumper cars," he said, making fun of her and lightly bumping her hip. "Your stomach can take that at least."

From the glint in his eye, Danny wasn't going to take no for an answer. "I'm a terrible driver," she joked as he led the way.

"I'm counting on it."

She had to admit, the bumper cars, or dodge-ems, were fun. There was nothing like slamming into complete strangers to get out a little aggression. Danny, she noticed, liked to sneak up and slam into her at the last minute. She turned the wheel, preparing to get him back, when suddenly Alanna was in a car coming straight for her. The look in her eye was unmistakable: unadulterated rage.

Tara's car took the blow, her head snapped back,

and her ears started to ring—or was that just the sound of Alanna's laughter echoing through her head? Alanna zoomed her little car after Danny. Tara stepped on the gas, even as her brain told her not to be so childish, and she made a beeline for the back of Alanna's shiny red bumper car. She slammed into it at the top speed allowed. "Good one," Danny said, flashing a smile, and forcing Alanna to laugh it off. "She needs to get you back for that sliver of glass in the salmon."

So he *had* mentioned it. Alanna's eyes widened as she stared at Tara. "Sliver?" Tara said. "It was a shard." Alanna continued to stare without a word. Adrenaline pumped through Tara. She was not going to get into it with the girl here and now. *Did she try to kill me?* She maneuvered her car to the exit and stepped out on wobbly legs. She glanced back at Alanna, who was zooming in on Danny again. The girl was absolutely obsessed. Did Danny realize the extent of it? Had they seen *Fatal Attraction* out here? That girl was one pot away from boiling a bunny. Maybe it was time Alanna found a new place to live. Tara didn't want to deal with her jealousy. Would it do any good to tell her that he just wasn't into her?

Probably not. Was it as simple as her being young and in love? Or had she been mucking about the mill at night? If so—why?

Her alibi would be easy enough to check—she claimed to be at cookery school. She remembered Johnny's notation in his book. Tara was going to have to visit her instructor, find out if Johnny had done the same thing, and why.

Danny caught up with Tara again, and tried to get her to go on the Ferris wheel. Tara looked up at the seat resting at the very top, swaying gently, and she thought about heights, and she thought about falling, and she thought about her son. She jerked her hand back, startling Danny. "No," she said. "Never." *I wasn't there to catch him.*

He took it all in, the flash of pain across her face. "Okay," he said. He put his hands up. "Sorry."

"Are you scared of heights?" Alanna belted out. Suddenly they were all standing behind her—Carrig, and Ben Kelly, and Alanna, and Grace, and Rose, and Danny. It was her turn to feel under the spotlight, to have sweat gathering on her brow.

"Leave her be," Danny scolded her. Alanna was stung, you could see it, but she didn't say another word. Tara was so grateful. Grief still had a way of grabbing her and squeezing hard, and even she was surprised at how it manifested. She felt always on the edge of a nervous breakdown. Now with her mother's death and the murder—

"I'm sorry," Alanna said, stepping forward. She took Tara's hand. "I've been so mean. I don't know why I'm like this."

It sounded honest. Had Tara been too hard on the girl? "That's okay."

Alanna put her hand on her heart. "And I'm so mortified about the piece of glass in your salmon."

"Oh," Tara said. "It was quite a shock."

"I was drinking a glass of wine. It shattered while I was cooking. I guess one of the pieces fell into the fish without me knowing."

"That's what Danny thought." *Exactly. Had they rehearsed the details?* She had to sit down on a nearby bench. She felt dizzy. It must be the heat. And that twirling Ferris wheel. *Make it stop.*

"I'll sit with you," Grace Quinn said. "Off with ye." Grace waited until everyone was gone to slip her something. Tara looked down. It was a letter. Tara started to open it. She felt Grace's fingers dig into her hand.

"Don't read it here," she said. "Put it in your hand-bag for later."

"What is it?"

"It's the last time I heard from your mother," Grace said. Tara's heart began to tap dance. Just the thought of a new letter written by her mother was like a little gift. Unless it wasn't a happy letter. When was it written? What did it say? Tara slipped it into her purse and scanned the fairgrounds.

"Thank you."

"What are you going to do if he doesn't come back? How long are you going to stay?"

Tara turned to Grace. "I hope you don't think me rude. But every time an Irish person asks me that—it feels like rejection. Like you can't wait for me to go home."

Grace sighed. "Your mother wasn't happy here," she said, patting Tara on the knee. "And you are your mother's daughter."

Tara was figuring out how to respond, and what Grace's true agenda was, when she saw a flash of long salt-and-pepper hair disappear into the fun house. This was her chance to talk to Rose.

"Nice speaking with you, Grace," she said. She gave a friendly wave and took off for the fun house.

Chapter 13

As soon as she entered the fun house, Tara was bombarded with her reflection in a wall of distorted mirrors. In the first panel, she was so thin it looked as if her skeletal body could slip through a keyhole. In the next, she was so fat, it looked as if she'd burst through the walls. She stared at her stretched-out cheeks, her enormous thighs. *This is me, but not me.* Definitely no more scones. Or scones every other day—that was reasonable. It was dark in the hallways between frights, and there was no sign of Rose. All she could hear were a few faint screams from within and the relentless drip of water. Striped colors swirled on the walls and the floor, making you feel as if the room had suddenly tilted. Tara stumbled. Piped laughter filtered through as she fumbled in the dark. A screech sounded as the shadow of a monkey suddenly swung along the wall. She put her hand on the rail and felt something squishy. Despite herself, she gave a little scream. The sound of thunder boomed, and for a split second the place lit up with what was supposed to mimic a flash of lightning. Hovering directly in front of Tara was a disembodied face, with flashing red eyes. She screamed again. These places had grown sophisticated since she was a kid. She tried to pick up speed, just wanting it to be over. She could see an exit sign up ahead. She bolted for it. Forget Rose, she'd find her at the caravan later. She was almost at the door with the exit sign above it when she sensed someone behind her. Before she could turn around, she felt a gloved hand slap over her mouth. She could smell the thick leather. Was it part of the act? They weren't allowed to touch people, were they? She immediately started to squirm, but the hand over her mouth tightened.

Why are they wearing gloves? She felt herself being pulled backwards, into the middle of the fun house. Tara wanted to scream, or bite, but the hand was clamped too tight over her mouth. She tried to kick but she couldn't without losing her balance. It was too dark to see a single thing. She stopped struggling until the hand over her mouth relaxed slightly. And then she bit the hand as hard as she could.

The hand jerked away, and the attacker shoved her, hard, into a new group of people swarming their way into the fun house. At first they thought she was part of the experience, squealing as her body stumbled in front of them, jumping out of the way. Tara landed on the sticky floor, slamming her lip into the concrete.

"Are you okay?" Someone grabbed under her arms and hauled her up. She stared into Carrig Murray's face.

"Someone attacked me," she said. Carrig was not

wearing gloves, but how had he gotten there so fast? Could he be her attacker?

"Hold on to me," he said. "I'll get you out."

She hesitated, then took his arm. She thought about running ahead, but it was too dark, her lip stung, and she'd twisted her ankle on the way down. By the time she got out of the fun house and caught her breath, whoever attacked her was either long gone or standing right beside her, pretending to be concerned. He nodded to her lip. "You're going to need some ice on that."

"Where were you," she asked, "the morning Emmet Walsh was killed?"

He laughed as if she was joking, then stopped. He took a step toward her. "You have a funny way about you," he said.

If she searched his pockets would she find a pair of gloves? Who had he been talking to when she came back into the theatre that day? *I didn't tell her a t'ing and neither will you* . . . What wasn't he telling her? What were several people not telling her?

"Enjoy the fun house?" She whirled around to find Rose standing in front of her, black hair blowing in the wind.

"I'll leave you to it," Carrig said, then hurried off before she could figure out a legitimate reason to pat him down.

"Someone attacked me in there," Tara said. Her hands were still shaking.

"I warned you," Rose said, adjusting a canvas bag slung over her body. "If you stay here, this is only the beginning."

Suddenly Tara thought of the cans of paint she'd seen near the caravan the first day she'd arrived. Was

Rose the one who painted GO HOME YANKEE on the barn? "I heard you were dating my uncle. I want to talk to you about him."

Rose's eyes darted around the fair. "Not now. Not here."

"When?" Tara asked. "Where?"

"My caravan," Rose said. "Tomorrow morning. I'll read your cards."

Was this a bait and switch? A scam? Rose looked genuinely frightened. And even if it was a scam, Tara would pay for a reading just to get a chance to talk to her. She did know things—real things—about her uncle. "I'll be there," she said. "What time?"

"Half eight," Rose said. "And not a minute later."

When Danny caught up with Tara, she was still shaking. Reluctantly, she told him what happened. "We have to call the guards," he said.

She shook her head. "I'm fine."

"It's not just about you. If there's someone hiding out in the fun house, waiting to attack women, we need to sound the alarm."

Oh, God, he was right. She nodded. Danny took out his mobile and called 999. He bought her a lemonade, and sat her on a nearby bench. "Wait here." He started to walk away.

"Where are you going?"

"Where do you t'ink?" He headed for the fun house. Tara sighed, leaned back and tried to ignore the flush of pleasure rippling through her from Danny morphing into the protector. She was no damsel in distress, but still, she'd been alone so long it was a nice feeling. Danny came back, shaking his head. "They're gone." They sat in silence until the guards arrived.

There were two of them and they started right in. "What kind of gloves?"

"Thick. Leather," Tara said. The memory gave her goose bumps.

"Just like everyone wears in the peak of summer," Danny deadpanned. He seemed to be taking this more seriously than the guards, although they did shut down the fun house, and nearby rubbish bins were being checked.

"There are no cameras inside," the guard said, "but we'll be posting guards there when it reopens and will tack a warning sign at the door so that no one goes in alone."

When they were done questioning her, Danny took her hand and led her to the waiting charter bus.

"You're asking a lot of questions around here," he said quietly. "Are you sure that's a good idea?"

"What if they never find my uncle? What if they never catch the murderer?"

"You can't control that."

"But everyone has made their mind up about him. The guards are only looking for him because they think he killed Emmet Walsh."

"And you feel—what? Some kind of family obligation?"

"Yes. I do."

"You won't be good to anyone if you get yourself killed."

"But it means I'm on to something—don't you think?"

"You're saying whoever attacked you has something to do with Emmet's murder?"

"Maybe someone is worried about what I'll find out if I keep looking."

"Even more reason to stop. You're not trained for this." Danny's voice was tinged with worry.

Maybe he was right. Maybe everyone was right. Maybe she should start thinking about booking a flight back home.

That evening, Tara settled onto the sofa in the cottage with her cup of tea and scone, watching the fire crackle, holding the envelope from her mother in her hands. She'd probably never get an opportunity like this again, a chance to connect with her mom by reading her own words. She noted the date on the envelope. It was mailed three years ago in June. It took Tara a moment to realize why the date was significant, and when she did she dropped the envelope onto the coffee table and stared at it as if it could strike out at her. She knew what the letter was. What it said. Why her mother had sent it. Had she sent one to Johnny as well?

Yes. She would have. Why was Grace showing this to her? Did her mother send a follow-up? Yes. She would have done that too. Tara couldn't face it, she didn't have to read it. Why were people so *awkward*?

She was tempted to storm over to the inn with the letter and confront Grace's cruelty. Was this Grace's last-ditch attempt to convince Tara to go home? She had another think coming. Maybe there would be a day, a year, a decade when Tara could bring herself to read it. Today was not that day. It took everything she had not to burn the letter in the fireplace. Instead she tucked it onto one of Johnny's shelves behind an old tin. She had her card-reading with Rose in the morning, then she planned on visiting the tattoo parlor and Alanna's cookery school.

Rain began to beat on the windows, making her sleepy. She heard a crack outside the window. Was there someone at the door? She looked around. There was no poker by the fireplace that could double as a weapon. Forty-six of them back at the warehouse and he couldn't bring one home? There were no cast-iron items either. Tara was forced to get a knife from the kitchen. She held it in front of her, heart pounding, as she headed for the window near the door. She turned off the inside lights, waited for her eyes to adjust, and peeked out the curtain. She saw the horselike body pacing in front of the door. She nearly crumpled with relief. "Hound." She unlocked the door and to her surprise he trotted right in, and immediately curled up on a rug near the fireplace. She double-checked the locks on the door, curled up on the sofa, and stared at the dancing flames until they, the beating rain, and the gentle snore of the wolfhound, swiftly lulled her to sleep.

Tara arrived at the caravan early. Most of the paint cans were still lined up where she'd first seen them. There were six in total. But there was a gap between the third and fifth ones. She walked over and peered down. All that was left was a ring where the can once sat, and a faint circle of black. Whoever had painted the side of her mill had taken the paint can from here. Anyone could have walked up and snatched one. Did that exclude Rose? Should Tara assume that was too obvious? Or was Rose flaunting the fact that she had done it? After all, the rest of the cans were still here, hiding in plain sight.

The door to the caravan swung open at exactly half eight. Rose led Tara directly to her built-in table, where a stack of tarot cards waited. The interior was filled with candles, and beaded curtains, and little pots of African violets. Tara slid into the booth and waited.

Rose had Tara cut the deck three times, then laid the cards facedown in the shape of a cross.

"Your mother is here," she said. The lines on her face looked like the road map of an interesting life.

The words startled Tara. "What?"

"I feel her around you."

Tara concentrated on her breathing. If Rose was a con artist, she was going right for Tara's wounds. She had to be careful not to let her anger show. Everyone knew by now about Tara and the fact that she had come here to spread her mother's ashes and meet her uncle. If she mentioned her son, Tara was afraid of what she might do. "What about my uncle?" she said, her tone coming out harsh. "Do you feel him around?"

Rose's eyes grazed over the cards. "Things are not as they seem."

"What does that mean?"

Irritation flicked across Rose's face. "A message," she said. "He's left you a message."

Her name written in blood on his wall. "What is it?" Tara wasn't going to give her anything, especially encouragement. This woman knew something, she was sure of it.

"You're not safe here." Her eyes flicked around the caravan as if someone might be looking. Except for the few candles and beaded curtains and violets, it looked like the inside of any RV a typical family planned on driving around the country. "I see a romance brewing," Rose said when she turned over the next card. "Is that what's keeping you here?"

Tara felt heat come to her cheeks. "Speaking of romance, I heard you were sleeping with my uncle."

Rose stopped moving, stopped blinking; she seemed for a time to stop breathing. When she looked up again there were tears in her eyes. "They did this."

"Who is they?"

"This town."

"The entire town did this?"

"All his enemies. Wanting him gone. Ben Kelly. Harassing him about the mill. Grace Quinn, always obsessed with the past. Carrig Murray and his blasted . . ." She stopped, as if startled she'd been speaking at all.

Tara leaned in. "Carrig Murray and his blasted *what*?"

Rose's lips moved but words did not come out. She shook her head.

"I'm trying to find my uncle," Tara said. "My blood. Do you understand?"

Rose nodded again. "Productions. His blasted *productions.*"

Tara got the feeling she was not talking about the all-female version of *Hamlet*. The reading of the cards had been abandoned. Rose knew something. She wanted to tell. Tara just had to find the right way in.

"The guards," Tara said. "They think Johnny murdered Emmet Walsh. What do you think?" Rose shook her head, fear stamped on her face. "Then *help* me. What do you know?" *What are you hiding?*

Rose swallowed. "Two days before Emmet was murdered, Johnny came to see me. He said he ran into Carrig and was shocked at the treatment he received."

"What treatment?"

Rose shook her head. "He was raving. Hard to understand. He thought everyone hated him and was plotting against him." She glanced around again. "I thought he was overreacting. Now it seems as if he was right."

"Are you saying Carrig killed Emmet?"

"I'm saying he has something to do with this whole thing. Somebody was out to get Johnny, or *several* somebodys. There are too many suspects."

"Who are the other suspects?"

"Ben Kelly is another. Plotting against him. Demanding Johnny sell him the mill."

Tara knew she would only get so far questioning Ben Kelly. But it was starting to look like another visit to Carrig Murray was in order. Or maybe she should speak with some of the actors in his play. Hamlet, for one. She stood to leave, then turned to Rose. "Did you know you're missing a can of black paint?"

Rose's face remained calm. "It's not my paint."

"Whose is it?"

"Danny O'Donnell's." Her head jerked to the side. "The gypsy painted on the outside of the carvan?"

"It's gorgeous."

Rose smiled as if she knew a secret. "That's Danny's work."

"Danny painted that?" She couldn't believe it. He never mentioned he was an artist. And quite a talented one. Was he doing anything with it? She knew so little about him. Rose's mouth was still turned up in a smirk. Tara wanted to slap it off. "Do you know if he came back for the black paint?"

"I wish he'd take the rest of it. The cans are barely covered when it rains. I don't like chemicals soaking into the ground."

Tara thought it should be the least of her worries, not to mention Rose wasn't answering Tara's question directly. Was that an answer in itself? Why would Danny paint GO HOME YANKEE on the side of the mill, only to be the one to power-wash it off? Was he playing some kind of game? Maybe Carrig wasn't the only devilish one in town.

The devil you know . . .

"I think you should go now," Rose said, gesturing to the door.

Tara sat back down. "Do you think my uncle is still alive?"

Rose pursed her lips, then nodded.

"Where do you think he is?"

"I don't know. I think he's hiding. I think he feels he's in danger here."

"His boat is missing. What if he died at sea?" The fear poured out of Tara before she could stop it.

Tears came into Rose's eyes. "I tried to warn him. Just like I'm warning you. Is it my fault if no one is listening?"

Her plea seemed genuine. And for the first time— vulnerable. "Tell me about the last time you saw my uncle. Leave nothing out." Shame crept into Rose's eyes. "Please," Tara begged. "I might be the only one trying to help him."

Rose sighed. "I'll put on the kettle," she said. When they were situated with tea and digestive biscuits, Rose began to talk.

Chapter 14

It was three days before the murder. Rose found Johnny Meehan pacing in front of her caravan. "He was wild-eyed with fury. Someone was stealing from his mill. He was sure of it. It started with a few minor things here or there. A poker for the fire. There were forty-seven in the collection. And then one day there were forty-six. A stained-glass window from Italy. One of his favorite pieces, one that would fetch a tidy sum. Missing one week after he'd hung it in a prominent spot in the mill. And then a lion's-head door knocker. He began to stay awake at the mill, never going home, never going to sleep, roaming the grounds like a deranged security guard."

"Why didn't he just get a security system?"

Rose shook her head. "It wasn't his way."

"Did he find anyone?"

"He caught Alanna tripping home with a lad one

night," Rose said with a shrug. "I suppose it's not against the law."

Interesting. Would Rose have told her if it was Danny? Or was it okay for lads to trip home to bed with a partner, just not the lasses? Sexism aside—did Alanna have a secret boyfriend? Or had this "lad" been the actress playing Hamlet?

"For a while everything quieted down. Until the banker from Manchester finally agreed to sell the pig. Johnny was over the moon. Traveled there himself. Why, I think that's the only time I ever heard of that Johnny Meehan set foot out of County Galway."

"Because Emmet paid him a lot of money for it?"

"That, and Emmet was obsessed. He was one of Johnny's best customers. Threatened to never buy from him again if he didn't get that pig. Johnny couldn't have that."

"Go on."

Rose explained how Johnny had put Emmet Walsh's cast-iron pig in his office. Right on the desk. He'd locked it up tight. When he returned, only hours later, it was gone. "By the time Johnny came to me, he was spitting mad. Even accused *me* of stealing it."

"Why did he accuse you?"

"He said I was one of the few people who knew about it. He was acting like a nutter. I told him so."

"Who else did he accuse?"

"Danny, of course. He was so angry he quit. Then he accused Alanna. And of course, her father."

"Do you know if he searched Alanna's room at the mill?"

"He did, of course. Didn't find a thing."

"Did he say what he planned on doing next?"

Rose pursed her lips, clasped her hands together tightly. "He was going to dig."

Tara wasn't sure she heard her correctly. "Pardon?"

Rose's eyes radiated fear. "He said he was going to dig and dig and dig until he caught the thievin' bastard." She exhaled. "I tried to read his cards. I've never seen such a sinister reading. Death all around him. But when I told him this—he flew into an even bigger rage. Accused me of purposely giving him a bad reading, bilking him out of his money. I charged him for the reading, 'course I did. But I'm no thief." She slumped in the booth. "I hate knowing our last words were so cross. I should have known something bad was brewing. I should have stopped him."

"Do you know where Emmet Walsh lived?"

"'Course I do."

"Can you write down the address?"

"What do you think you're going to do? Sneak into his house? You don't think the guards will be all over it?"

Tara sighed. Somehow this murder was connected to all the missing objects. She was relieved that Rose didn't appear to know that the head of the cast-iron pig had been reeled up in the Galway Bay. At least the guards were keeping some things quiet. "Do you know anything about the missing items from the mill? The pig, a cast-iron harp—"

"Harp?" Rose stood, hovering over Tara for a second, then turned and hurried to the back of the caravan. When she came back, slightly out of breath, she was holding a cast-iron harp.

"Where did you get that?" Tara said.

"It was a gift," Rose said.

"Johnny gave it to you?"

"No," Rose said. "That vile woman did."

"What vile woman?"

Rose dropped the harp on the table with a thunk, held her index finger up, then disappeared into the back of the caravan once more. Tara picked up the harp. It was awfully heavy. If someone swung this at a human head, the person would be dead. She hadn't touched it, but she imagined the cast-iron pig had been equally heavy. Was that the murder weapon? She wondered if the guards knew by now. She wished she knew someone there—

What about the young clerk at the Garda station? Breanna Cunningham. She seemed the friendly sort. Maybe Tara could pay her a visit, suggest a social activity. It would be nice to have a female friend of her own age around here.

As she thought through her options, Tara's eyes landed on the pot of African violets on the sill. There was something wedged behind it. She had to stand up to get a good look. There, tucked behind the pot was a pair of gloves. Leather gloves.

Do they belong to Rose? Had she been the one to attack me in the fun house?

Before she could pick them up, the beaded curtains swished and knocked, and Rose returned with a piece of paper in her hand.

Tara must have had a funny look on her face, for Rose stopped in her tracks.

"What the devil is wrong with you now?"

Don't look at the gloves. "Nothing."

"Out with it."

Fine. Tara snatched up the gloves. She smelled them. Unlike the ones in the fun house, these smelled like soil.

"My gardening gloves," Rose said. "What about them?"

"Whoever attacked me in the fun house was wearing leather gloves."

"And you think it's me, do you now?"

"I don't know. You were in there."

"You were following me."

"I saw you go in and I wanted to speak with you."

"You're starting to sound paranoid. Just like your uncle."

"I just think it's odd. Using leather gloves, in the summer, to garden." Tara paused. "When you don't even have a garden."

Rose laughed, a trilling sound that took Tara by surprise. She'd never even seen the woman smile. "I potted that violet m'self."

"I'm just going to come out and ask you. Did you come up behind me in the fun house with those gloves, and slap your hand over my mouth?"

Rose studied her. "I went into the fun house ahead of you. How would I suddenly be behind you, like?"

"It was dark and confusing in there. You could have turned around."

"And why would I do that?"

"Perhaps since I didn't heed your earlier warning, you were trying to drive your point home."

"If that's the case, I don't think it worked."

"You haven't denied it."

"Nor will I."

Tara sighed. This was getting them nowhere. She

glanced at the paper in Rose's hand. "What do you have for me?"

Rose thrust the sheet of paper at her. It was cream-colored stationery. Emerald letters were splashed across the top: Welcome to the Bay Inn. Next to it was a quaint sketch of the inn. "Danny sketched that as well," Rose said.

"He's talented." Tara wondered why he wasn't trying harder to make a living at it, or why he'd never mentioned it. Her eyes went back to the stationery.

"This came with the harp," Rose said.

Tara read the message:

An old harp for the old harpy.

Chapter 15

Grace Quinn was the vile woman. And not only was her harp not missing, she was the one who had given it away, then asked Tara to find it. One explanation, of course, the saddest one, was that Grace Quinn was going senile. The only other plausible explanation was that Grace Quinn was playing some kind of game. But why? And to what end?

Tara didn't want to wait to find out the answers. After leaving the caravan, she made a beeline for the inn. There was no one at the check-in desk. Rose had refused to give her the harp, but Tara had the note in her purse. She was dying to see what Grace would say about it and why she had lied. The parlor doors were shut. It was so silent Tara could hear the ticking of a clock coming from some dusty corner.

"Hello?" She stared at the cubbyholes. All she had to do to get her hands on the key to room 301 was slip behind the counter. "Hello?" she called again.

There was no reply. She would be quick. All she would do is look at the key. She hurried over to it before she could talk herself out of it. Now that she was no longer a guest, there was absolutely no good excuse for why she'd be behind the counter looking for keys. She reached her hand into the cubbyhole for room 301. It was empty. She glanced at all the other boxes. Had the key mistakenly been placed in the wrong slot? Someone could enter at any second; there was no time to search all the boxes.

Was there a guest in room 301 now? Were the plumbers back—fixing another leak? If the silence was any indication, there wasn't a soul in the inn at all. Tara returned to the other side of the counter. She stood there for a few more minutes, debating her options. None of them appealed to her, so she walked out of the inn and headed for her usual café. She would cut back on the scones. *Someday*. Today was not that day.

After a bite at the café, Tara headed for the salvage mill. The weather was holding out, but rain was predicted for the afternoon and evening. Tara was still ruminating over her meeting with Rose. Those leather gloves. Had she rolled them in soil after using them on her in the fun house? Had she left them out deliberately to confuse Tara, or had she forgotten they were there?

There was a note from Danny on the door of the mill. He'd taken Hound for a walk. Tara eyed the red bicycle. She could use some exercise too, especially while the weather was nice. She slipped into Johnny's office and opened his notebook.

Nun's Island Experimental Theatre—Carrig
Murray
Cookery—Talk to A's instructor
Tattoo Shop—Rose
Inis Mór—Talk to D

A trip to the Aran Islands was going to take some
planning. And she didn't want to pop into the cookery school while Alanna was there. So that left the
tattoo shop. But there had to be several in Galway.
Where should she start? She took out her smartphone and googled. There were indeed several to
choose from: Galway Bay Tattoo, G's Tattoo Studio,
Galway Tattoos—Inkfingers . . .

Should she call each one and ask if Johnny Meehan had ever come in for a rose tattoo? Given that he
was wanted for murder, wouldn't that raise a few eyebrows? She was being lazy. This wasn't New York City,
where it could take forever to get from one end of
the city to the other; this was a compact city where
she could easily visit every single tattoo parlor in the
span of a few hours. She would get exercise, be out in
the sun before the rain hit, and have a little ink ad-
venture. She jotted down the addresses, put them
into Google Maps, and planned her route.

The first two shops hadn't yielded anything but
glares and denials. But at the last one they'd pointed
her to one that she hadn't found through googling.
Tattoo Dreams. When Tara checked the address and
realized it was near Alanna's cookery school, her excitement grew.

The bike was hard to pedal, but at least she never

worried about anyone stealing it. She leaned it against the outside of Tattoo Dreams and entered.

The walls were covered with tattoo renderings. There were wolf heads, and geometric sleeves, and vines of flowers attended by a humming bird, and skulls, and the Galway hooker (which was a boat, not a tramp), and faces, and names, and sayings. It was clear this wasn't just body stamping, this was some-one's profession, someone's *art*, not a job. And his name was Stephen Kane.

He was in his thirties, skinny with a long black beard, slicked-back hair, earrings, and sleeve tattoos. A thin ring also pierced his lip. He was edgy, perhaps, or trying to be, but there was a salt-of-the-earth air about him and Tara liked him immediately.

"I care about attention to detail," he told Tara in between clients. "That's the most important thing."

Tara didn't have any tattoos, but standing here, she suddenly knew what her way in would be. She didn't want it to be large, but the more she thought of it, the more she knew. At first she imagined some-thing beautiful yet Irish, like a Celtic knot, or a Celtic cross, or even something written in the Irish lan-guage. But this wasn't for her—this was for *him*, and then she knew.

"Winne-the-Pooh?" he said. "Do you have a photo?"

She brought Winne-the-Pooh up on her phone. She pointed to the name *Pooh* on his red shirt. "I'd like this to say *Thomas* instead."

He raised his eyebrows and nodded.

She got it on her back, just behind her left shoul-der. There was pain, and the buzzing of his needle, and her eyes watered, but she welcomed it. He would be there now, on her back, always with her.

When he was finished, he asked if he could photograph it, then placed a protective plastic cover over the tattoo and told her to try and keep it there for the rest of the day.

"I'm sorry," he said, "if wee Thomas is no longer with us." Tears came to her eyes. She nodded. "I have three young ones m'self. I can't even imagine."

"No," Tara said. "Nor should you." She dug out her purse.

He held up his hands. "It's on me."

"I couldn't."

"I insist."

"Only if I can return the favor."

"Before you go too far, I'm a married man." He winked. "Notice I didn't say *happily.*"

She laughed. It was obvious from the numerous photos displayed throughout the shop, of a beautiful redheaded woman with three children, that he was joking.

"Come to Irish Revivals sometime. Bring the kids. Maybe you can find something you like."

"I wondered if you were any relation," he said.

Tara nodded. "My uncle. You probably know him. He owns the salvage mill."

"Ah. 'Course I do. You're not the first customer to come out of the salvage mill." He winked.

"I know," Tara said. "That's why I came to you."

He nodded, a grin spreading across his face. "I've been waiting to hear the verdict—was it a yes or a no?"

"I'm not sure either," Tara said. *What on earth was he talking about?*

"Did you see the tattoo?"

"The rose?" Tara guessed.

Stephen nodded. "The special-order rose." He winked.

She smiled, wondering what in the heck he was talking about. "I didn't see it."

"Oh. I assumed you had. But you know the story?"

"Bits and pieces," Tara said, still floundering in the dark. "Do you have a photo of the tattoo?"

"Aye."

He turned the album toward her. There was a rendering of a gorgeous red rose. But that's not what had her mouth open, staring. Wrapped around the rose was a glittering diamond ring and next to it a question mark.

This wasn't just a tattoo, it was marriage proposal.

Tara went straight to her favorite café for the second-best breakfast in Galway. It came with eggs, and toast, and potatoes, and rashers, and Irish sausages, and black-and-white pudding. She knew she'd never be able to eat it all—she didn't like the pudding, neither black nor white—but she hadn't decided whether it was more offensive to order it and not eat it, or ask them to leave it off the plate. So she simply ordered the Irish breakfast and decided to let the pudding fall where it may. She'd never be totally accepted here anyway; maybe they expected the Yank not to eat her pudding. Why did they call it pudding anyway? It was definitely not pudding. Did they not realize how odd it was to name delicious cookies *digestives* but pork meat and fat *pudding*? The Irish had a wicked sense of humor alright.

The rest of it though would be devoured. Suddenly,

her appetite was back in full force. She had to admit
that an adrenaline rush came with trying to figure
out a crime. Only when she was seated by a little table
near the window, with her mug of coffee and her
Irish breakfast, did she start mulling over what she
knew so far.

Had Johnny proposed to Rose before he disappeared? Maybe she had turned down his proposal
and he fled from the rejection?

That hardly made sense. Why didn't Rose mention this? *Because she's lying to you. Because she killed
him. Because she was bilking him out of money with her
doomsday predictions* . . .

Was Rose the one who left the thorny stem by
Johnny's door? Was it an answer to his proposal? Or
had it been Johnny himself—furious because she rejected him? Tara set the what-ifs aside. She could
only focus on the *facts.*

Someone had set out to whip Johnny Meehan into
a paranoid frenzy. And they had succeeded. He'd
burned most, if not all his bridges a few days before
the murder by upsetting customers with accusations
about missing items. He'd accused his employee and
tenant of stealing. And he thought Carrig Murray was
plotting against him somehow. And as Rose pointed
out—*someone* had certainly been plotting against him.
Maybe Johnny witnessed the killer deal the deadly
blow to poor Emmet. And then he ran for his life.
Was Johnny hiding somewhere in fear? Could he be
nearby? Watching it all unfold?

Those actions hardly sounded like a man who had
just gotten engaged. Either he hadn't proposed or
Rose had turned him down.

She hadn't gone into the cottage the morning

she'd found Emmet lying in the doorway. What if her name hadn't been written on the wall then? What if someone—her uncle—snuck in *later*? Because he'd seen her. He knew who she was. Or what if Johnny was in the cottage when she found Emmet? Crouching with the murder weapon . . .

No. The time of death was sunrise. Tara came in the late afternoon. Emmet had been dead for hours. If Johnny was still there waiting—what was he waiting for? Nobody would wait around in a tiny cottage with a dead body.

Maybe he had been hiding nearby. Had he planned on turning himself in—and then he saw *her*?

She had the Meehan look: dark hair and blue eyes. Her grandmother had it, according to her mother. It's possible that Johnny Meehan could have recognized her on sight.

Was the theory worth floating to the guards? Did it even matter? No matter what—Johnny wasn't there now.

If he had just installed a security camera, both at home and at the mill, maybe none of this would have happened. Or at the least he could have proven his innocence. Older people were so resistant to technology. To change. She could see that to a certain extent. Parts of Galway looked like what Ireland probably looked like a hundred years ago, and yet they were also a modern city with Internet, and iPads, and televisions in pubs. The blend of both was what made Galway, and probably all of Ireland, unique and magical.

She'd heard through the grapevine that the guards had searched the entire area where she had found the cap, and came up empty. Was the person who stole items from the mill selectively dropping them about town like secret breadcrumbs? Turning the folks against each other? Paranoia was a powerful tool. The killer was wicked smart. It almost seemed . . . scripted. But what in the world was the end game?

Bells jangled and heads turned to watch a beautiful young woman enter the café. She was tall and dressed all in black. Her hair was cut short and spikey, but you could have shaved her bald and heads would turn. Her cheekbones, her lips, her huge eyes. She was a stunner.

"There's Hamlet now," the café matron said with a big smile.

"Heya," the girl answered.

"To eat or not to eat?" the matron replied.

"Just tea and biscuits," Hamlet answered. "It's only a short break."

Tara had to force herself to look away before she was busted for staring. This was the star of Carrig's play. Alanna's friend. Or girlfriend. It wouldn't hurt to chat her up. See if there was any light she could shed on the mysterious Carrig Murray. And, if possible, see if she could get her hands on his mobile phone.

Tara threw money down for her breakfast and hurried out of the café after the actress. "Hamlet?" she was forced to yell when she realized the woman was going too fast to keep up with.

The woman turned and waited, with a patient smile, for her deranged fan to catch up. "Yes?"

"I'm sorry, I don't know your real name" The actress beamed.

"Good?"

She leaned in and whispered. "My name is Magda. I hate it. I prefer to stay in character as much as possible. Please just call me Hamlet." She winked.

"Will do." Tara held out her hand. "I'm Tara from New York."

Hamlet shook her hand, confusion stamped on her pretty face. "I love New York."

"I think New York would love *you*."

Hamlet laughed. "What makes you say that?"

"Are you kidding? You're playing Hamlet as a woman. You know. As opposed to a woman pretending to be a man. It's incredibly exciting." Tara realized as the words rolled out of her mouth, that she meant it. She loved the idea of a female Hamlet.

"Thank you. Are you coming to the show?"

"I wouldn't miss it. In fact. I'm planning a little surprise."

"What kind of surprise?"

Tara clasped her hands together. "We're planning a big surprise party for Carrig after opening night."

Hamlet's brow wrinkled in confusion. Tara imagined she was a great actress, her face was so expressive. "Who is we?"

"Some theatre friends of Carrig's from New York. We came to see the show and surprise him." The lie just rolled off her tongue. What was wrong with her? For a second even she believed it to be true.

"Are you an actress?"

Tara tried to imagine it. Standing on stage, under the lights, looking out at all those people. Nope. Nope. Could not do it. Even thinking about it gave her stage fright. "Me? Heavens no. I'm a designer." *When lying it is best to stick somewhat to the truth.*

Hamlet grinned. "That's so lovely. We adore our stage designers. Carrig will be thrilled."

Tara gently placed her hand on Hamlet's arm. "But there's one special guest we need to invite—only I don't have his number."

Hamlet looked more than ready to be in on the surprise. "Who is it?"

"George." Tara said the name confidently, as if assuming she knew who it was.

"George?" Hamlet's eyebrows raised. "What's his surname?"

"I'll be honest—I don't even know his name. I just know Carrig Murray was on the phone with him when I went to the theatre to meet with him."

"I don't understand. How do you know this person on the phone is a friend of his?"

Hamlet was no slouch. Tara leaned in, hating herself for the next part. "If the show goes well—it might travel to New York."

The actress's eyes popped open. She could see it all. Lights. Broadway. Her short pixie-cut the new rage. "Oh my God."

"You can't tell a soul."

She mimed zipping her lips and throwing away the key. "What does that have to do with the person on the phone?"

Tara glanced around as if she didn't want this information to leak out. "I think he was talking to a famous theatre critic. I think they got into a squabble on the phone."

"Really?"

"I know. It's none of my business. But you know how it is. Suddenly a personal argument bleeds into professional life—"

"And they'll drop the show."

"That's my fear."

"Is it because of the rumors?"

Rumors? "I can't say for sure. But yes, I'm sure they are a factor." *Tara was getting too good at pretending she knew what the heck she was talking about.* "Maybe if we could get this critic here for the party, and they mend fences—well then it's all back on." *I'm sorry,* she wanted to say. *I'm normally not a liar. I'm a good person. I'm just trying to find my uncle and catch a killer.*

"What do you need me to do?"

"Do you ever notice where he leaves his phone when you're rehearsing?"

"He puts it in the pocket of his suit jacket."

"Does he ever take the jacket off?" Eyes still wide, the woman nodded. Tara put on a dejected face. "Never mind. How silly of me. I don't know his password."

The girl beamed. "I bet it's Shakespeare's birthday."

"Really?"

Hamlet nodded. "It's 4-23-1564. He's Shakespeare-obsessed."

"I'm sorry. I shouldn't ask you to do this." Sticking her nose into this was one thing, she shouldn't drag innocent people into this.

"Are you kidding? It wouldn't be the first time I've played a spy" Hamlet winked. "I like the excitement if you must know. And I'm extremely good at it."

"Are you sure?"

"I insist. I'd do anything for Carrig. He's given me the role of a lifetime!"

Tara wrote down the date and time of the phone

call. "Here's the number I need. If you can get into the phone, it should be in his call history."

The girl bounced on her toes. "This is so exciting!"

"Just. Be careful."

Her smile faded. "Careful?"

Tara felt sick. Was this a huge mistake? "You don't want to ruin the surprise. And—I don't want him angry with you if he catches you."

Hamlet grabbed her hand and squeezed. "I can do it. He won't know a thing."

Chapter 16

"You did what?" Danny's stunned look conveyed her worst fear, and shame flooded her. She'd made a terrible mistake asking Hamlet to sneak a look at Carrig's phone.

They stood in the back garden behind the mill. This time the mini-oasis did little to soothe her. "I know. I'm not proud of it." Tara was sick over the lies she told Hamlet. Even reminding herself she was trying to find her uncle, and unmask a murderer, wasn't alleviating her guilt. "I'll just go see her again. Tell her it's off."

"No." Danny headed for the side of the building. "Come on." His long strides lengthened the distance between them and she had to hurry to catch up.

"Where are we going?"

"We're going to help her."

"How?"

"We'll distract Carrig long enough for her to get

the number and return Carrig's phone without any hassle."

"Okay. Okay. Good."

He stopped abruptly and once more she almost plowed into him. "On one condition." He held up his index finger.

"What?"

"This is it."

She tried to keep the irritation out of her voice. This wasn't Danny's fault, this was all her. "This is what?"

"This is the last thing you're going to do."

"That's a pretty broad statement."

"You know what I mean. We get the number—we find out who he was talking to. If it's important, we tell the guards and you wipe your hands of this. If it's not important, you tell no one and you wipe your hands of this. Do you agree?"

Tara nodded. She meant it too. She was in over her head. If she kept going she was likely to make too many mistakes. She was even torn about asking Danny about the paint cans at Rose's. Her uncle had made the mistake of accusing people without proof, and look where that got him. Mistakes could be fatal. At the very least she needed Danny's help. And whether she wanted to admit it or not, she didn't want Danny to be guilty of anything. She liked him. An image of Grace sprang to mind, hanging out her window, watching Tara and Danny on the sidewalk below.

Tara sighed. "I could also drop all of this right now. We could tell the actress the truth."

Danny shook his head as they crossed through the

mill and to the front door. "It's too late," he said. "Sometimes the truth is way more dangerous than a lie."

The Nun's Island Experimental Theatre rehearsal was in full swing when Danny and Tara entered. Hamlet was onstage in the middle of a monologue filled with turmoil. Danny and Tara waited in the back of the theatre until Carrig called a break, and only then did they step out of the shadows. "Danny," Carrig boomed when he saw him. Tara waited for him to yell at them to get out. "The set looks magnificent!" He pointed. Onstage were painted panels depicting a castle and rolling hills with fog coming in.

Tara turned to Danny and stared. He didn't meet her eyes. "You did that?"

Danny, she could have sworn, was blushing. Carrig strode up the aisle, beaming, and clapped Danny on the back. "Are you here for your check?"

"If you don't mind," Danny said, still refusing to look at Tara.

He doesn't want me to know about his artistic talents. Why?

Carrig turned to the actors. "Twenty-minute break." Tara glanced at the front-row seat where a suit blazer was draped, and then made eye contact with Hamlet. The actress glanced at the blazer, then she made eye contact with Tara. They were set. The three were nearly out of the theatre when Carrig stopped.

"Need the key to my office," he said. *Oh, no. Please let it be in your trouser pocket.* But Carrig whirled around and headed for his seat just in time to see Hamlet's hand stuffed inside the pocket of his blazer.

"Hey!" Carrig shouted. He started to run toward her.

She tossed him a set of keys. "I heard you," she said. "Thought I'd help."

"Oh." Carrig came to an abrupt stop. He stared at the keys in his hand, then at Hamlet. "Thank you."

She took a bow. It was all Tara could do *not* to applaud. Hamlet was awesome. Carrig returned to Danny and Tara, and they headed for the office. Hopefully while they were gone, Hamlet would find out who Carrig had been speaking with—or, to be more exact, who Carrig had been threatening to keep quiet—so that Tara could find out *why*.

Located at the mouth of the Galway Bay in the middle of the Wild Atlantic Way, and accessible only by boat, the Aran Islands were a treasure of three: the largest island, Inishmore (Inis Mór); the middle island, Inishmaan (Inis Meáin); and the smallest island, Inisheer (Inis Oírr). The twelve hundred residents primarily spoke Irish, and the rugged limestone rock islands boasted everything from ancient graveyards, medieval ruins, stone beaches, and a fort built in the Bronze and Iron Ages at Dun Aengus, on a cliff three hundred feet above the Atlantic Ocean. And, of course, shops, and pubs, and restaurants, and cows.

Tara wanted to see all three islands, but today she and Danny were setting out for the Inishmore to find George O'Malley, the man Carrig had warned not to tell Tara anything.

She'd heard the islands were a place stuck in time, a peek into what Irish culture might have been like long ago, a place where progress hadn't usurped culture. W. B. Yeats purportedly once said to John Millington Synge, "Go to the Aran Islands, and find a life that has never been expressed in literature."

Farming, fishing, and tourism were the main economic stays, along with artists, craftspeople, and musicians. Spiritualists were drawn to the islands too, perhaps to hear murmurings from long-ago ages, fossils buried in limestone, whispering their secrets. Tara could not wait.

The wind from the ferry ride blew Tara's black hair straight behind her and she stared out at the waves churned by the boat as the vibrations hummed through her body. Danny stood beside her. "Do you think Johnny could be hiding out in the Aran Islands?" she asked.

"Yes. Or he could be in London, Paris, or Rome."

"Wouldn't this be a bit closer and more in tune with his personality?"

Danny nodded. "It would indeed. Although it's still dangerous to hide this close to home."

In plain sight. "Only if he's guilty," Tara pointed out.

"He has to be guilty of something."

"What do you mean?"

"He's in hiding. What innocent person does that?"

"One who's terrified for his life?"

"You think he witnessed the murder?"

"It's possible, isn't it?"

"Why not go straight to the guards?"

"You know him better than me. Can you think of any reason?"

Danny frowned. "He's a stubborn man but not a stupid one. If he is innocent, witnessed the murder, and didn't go to the guards, then something has convinced him that he wouldn't be believed."

Tara stared out at the churning waves. "Or someone."

"Or someone," Danny echoed.

The ocean, so vast and powerful. In comparison humans are so, so small. For a moment Tara let all her worries fall into the churning waves. They were just temporarily sharing this bountiful earth, fooling themselves that they were in charge, had control. It was liberating to let go, even if it was for just a moment. The true inhabitants were the rugged cliffs, the soft peat, the blossoming heather, the thrashing ocean. Here, it was easy to remember the old adage: Don't sweat the small stuff. Here, Tara was reminded, she *was* the small stuff. Some might find that depressing; she found it enormously comforting.

Fifty minutes passed in what felt like seconds. Soon, the ferry's whistle sounded just as the edge of Innishmore appeared, green and rugged and welcoming. The ferry docked and the passengers filed out, following the hands that motioned the tourists to the road leading up to the official entrance to the island. There, tour guides waited with horse-drawn carts and minivans, and for those with stamina, a line of bicycles at the ready.

Pubs, and shops, and cafés were scattered among the breathtaking green grass and stone and sea.

Danny looked at his watch. "George O'Malley will be playing a trad session at three." He nodded to the pub visible in the distance, a white cottage with cheerful yellow trim.

"That gives us two hours," Tara said. She glanced at the bicycles. *No. Please, no. Riding my red bike around Galway city is one thing. But here it would be like trying to ride to the top of a mountain. Surely the bicycles are only here to terrify folks into taking the minivan tours.*

Danny scoffed. "Can you believe those lazy sods?" He stretched his arms wide. "It's a grand, fresh day for a bike ride." He gave her a long look. "Unless you're not up for it?"

She had a hard time breaking away from his twinkling eyes and teasing smile. "Are you kidding me?" *I am so not up for it.* She wanted to take one of the shuttle van tours. "You'd have to drag me kicking and screaming into a car. I'm team-bike all the way." *Enough. Too much. Please, please, drag me kicking and screaming into the van. Be a man—pretend it's your idea.*

Danny edged up to her and pointed at the hill rising in the distance. Whoever invented his cologne had *nailed* it. Like really nailed it. "What awaits is winding roads, and steep hills. Endless stretches of rocky roads. Not for the faint of heart."

Tara grinned. "I'm game if you are." *Please, please say you would rather ride in a vehicle.*

He winked. "Don't say I didn't warn you."

"I won't." *But I'm already thinking it.* She'd had enough of him torturing her. Best get it over with. She paid for a bicycle and hopped on, determined to get a head start. Tourists in the idling vans looked out the window at her, staring as if she was part of the tour. She could imagine the guide speaking: *Look at that eejit. Thought she was going for a little bike ride. We'll be picking her body off the hills the next time around . . .*

Tara pedaled harder. If a little engine could do it, so could she. It took Danny no time at all to catch up.

The roads wound around undulating green pastures and ragged cliffs, climbing up, up, up. The air was fresh and spiked with the taste of the ocean. Her heart and lungs hadn't exerted themselves this much in a long time. The tour vans rattled by, heads plastered in the windows with sympathetic looks and friendly waves. The remains of an old stone church came into view around the next bend. Danny, ahead of her now, pointed and nodded to it, indicating they could stop if she wished to visit the remains. "Yes," she shouted in the wind. They parked their bicycles so they could walk among the ruins. Tara loved being up close to such history. Around the next bend a lone cow lay in the middle of a patch of green with the ragged rocks, dropping cliff, and churning ocean as her background. Several times they had to stop to allow sheep to cross the road, their white and black wool colored with splotches of dye, the colors correlating with the farmer who owned them. She envied these animals. She wouldn't mind lying around here all day.

The first hour flew by and Danny suggested they head back. Tara was relieved there wasn't time to take the hike up the three-hundred-foot cliff to the archeological site of Dun Aengus. She was already feeling anxious this high up. Would she ever stop associating heights with her son's tragic accident? She had never been afraid before.

On the ride back, made easier since it was downhill, Danny told her how back in the day there was only one guard and one priest for all three islands. They would fly from one to another in a little plane, and when the guard was on one island, folks on the other two would be misbehaving.

The islands had also borne witness to devastating storms over the years. There was something so miraculous about such a rugged, isolated place still surviving, and thriving. As gorgeous as it was, Tara could hardly imagine spending her whole life here, as more than a few of the locals must have done. She could imagine the stark, bleak winters when the fog rolled in and the tourists sailed out.

After two hours of biking around the island, a pint of ale hit the spot. The musicians pulled chairs out from the corner, sat amidst the patrons at the round tables, and started in with a jaunty tune that lifted Tara's spirits. "That's him," Danny said with a nod to an older man in a wheelchair playing the guitar. An oxygen tank sat by his side. "That's George."

"How do you know?"

"After we got the number from the phone I asked around. There aren't many older musicians in wheelchairs on this island."

"That must be so tough here," Tara said. The terrain alone would be difficult to navigate.

"Everyone who lives on these islands are hearty souls, so they are," Danny said. "And I can only imagine it's even tougher if you've got a mobility problem."

Tara nodded, noting that Danny was an empathetic person and she liked that about him. They fell into a comfortable silence as they sat back and let the music take them away. An hour later, Tara had almost forgotten why they were there. Danny ordered them lunch, fat French fries that the Irish called chips, with vinegar and salt, and even mayonnaise to dip. Next came lump crab-cake sandwiches that were so good Tara felt obscene eating them in public. The musicians played all her favorites: "Dirty Old Town," and "The Irish Rover," and "Galway Girl." But she was even more delighted when they played "Fairytale of New York" and she found herself heartily singing along and wishing it were Christmas. Danny smiled beside her, and for a moment, they were just two people enjoying each other and the music, and, as they said here—the *craic*—or the fun. And she was having fun. She didn't want it to end. Several couples were dancing, and outside even the ocean seemed to churn in rhythm. When it was over—too soon for Tara's liking—Danny waved George O'Malley over, a fresh pint waiting for him at their table.

Before getting down to the real reason they were here, they let him know how much they enjoyed his playing and rich singing voice. He had a wide, doughy face and thick white hair, complete with trim beard and a joyful grin.

When he heard Tara's surname, his eyebrows shot up in surprise. "You wouldn't be related to Johnny Meehan, would you now?"

"That's why we're here," Danny said.

Tara nodded. "I'm his niece."

A scowl came over his face. "If he's after me light again on behalf of Carrig Murray, he can't have it. Not until I get what I asked for."

Danny and Tara exchanged a look. Carrig had mentioned something about a granite slab but that wasn't the primary thing on her mind. George

O'Malley was acting as if he hadn't heard about the murder and the fact that Johnny was missing, presumed on the run. It was plausible in a sense, that these islands could be protected from gossip—but given his phone call with Carrig Murray, they were pretty sure George knew everything that had happened to Emmet Walsh, and that Johnny was in the wind.

"Johnny Meehan hasn't been seen in days," Danny said. "He's a missing person." Suddenly he began speaking to George O'Malley in the Irish language. It was obvious from George's cascade of horrified facial expressions that Danny was recounting the murder. George's eyes flicked nervously to Tara.

"I'm sorry to hear dat."

"Thank you."

He took a long draw of his pint, set it down, wiped his mouth. "Why are you here?"

Tara recalled what Carrig had said to George. *What do you think I told her? Nothing! Exactly what you're going to tell her . . .* She asked, "We know Johnny paid you a visit recently. Can you tell us about that?"

George sighed. "I'll show you. *If* you buy me another pint and then roll me home."

Chapter 17

There wasn't much rolling to be done. George lived in a flat behind a souvenir gift shop, just down the path from the pub. The back entrance to his dwelling had been outfitted with a ramp, and it was a cheerful space, albeit a tad cluttered. Despite the gorgeous scenery, Tara bet there were days on end with nothing to do, especially if you weren't able to get physically active. She wondered why he stayed; there would be better services for people in wheelchairs in Galway, she guessed, but the answer was most likely simple: This was home.

He put the kettle on for tea and retrieved a box of chocolate digestives, and soon they were all sipping, nibbling, and staring at one another.

"He wanted *that*," George said suddenly, jerking his wheelchair around and pointing up. There, above the door to the restroom was a light the size and shape of your typical globe, set in wrought iron. "It's out of an old theatre in Dublin. Carrig Murray *just* sold it to me, then he turns around and wants it back. Insane! Haven't even had it long enough for a speck of dust to cover it. I wouldn't sell it back to him. Until he suggested a trade . . ." He wheeled his chair back around. "No trade, no light. No is no!"

"You told him you'd trade it for a stone slab," Tara said. "Granite with a female face carved into it."

"What?" From the tone of his voice, it was obvious Danny didn't like being left out.

George sighed. "There's a stone slab I want alright. Carrig got me to agree to a trade. Johnny told him he had a lead on it. I said that's a trade I would do and I meant it." He opened his arms. "But if Johnny had a lead, it must not have panned out. No slab." He seemed to invite them to look around as proof. "No slab, no light. Last time Johnny was here on behalf of Carrig, I told him so m'self."

So many folks were either waiting for objects from Johnny or missing them. This was important, Tara could feel it. She just didn't know how it fit in to a bigger picture and what, if anything, it had to do with Emmet's murder and Johnny's disappearance.

"Did Johnny get upset with you?" Danny asked gently.

"With me?" George wheeled back to the table. "Who would get upset at an old man in a wheelchair?"

"When did he pay you this visit?" Tara asked.

"It was a Friday. He showed up at the noon session. Wanted to see if there was any other way to get the light. As you know, he left empty-handed."

The day before the murder. How badly had Carrig wanted this light? Was he angry enough to kill for it? Why sell it and then turn around and want it back so desper-

ately? It didn't make sense. And even if he wanted it bad enough to kill—it wouldn't have been Emmet he wanted to kill. He would have killed George for it. Every time Tara felt like she had just picked up a thread to this mystery another one unraveled. "Are you sure Johnny made the ferry back?"

"I didn't follow him out to the boat, mind you. But I didn't see him again. If he's hanging out here, luv, someone would have spotted him." George's hands began to tremble. He smacked his lips. He was nervous, but maybe he just didn't like strangers in his flat.

"When's the last time you spoke with Carrig Murray?" Tara's voice came out more singsong than she meant it to. Danny shot her a look. They hadn't exactly agreed on their approach to this question.

George rolled his eyes up and around as if turning the pages of a mental calendar. "I'm not sure. Why?" His eyes narrowed.

Danny cleared his throat. "Tara overheard a recent conversation between Carrig and yourself. Carrig warned you not to say anything to her."

George's eyes were now barely slits. Tara didn't know the human eye could do that. Now she wasn't sure they *should* do that. "How did you know he was talking to me?"

"I saw your number flash on his screen." Actually, *Hamlet* found his number in Carrig's phone, but George didn't need to be bogged down in the minutia.

"How did you know it was my number?"

"It's a smartphone," Danny said gently. "Your name was programmed into the phone."

"Outrageous!" George said. "Big brother is watching! Too much drama. I live all the way out here to avoid drama."

"We meant no disrespect to your privacy. Tara is trying to find her uncle."

"Please," Tara said. "What is Carrig hiding?"

George wheeled away from the table to a nearby window. He parted the curtains. The view looked out on a hill, the path from the ferry, and the thrashing sea. "That wild batch of water is all the drama I need."

"I'll keep looking for the slab of granite," Tara said. "And you can keep your theatre light."

"Emmet Walsh has my slab of granite," he said. He caught himself. "*Had.*" He rubbed his chin. "I reckon it's in his fancy castle."

And just like that, a little piece clicked into place. Perhaps Carrig had murdered Emmet. *Maybe they argued over the granite slab. Was it possible?* Danny and Tara exchanged a look. "How do you know Emmet has it? *Had* it?"

"Because he was heard bragging about it one minute, then claiming it was missing the next. Emmet Walsh was a snake of a man. He should have been run out of Ireland by Saint Patrick himself."

Tara was starting to see where this was going. "Emmet either couldn't hand over the slab because it was missing, or he wouldn't hand over the slab because Johnny hadn't given him his pig," she said. It all came back to the blasted pig.

George nodded. "Can ye imagine? All this over a little piggy." He shook his head. He looked at the sky. "A storm is coming in. The two of you best be on the next ferry."

Danny stood. Tara did too, but reluctantly. "I still don't understand. What's the big secret?"

George folded his hands into a steeple and looked thoughtful. "Did ye know Carrig is doing an all-female version of *Hamlet?*"

"Yes," Tara said.

"Imagine that."

Tara waited.

"He brought in some fancy talent out of the Edinburgh Festival. And he's hired a fancy set director."

Tara glanced at Danny. "I thought you painted his set."

George's head jerked to Danny. The two men stared at each other for a long time.

"What's going on?" Tara said. The spell broke, the men backed away and averted their gazes. In that instant it was clear, the two of them were now keeping a secret. Tara stepped forward. "Danny?"

"I did paint his sets," Danny said. "He never mentioned another set designer."

"'Course he didn't," George said. "Except on paper."

Tara sighed. Why didn't people just get to the point? Why was Danny lying to her now? Or was she misreading the room? "So Carrig is inflating his budget. What's that have to do with Johnny?"

George turned and challenged her. "Is that the question you should be asking?"

Tara chewed on it. *Inflating his budget. Collecting more money than he's spending.* "What's he doing with the money?"

"Yes, chicken," George said. "What is he doing with the money?"

Chapter 18

Was Carrig Murray skimming from the theatre? How much? And yes—what was he planning on doing with the money? Did it even matter? George seemed to be hinting that it did, and Tara was convinced he knew more about it, but it was clear that was all they were going to get. The ferry ride back was choppy, and silent. Tara didn't want to accuse Danny of withholding, but that's exactly what he was doing. The two of them stood at the rails of the ferry, moving up and down with the boat, neither of them saying a word. Maybe she was wrong to be investigating this with him. After all, he was a suspect too. What if he was only going with her to keep her from getting at the truth? What if she was going around with a killer? Did he see her as the enemy and he was keeping her close?

The silence continued during the bus ride back to Galway. A few minutes after the bus started moving,

Tara nodded off. By the time she heard the screech of breaks, and the belch of the engine as it shut off, she was startled to find her head on Danny's shoulder. Oh, God. Did she just drool on him?

She jerked up and apologized. He laughed, a low, comforting sound.

"No, really. I'm so sorry."

"I've had worse bus rides," he said with a wink. She laughed. She couldn't be wrong about Danny. He was so *nice.* But weren't murderers capable of being nice?

After filing off the bus, and making their way back to the center of town, they eyed each other like teenagers on a first date.

"I'm not going to snoop into Carrig's financial records," Danny said.

"No," Tara said. "Of course not."

"Don't give me that. We just stole his phone records."

"I know. But you're right. We don't know what we're doing. Either of us. I'm going to stop." Danny didn't look as if he believed her. "You and George exchanged a look when he talked about the fancy designer Carrig had on his books. Why?"

"Because I'm the designer, I'm not fancy, and the pay wasn't above standard."

"What do you think he's up to?"

Danny looked away. "I have no idea." He looked into her eyes. "Please. Let's leave this to the guards. Will you promise me that?"

Tara resisted the urge to kiss his cheek. "It's been a long day," she said. "Let's both get some rest."

*   *   *

Tara and Breanna met in Eyre Square near the fountain. The rectangular public park was centrally located, adjacent to the train station, and littered with college students and tourists. John F. Kennedy had visited Galway shortly before his death and made a speech in the park, so it was also known as the John F. Kennedy Memorial Park. Tara had packed a picnic lunch and staked out a spot on the grass. She laid out a blanket she bought in town. It reminded her of the one she always took to Central Park. Breanna Cunningham was all smiles. When she sat down a few people moved away from them. It was the guard uniform; it made folks keep their distance.

"Does it bother you that people see you coming and get out of your way?"

"No," Breanna said, with a smile and a wink. "I consider it one of the top perks of the job."

Tara laughed. She did like this woman, even if she also wanted some information. Tara brought out the mini ham-and-cheese sandwiches she'd made, along with her homemade potato salad. She'd had such fun spending a day at the shops, then making the picnic back at Johnny's cottage. She was starting to fall into a rhythm here, walking with Hound, going through the salvage mill, relishing the historical objects, and finding stolen minutes to pretend she was just here on holiday. Today felt like one of those days. She waited until they had finished eating and exhausted getting-to-know-you talk, to gently swing the subject around to the investigation.

"Do they think it's silly that I brought in that cap I found?"

"Oh, no," Breanna said. She stopped after that but her eyes had lit up for a second.

"Did it help in any way?"

Breanna nodded. She looked around. Then leaned in. "Traces of blood were found on the cap. It's Johnny's cap alright."

"His blood?" Tara said. The alarm was evident in her voice. Breanna put her hand out.

"Don't worry. Just trace amounts. It's not an indication of any major harm to him—but it does tell us that at some point he was wandering the grounds."

"Is that unusual?"

Breanna shrugged. "When you're investigating a murder, you'd best treat everything as if it's unusual, like." *Perhaps he'd seen the murderer . . .* "But we've combed the patch and there's not a single other bit of evidence, so I'm afraid it doesn't help much."

Tara sighed. "I was hoping it would."

"We're sending cadaver dogs to the area just in case." Tara shivered. She prayed they wouldn't find anything. "If he does turn up, I hope you're not going to be too disappointed."

"What do you mean?"

"Johnny Meehan was an odd one, and take it from me—this is a city so full of odd ones that you really have to stand out to earn that moniker."

"He's still family. I don't need him to warm up to me even—I just want to make sure he's okay."

"What if he killed Emmet? Will you stand by him?"

"I'm not even sure what that means."

"Visit him in jail, like."

"Oh." Tara hadn't thought of that. "I'll probably be back in New York."

"Ah, tell me what it's like," Breanna said. "Paint me a dream of New York so I can imagine m'self there."

Tara laughed, was happy to turn the conversation away from her uncle, and for once talk about something other than murder. "Well. On a beautiful Saturday morning, my favorite thing is to buy a latte and go for a stroll in Central Park . . ."

Tara was in Johnny's office straightening out his papers when the phone on the desk rang. She jumped and then laughed. *Afraid of phones now, are we?* She felt a tingle of excitement as she picked it up. Maybe it was a customer. She was dying to "source" something for someone. "Irish Revivals," she said into the phone, feeling slightly guilty that she was answering it instead of Johnny. "How may I help you?"

There was a pause. "Is Johnny in?" It was a male voice with an Irish accent, but beyond that she had no idea who he was.

"No." The question startled her so that she didn't know what else to say at first. There wasn't a soul in Galway and probably half the neighboring towns who didn't know about the murder and Johnny's disappearance. She was pretty sure the betting shops in Galway were taking odds on whether or not Johnny was the killer, whether or not Johnny was alive, and whether Ben Kelly was going to get the boxing ring. Tara was going to do her part to make sure that last one didn't happen on her watch. "Who is calling?"

"I sold an item to Johnny a while back. I just wanted to see if it met his needs."

"Oh?" She tried to keep her voice light. "What was the item?" Tara took a sip of her coffee.

"A cast-iron pig." Tara choked on the hot coffee,

nearly spitting it out. "Are you alright?" the man asked.

"You're calling from Manchester?" Was this the banker?

"Manchester?" He sounded alarmed.

"Sorry. I mistook you for—"

"The original?" the man filled in with a laugh.

"Yes. My apologies." *The original?*

"Ah, no worries. I'm in Donegal, luv."

"Right. It's all coming back to me now."

"Are you an employee at Irish Revivals?"

She sensed there was something he wanted to say but he didn't know if he could trust her. "I'm the owner's niece. From New York. And the one running it at the moment."

"Are you aware of the situation?"

What situation? *Darn it.* She had to play along. "Oh, yes. Believe me. I am aware."

"Perhaps I'm foolish to call. But after that much effort I just have to ask. Did the client believe it?"

The client: Emmet Walsh. *Believe it? Believe what?* "I'm afraid the client passed away," Tara said. "Before he could receive it."

"Ah, so we'll never know."

"No. Sadly." She stared at a mug of pens on the desk, trying to figure out how to get him to spill what they were talking about without revealing that she had no idea what they were talking about. "Do you think he would have believed it?"

"I should say so. I know that doesn't sound very modest of me."

"I totally agree," Tara said. "He would have believed it."

"The irony. Him passing away when I went to so much trouble."

Yes. So sorry for your trouble. "Right," Tara said. The longer she talked to this man without knowing what he was on about, the higher the chances she would slip and say something that alerted him to her charade. "It must have been difficult," she said, still tripping in the dark.

He laughed. "Now you see why I'm calling. It was a real work of art. I even got the patina around the ears right, wouldn't you say, now?"

An image of the pig's head resting on the fisherman's palm sprang to mind. Followed by Emmet on the floor, staring up with his glassy eyes. She pushed the image away. Johnny Meehan had hired this man to replicate the cast-iron pig that had belonged to a princess.

"Did you happen to get a look at it?"

Tara bit her lip. Was the pig she saw the replica or the original? Her best guess was the former. It was harder to imagine someone tossing the original away. The question still remained, why toss it in the first place? One good reason leapt to mind. It was the murder weapon and someone wanted to get rid of evidence. Either way, this man had no idea that his item could have been used to murder the client. She had to keep that in mind. He was greedy and taking pleasure out of cheating someone out of something— which was horrid—but he did not know the entire story. "Yes." Tara could not wait to end this conversation.

"I think in the end it looked exactly like the photo Johnny sent me."

"I'll make sure Johnny knows you called."

"Anyway, I'd be happy to work with Irish Revivals again. Please keep me in mind."

She hesitated. "May I have your phone number?"

"Doesn't Johnny have it?"

"I'm sure he does. But just in case."

He gave her his name and number. She was going to have to turn it over to the guards. At this point getting to the truth was more important than any shady business practices Johnny might have been involved in. If he had done this before—cheated a customer out of an authentic item—why then, any past customer could have wanted him dead. Why did Emmet Walsh wind up being the victim?

Was my uncle the intended target and Emmet just got in the way? Or did Emmet find out Johnny had the pig replicated and he stormed up to the cottage to confront him? It would have destroyed the reputation of Irish Revivals. Ben Kelly would get his boxing mill. The deception was a dark secret—a powerful weapon that could have easily been used against Johnny Meehan. And Tara had to face it—Johnny may have killed to keep the secret. Under normal circumstances maybe Johnny would have just confessed that the pig had been stolen and let the chips fall where they may. But Emmet Walsh was no ordinary customer. He was Johnny's best customer. So Johnny went to extremes to satisfy him. Illegal and unethical extremes. *Oh, the tangled web we weave . . .*

Her mother wouldn't have done a shady deal like that, no matter what pressure was being brought to bear. Maybe it was the first time he'd done it. Maybe Emmet was putting too much pressure on him and he cracked. With the relentless campaign of Ben

Kelly to get the mill, combined with his biggest client threatening never to buy from him again—

Everyone seemed in agreement that Johnny had purchased the original pig from this banker in Manchester. When it disappeared he commissioned the artist in Donegal to replicate it. If the one tossed in the bay was the forgery, then where was the real pig? Did the murderer have it? The more she dug into this case, the more questions she unearthed.

The weather had taken a nasty turn, and it was predicted to last all week. "It's going to be lashing rain," the woman in the Galway Café told her. "We're going to have to watch for floods."

Tara sat by the window watching the wind whip down the street. Soon the rain began to fall, splattering the pavement, fogging up the window. The bell dinged and an old man whisked in, shaking off droplets. It took Tara a minute to realize it was the fisherman who reeled up the head of the pig.

"How ya, Richard," the woman sang out. "The usual?"

"Ah sure lookit," he said, and sat down. That must have meant yes, for the woman nodded and disappeared through the kitchen door. She returned shortly thereafter with tea and porridge.

"You won't be out on the boats today," she said.

"T'ank God," he said. "I was supposed to take the coppers out today."

"Were you now? What for?"

"It seems dat little piggy head I reeled up is what killed Emmet."

The woman gasped and so did Tara. "Is it now?"

"Seems the indentations on his poor head are an exact match for the ear or something like dat. I'm not supposed to say a word."

"I didn't hear a thing." Suddenly the two heads snapped toward Tara, as if just realizing she was there.

"Nasty weather," Tara said.

They nodded, then looked away, this time speaking in whispers. Tara's mind was reeling. The pig was the murder weapon. Another piece in place, yet it still didn't add up to a whole.

Chapter 19

"I'm afraid if you don't sign the lease today, you are going to lose the deposit." Tara listened three times to the voicemail left for Irish Revivals, then finally jotted down the address left by the female real estate agent. What lease? She was starting to grow weary of all the shoes dropping. If only they came in pairs and were her size. It was nearing the point in her day when she would normally take a walk. She would visit this real estate agent face-to-face, and get some fresh air at the same time. She'd tried to reach Carrig Murray, but he hadn't returned her calls. Had George O'Malley told him of their visit to the Aran Islands? Maybe she would stop at the theatre before setting off for the real estate office. She would take the rusty red bike. She was starting to grow fond of it.

* * *

Carlene O'Connor

The theatre had a sign on it: IN REHEARSAL. DO NOT DISTURB. There weren't any fencers in the tiny yard. She tried the gate, mainly out of curiosity, but it was locked. She imagined Danny finding out she was here after she'd sworn she was done investigating. The call from the artist in Donegal and from the real estate agent had stirred up her interest, making it nearly impossible to stop. She wasn't hurting anyone, and she wouldn't put herself in any danger. She wouldn't steal anyone's phone again, or push too many buttons. But she could hardly ignore it when people were reaching out to her. She pushed on, heading for the real estate office, following the Google directions.

A slim woman with red hair was just coming out of Galway Properties when Tara hurried up to her, ducking her head so that the hood of her raincoat wouldn't blow off in the harsh wind. "I'm Tara Meehan," she said to the woman. "I work at Irish Revivals."

"Heather Milton," the woman said. "Let's get inside." Tara propped her bike against the building and followed Heather into her office, where she opened a drawer in her desk and set a plain file on top of it. "The owner didn't want to wait any longer, and I can only imagine what you're going through," she said. "But I think you're doing the right thing. It's a fantastic spot and I wouldn't want you to lose the deposit."

"Right," Tara said. She was getting way too adept at faking her way through conversations.

"We'll need the first and last month." She pushed the file toward Tara.

"I'm sorry," Tara said. "But I have no idea what my uncle put a deposit down on exactly."

"Oh," Heather said. "Silly me. I just assumed his employee filled you in."

Tara felt a bit of a jolt. His employee? *Danny.* Tara's mind flashed to Danny telling her all about his idea for opening a retail shop. Had he actually taken steps to do that behind Johnny's back? Heather was looking at her sideways. "I'm sure someone did," Tara said, flashing a smile. "I must confess—sometimes it *looks* like I'm listening but I'm drifting off, worried about other things. I heard mention of it, I'm sure. But I'd love it if you'd refresh my memory."

Heather tilted her head. "It's a lease for a retail space on Quay Street." She said it slowly, as if Tara were a troublesome child.

"And my uncle wanted to rent this space?"

"I already told you. He didn't come to me personally—"

"I understand—"

"I said we needed Johnny's signature. But yours will do, seeing as how you're an owner." She returned a smile. "Unless those are just rumors?"

Tara was not going to confirm nor deny. "Did you ever talk to Johnny about this?"

She shook her head. "This all happened the day before he went missing."

"The day before?"

"I was first contacted a few weeks prior—I'm not saying there's any correlation between the events. I'm only stating that we were waiting for very specific spots. This the first opening in a high-traffic area. Not far from here."

Had Danny mentioned this to Johnny? Or maybe Johnny had found out and—

Danny kills Emmet? No. None of this made any sense.

"I'd like to see the space first," Tara said.

"Of course." She opened a drawer and removed a set of keys. "Are you ready to brave the rain again?"

"After you."

As they neared the space for rent, Tara had to admit that Danny had picked the perfect location, sandwiched between a pub and a gift shop. It had a green door with a gorgeous lion's-head knocker, and the façade was limestone. Tara could already see a sign hanging above: Irish Revivals. Five hundred square feet of open space lay before her, and every inch looked usable, a decorator's dream. French doors along the back wall led to a small garden. A fireplace accented the back wall, its poker leaning next to the empty mouth like a fork snuggled up to its plate. Excitement zipped through her as she imagined selecting her favorite pieces from the warehouse and catering to tourists. She could imagine the garden filled with sculptures, fountains, and seating, customers mingling freely among them.

"It's lovely," Tara said. She had been going over the operating budget. They would probably have to take out a loan to make this second location work. There were still monies in reserve, but at the moment there were no new clients. Although . . . she could open this shop right away. It was summer, a busy time for tourists. At the least she could probably generate enough to keep up the rent until they found Johnny or . . . didn't . . .

But that still didn't explain why Danny had kept this from her.

"We have to get the lease signed today or we lose it," Heather said.

"I'll sign."

"Good. I didn't know how you were going to get *that* thing out of here."

Tara had no idea what she was talking about until Heather Milton stepped to the side. Behind her, in the farthest corner of the store, was a giant stone slab with a face cut into it. Unlike the male face she'd seen in Carrig's garden, this one had eyelashes. Her mouth dropped open.

"Who brought this here?" she asked. *Please don't let it be Danny.*

It was Heather's turn to look startled. "I assumed someone from Irish Revivals did."

"Did you see the person who brought this here?"

"No. I only noticed it the other day." Her eyes flicked around the space. "To be honest, you were going to get an earful about it if you hadn't signed the lease. I can't have clients breaking into properties."

"This item has been *missing* from our inventory. I don't think it was put here for us. I think someone was trying to hide it from my uncle." *Slowly torturing him? Making him think he was crazy? Ruining his reputation?* Tara didn't know that for sure. She just didn't like this woman jumping to the worst conclusions. "Did you give an employee of Irish Revivals the key to this shop?"

"I did not."

"Then you're right. Someone must have broken in."

Heather sighed. "It's possible one of my employees was a bit careless with the key."

"Careless how?"

"He gave it away when I was out of the office. Clients are always asking for early access to measure, take photos, plan. If we trust them, we often say yes. He said he didn't realize the contract had yet to be finalized." She gave a tense smile. "No harm done. As long as you're taking the space."

Tara continued to take in the space. The gorgeous stained-glass window high above the fireplace: intricate flowers and geometric shapes in vibrant colors. *Lion's-head door knocker. A fire poker. Stained-glass window. The granite slab . . .*

These were all the missing items Rose had rattled off. She'd almost forgotten. The ones that Johnny had been raving about. *Oh, Danny. What have you done?*

Heather Milton's high heels clicked as she walked to the French doors and threw them open. "As I thought." Tara inched forward as Heather turned to her. "Last time I was here, the previous real estate agent had left the French doors unlocked. That is why the owner should have listed exclusively with me. I'd never be so careless."

"Anyone could have snuck in," Tara said. *It wasn't necessarily Danny. But the items were from the salvage mill.*

Heather stared at the sculpture. "I just assumed this item belonged to Irish Revivals." Her gaze fell on Tara. "If it doesn't—I'll make sure to have the owner remove it."

"It's ours."

Heather looked at the slab as if it was a personal affront. "Hideous, isn't it?"

"I have a client who's eager for it," Tara said, quite liking it. "In a garden perhaps." If she could get the slab to George O'Malley maybe she could find out why Carrig Murray was after the theatre light. That had been bothering her. Why sell the light then be desperate to get it back? George said he'd barely had it. Dust hadn't even settled on it yet. It wasn't as if Carrig had his own theatre in which to display it. *Desperate* was the word he'd used with her. The question was why.

"Yes, yes, I can see it in a garden." Heather nodded with the look of a person weary of trying to understand the strange tastes of other people. "Let's zip back to the office and get her done."

"Yes," Tara said. "But first things first." She stepped toward the French doors and turned the lock with a decisive click.

Tara was walking back to the warehouse with a copy of the signed lease in her purse when someone stepped up, blocking her path. Alanna stood in front of her, hair tucked into a baseball cap, decked out in a tracksuit.

"There you are," Alanna said. "I have to talk to you."

"I'm on my way back to the warehouse," Tara said. "Do you want to talk there?"

"Actually," Alanna said, "I think we should go to the inn."

"The inn? Whatever for?"

Alanna took Tara's arm, whirled her in the other

direction, and started walking. "There's something I have to tell you."

"I got that already."

"Remember when you first checked in and Grace was going to give you room 301?"

"Yes." The key flashed before her, blood on the stem.

"There wasn't a leak," Alanna said just as the memory came back to Tara.

"Okay . . ."

"Carrig Murray had stayed in the room the night before, and I hadn't had time to clean it."

They entered the inn, and Alanna snatched the key to room 301. Why hadn't it been there when Tara tried to get it? She could hardly ask, given the fact that she shouldn't be trying to get her hands on hotel keys that didn't belong to her. They headed up the stairs. Tara tried to glance at the key to see if there was still a red splotch on it, but it was tucked into Alanna's palm.

"I know you were there when the fisherman pulled something strange out of the bay. What was it?" Alanna asked.

Tara wasn't the only one trying to get answers. "The guards have asked me to keep that information private."

"Rumor has it it was the head of the cast-iron pig. And that it's the murder weapon."

"Again. I can't comment."

"I'm just saying that the reason I haven't come forward with this earlier is that I had no idea the wee pig was a murder weapon. It didn't look sinister then— only a tad strange. But Carrig is a theatre director, he's always been a tad strange."

"Why did he stay here that night?" They were almost to the third floor.

"I wasn't even on duty," Alanna said. "I'd left one of my schoolbooks here, so I was at the desk early to fetch it."

Is that why Grace insisted they were both at the desk that morning?

"Okay. And?"

"Carrig hurried in when Grace was in the kitchen. He was a mess." Alanna stopped at the door to room 301.

"A mess—how?"

"He had streaks of dirt on him—and . . ." She swallowed. "What looked like blood on his shirt."

That would explain the blood on the key. "Did you ask him what it was?"

"Oh, yes. He said it was fake blood. That made perfect sense—they're doing *Hamlet.* I mean, there's a lot of bloodshed in plays by the Bard."

"There is indeed." If Tara knew anything about theatre types, they were night owls, not morning people. "Why was he here so early?"

Alanna shrugged. "Theatre people have their own way about them. For all I knew, they pulled an allnighter." She opened the door. It was neat. Identical to room 305 except the windows overlooked the building next door. There was no one who could see in.

"Why did you make up this business about a leak?"

"What was I supposed to say? Grace would have been on my case about not cleaning it. I'm doing my best balancing cooking school, and work, and boxing." Alanna went to the dresser and stood in front of it. She turned back to Tara. "I think we're going to need to call the guards, but I need you to *promise* me something first."

"I can't make promises until I know what you're on about."

"I just don't want them to know I've known about this for a while," Alanna said. "I mean, they'll figure out that it was left after Carrig stayed—but can't we just pretend that I just discovered it?"

Tara took a step forward, although she was somewhat afraid of what was waiting in that drawer. "Discovered what?"

"If I get in trouble, me da is never going to let me box again."

Tara pushed past her and opened the dresser drawer. There, sitting on its bottom with hands and legs splayed out, was a cast-iron piggy, missing its head, covered in blood.

Chapter 20

"This afternoon?" Tara repeated when Alanna clicked off her mobile and gave her a look. They were standing outside the inn, as if to separate themselves from the grisly discovery in room 301. Alanna had just phoned the guards, and apparently they were in no hurry to rush over and investigate.

Alanna threw up her hands. "That's what they said."

Tara knew they had other cases, but she wanted them to hurry over straightaway. "You're going to wait here for them?"

"Yes. I had to cancel class, but the guards want me here."

When Alanna was putting the key to room 301 back into the cubby, Tara was finally able to ascertain that the splotch of red was still visible. If the guards could prove the blood belonged to Emmet, and Alanna could prove that Carrig had handled the key, and the rest of the murder weapon was found in room 301, this case was solved.

Except for the "why" . . .

Why on earth would Carrig Murray kill Emmet? *Over the granite slab?* Had Emmet learned that Carrig was inflating the budget? Was Carrig simply pocketing the extra money? But how would Carrig know that Emmet was at Johnny's cottage? Perhaps Carrig found out Emmet was coming to collect his pig that morning. He could have sent Johnny off to fetch an item. Left the note on the door to the mill, only to lie in wait for him at the cottage. Far-fetched for a normal person perhaps. But Carrig Murray thrived on drama.

It was also Carrig who had mentioned the stone slab—and warned George O'Malley that Tara would be coming. Had Carrig hidden the stone slab in the retail shop? Why? She didn't have all the answers. Why were the guards going to wait so long to come check it out? What if Carrig somehow got wind of this discovery and skipped town? The Irish grapevine was swift.

The stone slab. Tara had the perfect excuse to pop in and visit Carrig Murray. She would let him know she'd found the slab.

"Are you going to keep my secret?" Alanna said.

"If someone asks me I'm going to tell the truth," Tara said. "But I don't think the guards are going to go squealing to your father. You didn't know Carrig was doing anything wrong. I can see how you would believe it was fake blood." Tara reached out and patted Alanna's shoulder.

"I've worked too hard to lose my progress," Alanna said.

"You're a grown woman," Tara said. "Your father can't stop you from boxing. He can't make you finish cookery school. You made an honest mistake. Believe me. The best thing you can do is tell the whole truth."

Alanna nodded, but she still looked ambivalent. "Do you think I'd be in any trouble? For *not* saying something?"

"Again. You didn't know about the murder, the time of the murder, or the murder weapon until now—right?" Alanna nodded. "But as soon as you did—you said something. I don't see why you'd be in any trouble."

"Thank you." Alanna took an awkward step, and then threw her arms around Tara.

As soon as the hug was over and Alanna was still looking at Tara with fondness, she cut in. "Did you paint 'Go Home Yankee' on the mill?"

Red blotches broke out on Alanna's pale face. "I'm sorry," she whispered. "I was such a jerk."

"Where is it now?"

"Where is what?"

"The paint and the can?"

"In my room."

"Don't do it again." Tara took off down the footpath.

"Where are you going?" Alanna called after her.

She was going straight to the theatre to confront Carrig Murray. She wasn't about to tell Alanna that. "Back to the mill. Call me when the guards are finished."

The red gate at the theatre was standing open. But when she reached the front door, a typed note awaited her:

REHEARSAL CANCELED DUE TO
PERSONAL EMERGENCY

Tara stopped and stared at it. That was odd. There was no way Carrig could have known Alanna had called the guards, was there? She expected the door to the theatre to be locked, but when she pulled on it, it swung open. She headed for the stage. As soon as she crossed the lobby, she knew something was terribly wrong. The red velvet curtain at stage-right lay crumpled on the stage, forming a little hill. Tara hurried down the aisle. As she drew closer, she saw an arm and a leg sticking out of the curtain. "Hello?" She ran toward it, taking the stairs up to the stage two at time. Sticking out of the fallen curtain was the handle of a large knife. She threw her hand over her mouth. A large head protruded from underneath the curtain. Carrig Murray. Stabbed in the back from behind the curtain. Whoever the killer was, he or she was a coward, preferring not to look his or her victim in the eye.

The only time Tara had seen a knife this big was when she watched the juggler on the unicycle. Was that one of his knives? If it was, and if Tara were a detective, she would eliminate him immediately. No one in his right mind would leave such a recognizable knife in a person's back unless they wanted to be arrested for the murder.

She didn't notice the business card or the blood until she drew closer. The blood had blended in with the red velvet curtain, his final cloak of death. The shocks kept coming. Lying on top of Carrig's head was a business card. Tara leaned in to read it:

IRISH REVIVALS
JOHNNY MEEHAN—OWNER

Tara gasped and turned away. Her uncle hadn't done this. Had he? If he had, he was insane. Taunting the police. Maybe it *was* him. Everyone said he hadn't been right in the head, she just didn't want to believe it. Her own mother hadn't gotten along with him, and Margaret Meehan's huge heart had welcomed almost everyone into her life.

Margaret Meehan had also had a huge brain. She read. A lot. She loved the Bard. When other children were being read rhyming books, Tara was getting lulled to sleep by Shakespeare. In *Hamlet,* Polonius had been stabbed from behind a curtain—by Hamlet. Although Polonius believed it was Claudius, spying on him. Was this one of his cast members? Was it Hamlet? Had she come in early, stabbed him, and then put the sign on the door? What on earth would be her motive? She was the one who said Carrig had given her the role of a lifetime and she'd do anything for him. Someone was keen to throw suspicion on everyone and anyone . . .

Why leave Johnny's business card? Another attempt to throw off suspicion?

She stared at the card. All it would take to make it disappear would be to lean over the body and gently pluck it up with her fingertips. This was an older theatre, it probably wasn't decked out with surveillance cameras. *To leave the card or take the card. That is the question. Whether 'tis nobler to be honest . . .*

Stop. Of course she wasn't going to mess with a crime scene even if she suspected the crime scene had been deliberately doctored to make Johnny Meehan look guilty. *Again.*

She backed away, slowly, clutching her cell phone, and raced up the aisle, waiting until she burst through the entrance doors and was outside to call the guards. She hesitated just a second, knowing what she had to do but dreading it. It wouldn't look good, her discovering the second body. Couldn't she just wait for someone else to find him? Couldn't she just say she had come by but turned away when she saw the sign on the door? Why did she open the door at all? They were also going to find out that Alanna had just told her about Carrig Murray staying at the inn and leaving behind the body of the pig—the first murder weapon. Yet instead of minding her own business, Tara had gone straight to the theatre. That probably wasn't going to sit well either. At this point it was looking like the best scenario was that Johnny Meehan was in fact the killer. Otherwise, the killer could be anyone, and she was going to be under an intense spotlight. For a second all she wanted to do was board a plane back to New York.

Enough. Another man had been murdered. She braced herself to be a suspect again, not to mention a target of gossip, and called 999.

She called the inn while she waited for the guards. "The Bay Inn, how may I help you?" Tara was relieved when Alanna answered right away.

"This is Tara. Something awful has happened."

"What?"

"Nobody knows yet. The guards are on their way. You have to promise . . ."

"I promise."

"I came to the theatre to find Carrig."

"Oh, Jaysus, why did you do that?"

"Just wait—"

"You didn't tell him what I'd found, did you?"

"No."

"You didn't tell him I called the guards?" Her voice was laced with panic.

"Listen to me."

"I can't believe you."

"He's dead."

Finally, there was a moment of silence. "You're jokin' me."

"No. He's lying facedown on the stage—there's a lot of blood." Tara wasn't going to mention the knife.

"Oh my God."

"I called the guards. It's going to look bad that I'm the one who found him. But it will be even worse if—"

"They knew you were just here and learned that Carrig had been hiding the murder weapon and you went to confront him."

Tara sighed. This was bad. "Yes."

"Does that mean Carrig is not the murderer? Or did Carrig kill Emmet and we have two murderers running around the city?"

"I honestly don't know."

"I won't mention you were here," Alanna said. "As long as you keep my confidences as well."

"I'm not going to lie," Tara said. "And neither are you. However . . ."

"We should only answer the questions they think to ask, not the ones they don't?"

Tara hesitated. That was exactly what she meant. Was it a mistake? "Yes." She sighed. "Do we agree?"

"We do."

Tara hung up. She glanced past the red gates, where a guard car was pulling up. Sergeant Gable got out, slamming the door, already glaring at her. Tara had to remind herself that she'd done nothing wrong. It didn't help to quell her nerves.

Detective Gable walked up to her, flanked by two other guards. He stopped, hands on hips. He glanced at the theatre door. "You're saying that Carrig Murray is inside . . ." He pointed. "And he's dead?"

Tara swallowed and nodded. "Stabbed," she said. "In the back."

His eyes turned to angry slits. "What are you doing here?"

"Carrig asked me to be on the lookout for an item he wanted. It's a stone sculpture. A granite slab." She was rambling. "I was coming to tell him I'd found it."

Gable shook his head. "Dead bodies seem to follow you around."

"Please don't even joke about it," Tara replied. "I'm traumatized."

He bowed his head, then nodded. He put on gloves and Tara watched as the other two did the same. They headed for the door. "Don't leave town," Gable called out without turning around.

Tara scrambled away before he found Johnny Meehan's business card at the scene.

Chapter 21

Rose was the only person Tara could think of who would understand the horror of what she just witnessed. She had to tell *someone* besides Alanna. Keeping it bottled in was not healthy. She'd love to have friend time with Breanna, but that wasn't smart given where she was employed. Danny came to mind, of course, but when she saw him she'd have to confront him about renting the retail space behind her back, not to mention stealing and storing items there, and she still hadn't worked out all the possible implications of those actions. What if he was trying to steal the business out from under Johnny, and now her? He had seemed like the only man in town who cared about Johnny, but what if that was just an act? What if all his Irish charm was actually deadly?

She had two missed calls from him. She would call him back when she figured out what she was going to

say. She jumped on her bicycle and rode to the caravan. Just as she reached it, she saw Rose hopping on
a black bicycle and wheeling down the street along
the bay. Tara wondered where she was going. It was a
natural instinct to follow Rose. She told herself it was
out of a sense of duty; once she caught up to Rose
she would tell her that Carrig had been murdered.
She would warn her, that if she was in touch with
Johnny—he could be a killer. Or did she already
know that? Was she an accomplice?

The terrain grew bumpier, the houses and businesses were farther apart, the bay spread out before
her. Rose was still ahead, peddling away, without a
single glance behind her. When she turned off onto
a narrow street, Tara hung back until she could
barely see Rose's black hair flying straight behind
her. Tara took the street, keeping up just enough so
she could see which way Rose would go.

Rose finally stopped at a stone building in a field
set back off the road. There were no other homes or
businesses flanking it, and no sign above the door to
indicate what kind of business it was. Or *used* to be.
The doors and windows were dark. There was a chain
across the front door. Rose hopped off her bicycle
and walked it down the stone passageway that hugged
the side of the building. She parked the bicycle behind a rubbish bin and disappeared down a set of
stairs. Tara parked her bicycle across the street, then
hurried over just in time to hear a door slamming
and then the sound of a lock being turned. Darn it.
Now what? They wouldn't answer a knock on the
door, would they? Was she going to have to wait until

Rose came back out? Tara hugged the side of the building and inched her way toward the stairwell.

There were only six steps. She bounded down them, then tried the door. Just as she suspected, it was locked.

Tara sat down on the steps and waited.

The door opened with a screech and Rose exited. It took her two steps before she looked up to find Tara. Rose screamed.

"What's the matter?" The male voice came from inside the building.

And then there he was, a man with black hair and blue eyes like her, tall and broad, in his sixties, and there was no mistaking it—he was her mother's brother. He came to a dead stop when he saw Tara, and she saw the same instant recognition in his eyes. She was shocked to see tears come into his eyes. "Margaret's daughter," he said. Unexpected grief clogged Tara's throat. She could barely manage a nod. Johnny Meehan hung his head for a moment, then looked up again. "I'm so sorry."

"She was too," Tara said. "She wanted you to know she forgave you. She wishes . . . things hadn't turned out this way."

He nodded.

"We can't talk out here in the open," Rose said.

"Come on." Johnny turned and headed back into the building. Tara didn't hesitate to follow. She had looked into his eyes and had seen a family member. She was not afraid of him. If he'd murdered others she would turn him in, but she was going to speak with him first.

* * *

Tara found herself in the middle of a storage room, damp, with a moldy smell. In the corner were several overturned wooden crates that Johnny seemed to be using as a chair and table. He was huddled there now. His beard was scraggly, and his eyes bloodshot.

"What is this place?" Tara said.

"Used to be a pub in front. This was the storage room."

Right. That explained the scent of yeast lingering amongst the mold. Johnny headed for one of the crates. His back had a curve to it, as if it hurt to stand up straight, and he was walking with a limp. He sat down and motioned for her to sit on the other crate. Rose leaned against a wall, giving them some space.

"Look at you," he said. "You're a lovely vision." His voice was thick. He swallowed. "I wish I could offer you a cup of tea."

Tara offered a soft smile. "It's the thought that counts." She took a deep breath. "Did you hear about my mother?"

He maintained eye contact and nodded. His vulnerability was etched in his face, in the shaking of his hands. She had an urge to care for him, protect him. She had to remind herself he could be a killer. "I'm in a bit of a mess."

"I've heard."

"I told him you moved into the cottage," Rose said.

"Oh." Tara slapped her forehead. "I did. I'm sorry. I should have—"

"No, no, pet. What's mine is yours."

"It's been professionally cleaned and . . ." She

stopped. Now was not the time to talk about her decorating ideas.

"I'm so sorry about the mess," Johnny said. "I'm ashamed."

Rose approached and set a canvas bag by Johnny's feet. "There's your supper. I'm away." She turned and headed for the door without another glance at either of them. Once it was closed they were in the dark.

"Is there a light?" Tara said.

"It's by the door," Johnny said.

"Will it attract attention?" She felt silly asking, because there were no windows. But there must be some reason they were here in the dark.

"I'm sorry, it hurts me eyes," Johnny said. He bent over and a minute later a small lantern illuminated the space just enough to see his face. It struck her that she could be in here, in the dark, with a murderer. But she didn't feel afraid. Was she naïve or was that the power of family? Of course he could be both family and a murderer, but that's not how she felt in her gut. If she was wrong she would certainly pay the price.

Johnny clasped his hands and leaned forward. "It's not safe for you here."

"I wasn't followed," Tara said. "I checked. And I hid my bicycle."

"I don't mean here. I mean in Galway. It's not safe yet."

"You saw who killed Emmet, didn't you?"

Johnny bowed his head. "I saw Emmet alright. Lying dead in me doorway." He crossed himself. "It was a message to me." *Is that why the body had been dragged to the doorway?*

"What kind of a message?"

"If I come back, I'll be arrested for murder. Whoever did this wants me gone."

Tara didn't know whether or not he was withholding information. If he had seen the murderer, would he tell her? Or was he trying to protect her? The burdens and bonds of family love were so very complicated. "Why haven't you gone to the police?"

"He was killed in me doorway with a cast-iron pig that has my fingerprints all over it."

"Wait. You saw the murder weapon?"

"'Course I did. It was lying right next to his poor head." Johnny put his head in his hands and moaned.

It wasn't next to the body when the guards went in. If Johnny was telling the truth it meant someone came back for it. *The killer?*

"Why did you write my name on the wall?"

Johnny's head snapped up. "What are you on about?"

"My name was written on the back wall in blood."

Johnny stood. He took a step and stumbled. "My God." He shook his head. "I never saw that."

"You didn't write it?"

"Me? Course not. What a thing to do."

"I noticed you were walking with a limp. What happened?"

"Running away from the cottage. I slipped on the grass, lost me hat."

"Hound found it. The guards have it now."

Johnny perked up. "How is Hound?"

"He's fine. Danny and I are taking care of him."

Johnny nodded his thanks. "The killer came back," he said, almost a whisper, mostly to himself.

"Come with me to the guards," Tara said.

"They won't believe me. I'll go to prison for the rest of me life." He turned. "I'd rather die."

"Who do you think did this?"

"The question is . . . will this end with Carrig Murray?" Johnny stood and began pacing along the back wall. He must have been doing a lot of that lately. Tara could not imagine hiding out in this place for so long. She was already itching to get out. Ironically, it would be even worse in prison, and that's why Johnny was here. Only a fool thought that innocent people didn't go to prison. But hiding from the truth—especially when there was a murderer out there—how could that be justified?

One thing was obvious. Rose knew about Carrig's murder, and she had ridden off to tell Johnny straightaway. "Why do you think Carrig was killed?"

"He and Ben Kelly were in cahoots. This was all about driving me out of the salvage mill for good." He took a step toward Tara. She stood. He grabbed her hands. "Please. I can't have you in danger. I can't. You have to leave. *Today. Right now.*"

"No. I want to help you."

"My time is coming. I can feel it. It's too late for me." He withdrew his hands.

"Whoever killed Carrig is a fan of Shakespeare."

"Rose said you were investigating. Please. Don't. Go back to America."

"Enough. I've heard 'go back to America' in one form or another from almost every Irishman and -woman I've met. I'm going to figure out who is doing this, we're going to have a long talk about family matters, and then I'll decide whether or not I'm going back to America. But you're a fugitive, and just being here makes me an accomplice. I have to call the guards."

"I won't stop you," Johnny said. "I wouldn't be wanting you messed up in this, now."

She reached into her bag. Her cell phone was gone. Rose! "Rose took my phone." Tara didn't normally swear, but the fact that the fortune-teller had played her really stoked her temper. She let out a string of colorful words. There was silence, Johnny's deep laugh rumbled out. "What?"

"I wasn't sure you were your mother's daughter," Johnny said. "Until just now."

The killer came back. The thought kept circling through her head as she pedaled for the Garda station. By the time they arrived at Johnny's hiding place he would be long gone. She knew it, Rose knew it, and Johnny knew it. Would they believe that her phone had been stolen? Since she couldn't control what the guards said or did, she went back to mulling over the case. The killer came back to get rid of the murder weapon. He or she had either panicked and had forgotten to take it as he or she fled, or someone had interrupted him or her, forcing a return to the scene. She knew killers often returned to the scene of the crime, but not when the body hadn't even been discovered. Wasn't that too great of a risk? When the killer returned he or she also wrote Tara's name on the wall in Emmet's blood. That meant the killer must have come back *after* Tara arrived in Ireland, but before Tara discovered Emmet's body. There was no other explanation for her name to be on the wall. This could be an exciting development.

Where would Johnny run next? Tara couldn't blame him. Emmet Walsh had been a wealthy and influential man, and his death would not go unpunished. Even if they punished the wrong man.

Up ahead the road twisted into a narrow curve. Tara couldn't imagine how cars had enough room to pass each other, and just as she had the thought there was a car behind her, so close she could feel the heat from the engine, and a whisper of hot air on her ankles. She was on the edge of a steep, rocky slope. It was too low to call it a cliff, yet there was a steep drop to the bay. If she took a tumble, it could kill her. There was nowhere for her to go. She kept her bicycle steady, waiting for the car to pass. She turned to look, and got a glimpse of a dark hood, oversized sunglasses, and a black bandana. Tara screamed. The driver gunned the engine and the car cut to the right, just enough to bump her leg. *I just got hit by a car.* The bike tipped over, and although her brain was screaming, it was too late for her body to react. Immediately she and her bicycle were airborne, falling over the rocky side, her screams lost in the wind. The driver accelerated and screeched away. She let go of the handlebars of the bike, and soon it was falling away from her, bouncing against the rocks, her body sailing past it. She was falling too fast to think, but then there was a tree, with a branch sticking out, like a gnarled arm. Tara reached with both hands until she was grasping bark, hanging on to the branch with all her strength. For a second she didn't do anything but squeeze tight and breathe. *Calm down, this is life or death, just hold on.* She took one more gulp of air, and looked down. Jagged rocks weren't her biggest fear; it was the road below, cars bouncing over her red bicycle, mangling it to bits until they could come to a stop. Cars swerved and horns honked. *Please don't let it cause an accident.* She would rather suffer injuries or death herself than have an innocent motorist die because of this. If she let go, that would be it for her. If the fall didn't kill her, a car would. Her fingers started to grow slick with fear. She held on, mouthing prayers, her sweaty fingers the only thing between her and plummeting to her death.

Inch by inch, she slid across the branch. She suddenly saw Thomas in her mind's eye. He had died from a fall. Should she just let go? It would be so nice to be with him again. *Hold on.* She felt as if she could hear his voice clear as day. He would be with her mam now, and they would want her to survive. It took all her focus, and what felt like a very long time, but soon she reached the trunk of the tree. She wrapped herself around it, and slowly slid down. She was so happy to reach the bottom, she let go too fast. She was still trembling with fear, and soon she was rolling down the rest of the rocky incline, large stones cutting into her as her body picked up speed. She felt a deep scrape on her side, and then wetness spread through her. She was bleeding. She hit the bottom, near the road, just managing to land short of a passing car. She crawled to the safest edge, and waited to flag down any vehicle that would stop.

"A dark hood? Sunglasses. And a bandana." Detective Sergeant Gable stared at Tara, still in the hospital bed despite insisting she was fine. A sharp boulder had sliced her side and she had seven stitches, and more scrapes and bruises than she could count, but she would heal.

"Yes."

"But no make or model of the car?"

"That's correct. I was too close to it, and right after I saw that—hood—I fell."

"Where were you coming from again?"

He was asking her everything twice. Trying to catch her in a lie? "I saw Rose—"

"Rose Byrne?"

"The fortune-teller."

"Rose Byrne. Johnny Meehan's other half, isn't she?"

"They're not married and I'm no authority on his romantic life." She wished he would stop interrupting so she could finish her story.

"Go on."

"I saw Rose Byrne heading off on her bicycle and I followed her."

"I need to know exactly where she went."

"And I already told you. I might be able to find it if you drove me there, but I wasn't looking at street signs. It was an abandoned stone building about twenty minutes from town. Johnny said it used to be a pub."

Gable shook his head. "You could have caused a serious accident." If he knew the building, he wasn't going to let her know.

"Excuse me?"

"Your bike landed in the middle of a busy road. You're lucky no one was killed."

"I'm lucky I wasn't killed!" Tara was yelling now, and she didn't care.

"Why do you think this—hood—tried to run you off the road?"

"How would I know?"

"You wouldn't be going around accusing the people of my city of murder, would you now?"

"Is that your working theory?" Tara swung her legs over the bed and spotted her clothing on the chair behind Sergeant Gable. She pointed. "You can either hand those to me and leave or I'll jump off this bed with my backside hanging out and get dressed in front of you. Your choice."

He glared at her, and she glared back.

"When are they releasing you?"

"This afternoon."

"You don't suppose Johnny is just going to wait for us to show up in his little hidey-hole?"

"No. I don't suppose he will."

"And you're certain that Rose stole your mobile phone?"

"I know I had it in my purse when I went in, and it was gone when I reached for it a few minutes later."

"I'll pay you a visit at the mill tomorrow morning," he said. "Maybe something will shake loose by then. In the meantime, if I hear about you going around and chatting up any more folks in this town about your uncle, or anything related to my case, I'll have you arrested for interfering with an ongoing investigation."

"I've taken over my uncle's business until he gets back. I'm only talking to people about items they are looking for or items they might have for sale."

"Not anymore, you're not."

"You can't stop me from conducting business."

"Watch me." He tipped his hat and was gone.

Chapter 22

Tara just wanted a scone as big as her head, a mug of coffee, and to her surprise—Hound. She wanted his comforting presence by her side, his gentle whine. She wanted to sit and drink her coffee, and eat her scone, and touch a dog while she gazed out at the bay. She had almost died. It wasn't the big dreams she wanted now—success as a designer, or lavish homes, or trips—it was the little things. The miraculous everyday. The things she often took for granted. And Danny. If she was honest with herself, she wanted to see Danny's smiling face, hear him say something sarcastic. And find out once and for all whether she could trust him. She so wanted to trust him.

She took a taxi from the hospital and had the driver drop her off a little ways from the mill so that she could walk along the water and breathe. Listen to the birds cry overhead, hear the lap of the water. When she reached the door of the mill she felt a tug of happiness. That is until she saw something tacked to the door. Make that two somethings. There were two official-looking sheets of paper nailed to the door. What now? More threats? She drew closer, and saw that the two notices were from the city:

FINAL NOTICE OF VIOLATION
NOTICE TO EVACUATE THE PREMISES

Final notice of violation? How many had Johnny received? What had he done with them?

Didn't they own this building? Was there a loan out on it?

Tara reached for her purse to call Danny when she remembered. Her phone was gone. She was going to have to buy a new one. Danny hadn't visited her in the hospital. Had he tried to call her? He had to know what had happened to her by now. She couldn't worry about her relationships, she needed a lawyer. She stood in Johnny's tiny office, worried about what to do. If he had received other notices he hadn't kept them.

The notices were full of legalese. She had thirty days to pay a ten-thousand-euro fine for the violations. Ten thousand euro. That was impossible. And ridiculous. For the evacuation, she also had thirty days to "restore the account to good-standing." What did that mean? Who did Johnny owe, and how much? She didn't suppose there was any chance Johnny hadn't run again, that he was now in the custody of the *gardai*, where she could visit him and help him, and get to the bottom of this . . .

No, he would have run. He said he'd rather die.

Ben Kelly was behind this. He had to be. She had half a mind to storm over to his place. First, she was going to get her darn scone and coffee, and make sure Hound was okay. The elation she'd felt at being alive, and the miracle of the everyday, was already being replaced with annoyance. This was life. A fragile balance of yin and yang, dark and light. If only the light would last longer.

The café was busy and welcoming. Tara loved all the sounds—plates clinking, bells tinkling, customers chatting. The smells of breakfast were as comforting as sliding into a warm pair of slippers on a cold morning. Maybe they would let her move in. She could sit at the table near the window, use the restroom when needed, and take naps under the table in between meals. She would sit here until the murderer was caught, and the people of Galway accepted her as one of them. She would eat her weight in scones, and have coffee running through her veins.

"Hello, luv," the woman sang. "Coffee?"

Tara wondered if ambushing the woman in a hug and breaking into tears would seem out of the norm. She smiled instead. "And a scone, please."

"Headed off to Carrig Murray's funeral, are you?"

"Oh." Was that where everyone was? No one had told her about it. "Yes," she said. She glanced left and right and then leaned in. "But I'm so embarrassed."

"What's wrong, luv?"

"I forgot which funeral home."

"Mass is at noon, then they're bucking tradition and having his funeral at the theatre. He had it all scripted, if you can believe dat."

Tara could believe it. For a second Carrig's larger-than-life figure loomed in front of her, immediately followed by an image of the knife in his back. "It's still such a shock."

"I would have thought it was one of the actors who done it," the woman said. "But others are saying we've got a serial killer on the loose."

A serial killer. Or a killer forced to kill again to cover his or her tracks? "What time is the service again?" Tara asked.

The woman glanced at the clock. "I'd say it's already started."

The actors all wore long, black robes. There was a small choir that sang and echoed sentiments. The weather was mild, so it was held in the back garden as Carrig had requested. Tara soon learned there was no need for a burial, for the guards still had his body. A murder investigation and autopsy took time. But before all the actors flew home they were going to have the send-off that Carrig had morbidly planned some time ago, just in case. Standing here in the black dress she'd planned on wearing for her mother's send-off, she realized her mother had been right. *Funerals are for the living.* Although in this case, it was clear Carrig's ghost was hovering around, trying to direct the action. She'd missed the mass, and more prayers by the priest in the garden, and by the time the choir finished, the service was done. The crowd was headed to O'Doole's for an informal wake. She found Danny in the crowd standing next to a woman in a black dress so short it looked as if she were going to a cocktail party. Tara had no idea until the woman turned around that it was Alanna. Her hair was down and straightened, her makeup just so. She was holding on to Hamlet's arm. The young actress looked equally stunning in her little black dress.

Danny caught Tara's eye, extricated himself from the pair, and headed her way. Concern was stamped on his handsome face.

Danny took Tara's arm and steered her to a private corner. "Are you okay?"

"Oh," Tara said. "You heard."

"I came to the hospital."

"Funny. I didn't see you there." That came out way too bitter.

"The guards were questioning you," Danny said. "They wouldn't let me in."

She bit her lip and nodded. It wasn't his fault. And Carrig's funeral wasn't the right place to get into any of her probing questions. Questions like—did you open a retail shop behind my uncle's back? Have you been plotting to take over the company?

"Did you get a look at the driver?" he asked.

"I told the police everything I could," Tara said. Until she knew who she could trust, she needed to leave everything as vague as possible.

"Rumor is he was wearing some kind of a mask?"

"Not exactly a mask," Tara said. "I don't want to talk about it here."

"I'm sorry." He placed his hand on her lower back. She wanted to lean into him. Instead, she pulled away.

"I won't grill you," Danny said. "But you don't look like everything is alright. I want to help."

Tara removed the violation and eviction notices from her handbag and handed them to him.

He looked them over then gave a low whistle.

"He must have received other violations," Tara said. "Did you ever see any?"

"No," Danny said. "He kept this to himself. What about his office?"

"I didn't find a single one."

"Leave these to me." Danny tucked the notices into the inside pocket of his suit jacket. "There's a solicitor we've used a couple of times. I'll have a word with him."

"Can you set up an official meeting for the two of us?" Tara asked. "I'd like to be there."

"Of course."

"The notice says thirty days to respond."

"I'll call him after the wake."

Would he be drunk then? Tara stopped herself from asking.

Danny touched her wrist. She turned. "You could have been killed."

"Were you really at the hospital?" It slipped out before she could catch herself.

Danny squeezed her hand. "'Course I was. Gable wouldn't let me in. I waited in the lobby. By the time I checked with them again, they said you had been discharged. I called you several times. You never called back."

"I lost my cell phone before the accident." *It was stolen. By Rose Byrne. Who was also hiding my uncle. I met him. I don't think he's guilty.* There were so many things she wanted to tell him.

"What happened?"

"I'm going to need a drink."

"Lucky for you, that's what wakes are all about."

Carrig had a lot of theatrical friends, and that included musicians. A trad band was playing jaunty tunes when Tara and Danny walked in. She spotted Ben Kelly at the bar and to Tara's surprise he was speaking with Grace Quinn.

"I think he has something to do with the eviction notice," Tara said.

"That's probably true, but don't confront him here. Despite the drinking and the *craic*, this is still a wake. You'll cause a much bigger stir if you try to turn it into an interrogation."

"I won't. I swear."

He handed her a pint. "Drink this."

She was drunk. And having a good time. Dancing with Danny O'Donnell. Lifting her pint every time someone made a toast to say something nice about Carrig Murray. Singing when they sang. It was a celebration of his life. Before she knew it, she was weeping and Danny had his arm around her.

"I was going to do this for my mom. When I found my uncle."

"There, there." He kissed her cheek.

"It was going to be so lovely. I imagined everyone standing by the water with roses. I had a speech." Her own speech, the sober part of her brain noted, was slurred. "It would have been beautiful."

"You can arrange one later."

"Yes. I will. I will do that. If only Johnny had come out of that miserable hidey-hole." She heard herself say it and she froze. Too much alcohol! Maybe he didn't hear her.

"What did you just say?" His pint was down, his eyes were alert and pinned to hers.

"I'm drunk," she said.

"What hidey-hole?"

"It's an expression. You don't have that expression here?"

"I think I should get you home," Danny said. He looked around. The pub was mobbed.

"I'm having a good time." She heard the words come out of her mouth and gasped. What kind of person had a good time at a funeral? It wasn't her fault, it was this darn Irish culture. The music, the drinks, the toasts. "I don't mean I'm having a good time," she faltered. "I just mean I don't want to go home."

"You're in no state to be here. You have to be very careful about what you say, who you say it to."

"It was just an expression. In his hidey-hole. It means, missing—and *presumed* to be hiding out somewhere. I don't know where. It might not be miserable at all. He could be anywhere."

"Where did you go on that bike of yours?"

"Just for a ride." He was asking her the same questions the guards asked her.

"Let's get out of here."

"I want Hound."

"Maybe he's back at the cottage."

Danny stood. Tara grabbed his arm and pulled him back down. "I didn't get a chance to question Ben Kelly."

"This is not the time or the place."

"Some of the actors—they had been working out at Kelly's gym."

"Practicing for the fencing scenes."

"Exactly." Tara hit Danny. He rubbed his arm. She laughed. "Do you get what I'm saying?" *The hood. It looked just like the hoods the actors were wearing.*

"You're langered," Danny said. "I don't even think you get what you're saying. That's why I'm taking you home."

"Ben Kelly could have learned a bit about Shakespeare from *them*." Tara knew it was no mistake that Carrig had been stabbed from behind a curtain just like Polonius was stabbed from behind a tapestry by Hamlet. Could it be the actress who played Hamlet? What on earth would be her motive? Tara remembered her saying that playing Hamlet was the role of a lifetime and she would do anything for Carrig . . .

"You're assuming Ben Kelly knew nothing about Shakespeare before that?"

"He's a jock."

"He's Irish. We all know our Shakespeare, Miss America."

"Maybe they were practicing the sword thingy—"

"Fencing?" Amusement danced in Danny's eyes.

"Yes. Perhaps it was when they were fencing with those sword things that he got the idea." Tara thrust an invisible sword. Danny swatted it down.

He grabbed her around the waist and hauled her up. She really was drunk. It was all this stress. She always drank fast when she was nervous. Normally she knew when to stop. But here, it was like the pints just kept *flowing*. And the music. She loved the music. And the people . . . well . . . she loved some of the people. "I think I should get some things straightened out before we go," Tara said as she tried to keep up with Danny. He was pulling her through the crowd toward the door.

"Not today."

Tara couldn't believe she had to leave and they were all staying. They were drinking just as much as she was—more, even—and they were all still standing. "Why aren't all of you drunk?"

"Because we can hold it," Danny said. "You, on the other hand, are a mess."

"It's probably because I almost died," she said. "When my bike went over that cliff." She started to laugh. It hadn't been funny in the moment, but for some reason it seemed funny now.

"Jaysus," Danny said. "I don't think you're Irish at all." She stumbled outside, Danny holding her up. The fresh air immediately soothed her.

"It's so beautiful here," she slurred, trying but failing to walk straight. *I am so drunk.* Danny was an excellent minder, which was much needed considering the closer they got to Johnny's cottage, the rockier the terrain. Not easy to stumble home in this condition. Without Danny she probably would have tripped in a field and been woken up by cows. "Moo," she said. "Moo."

"Jaysus," Danny said.

The next thing she knew, she was being lowered onto the sofa in Johnny's cottage. Danny had handed her water that was fizzing. "Alka-Seltzer?"

"Solpadine. Trust me, your head will thank me in the morning."

His last words echoed through her head as she fell asleep. *Trust me* . . . Could she?

Chapter 23

Danny was nowhere in sight when Tara woke the next morning. Her neck was stiff but she was surprisingly okay otherwise. That little fizzy drink he'd given her had done wonders. The rain was coming down, whispering at her to stay on the sofa all day, and for a few serious seconds she considered it. A cell phone rang. It made her jump. She didn't have a cell phone. There was one sitting on the coffee table. She answered it, perplexed. "Hello?"

"How's the head?" It was Danny.

"Whose phone is this?"

"It's yours now. Grabbed one for you this morning, I did."

"What time is it?"

"Half eleven."

"Oh my God." Tara couldn't remember the last time she'd slept until almost noon.

"The head?" Danny asked again.

"Thanks to you, it's great."

He chuckled. "No more wakes for you."

"Here's hoping."

"Jokes aside, I just spoke with our solicitor. Apparently, there's been a report to the city planners that our building is not up to code."

"What do we need to do?"

She heard him sigh. "I'm still trying to get the details and the potential cost."

"Is this Ben Kelly's work?"

"That's the rumor."

"Do you need help?"

"I need Johnny."

"What?"

"If Johnny has paperwork that grandfathers the building in before this code was written, we could make this all go away."

"Have you searched his office?"

"Top to bottom." Was Danny hoping Tara would run off to ask Johnny about this matter and lead Danny right to him? She hated this. Warming to him one minute, suspecting him the next.

"I guess we keep looking."

"For Johnny or the paperwork?" he asked.

"Both."

As she hung up the phone, she thought of Johnny huddled in some other dark storeroom on this rainy day. Emmet and Carrig in early graves. With each thought, her motivation to move lessened. She snuggled under the blanket. Just a few more minutes.

Tara was reaching for the door to the mill when a figure emerged from around the corner. She jumped and let out a little yelp, even as she processed Rose standing in front of her, black-and-white hair blowing in the wind. The rain was coming down, but Rose stood there, dripping and staring.

Rose almost smiled. "Put the heart in you crossways, did I?"

"If that means you scared me half to death, then yes." Tara pushed open the door and waited for Rose to enter. She flicked on the lights, still shivering, as the wind slammed the door against the rain.

"I heard what happened to you on your way home," Rose said, her voice barely a whisper. Tara glanced up at the second floor. Alanna was probably at cookery school, but like Rose, she didn't want to take any chances. She gestured for Rose to follow her to her office. Once there she cleared papers off a chair for Rose and sat behind Johnny's desk.

"Someone tried to kill me," Tara said. It was the first time she'd said this to anyone other than the guards.

"That curve is deadly. Are you sure it wasn't just a close call?"

"I'm sure. The person was wearing a hood and large sunglasses *and* a bandana around the mouth. And he or she deliberately cut me off and bumped my bike."

"I tried to tell you."

"That death was all around me?" Tara asked. Rose nodded. "I don't suppose you're going to tell me where my uncle is this time."

"I don't know where he is," Rose said. "He must have left shortly after you did."

"I thought you'd be angry with me," Tara said. "For telling the guards."

Rose wiped dust off the desk with her finger. "I knew you would tell them. I think it's for the best that he comes out of hiding. He won't listen to me."

"You wanted me to follow you," Tara said. "Knowing I'd have to report it."

Rose sighed. "I won't admit to dat. But I wish he wasn't so stubborn. He's going to be in trouble now, even after they unmask the true killer." Rose leaned back in her chair. "Do they know what time Carrig was murdered?"

This threw Tara for a second. "Yes. They were able to narrow it down from the end of rehearsal to the next morning."

"As I thought. I was with Johnny the entire time."

"If you're his alibi, why not go to the guards? He's getting himself in worse trouble by hiding."

"I'm his lover. And not exactly loved in this town. They would never just take me word for it."

"I don't like keeping this from Danny."

Rose's eyes widened. She clasped her hands. "You must."

"I need to get a question to Johnny about an eviction notice we received."

Rose gasped. "Ben Kelly," she said. She clamped her lips and shook her head.

"I suspect," Tara said, "*someone* has reported a supposed building violation to the city planners. We have thirty days—well, twenty-nine days—to respond. Danny thinks Johnny might have paperwork that proves something about being grandfathered in—to whatever this violation is—but we can't find it."

Rose nodded. "I told you the truth. I don't know where he is."

"Do you know where my cell phone is?"

Rose had the decency to look ashamed. She reached in her bag and plunked it on the desk. "I had to give him a head start. What I didn't count on was you almost getting killed."

"You have to promise me—you'll tell me if you hear from him," Tara said.

Rose nodded. "You have me word."

Just as Tara was about to leave to walk Hound, the black phone on Johnny's desk rang, sending her heart fluttering into her throat once again.

"Hello?"

"This is Dawson Securities, may I speak with Johnny Meehan?"

"He's not in." Tara kept her voice steady. The caller either knew full well Johnny was missing, or he was not calling from Galway.

"May I speak with someone in charge of your security system?"

Dawson. That's why she recognized the name. That was the company Danny hired to set up the security cameras.

"This is Tara Meehan, you can speak with me."

"We just got an alert that all your cameras have been disabled."

"Disabled? How?"

"That's what I'm trying to ascertain. Are you near a camera now?"

Tara glanced at the ceiling. There in the corner, pointed directly at the desk, was one of eight cameras that had been installed. "Yes."

"Is there a red light flashing or a green light?"

Tara stepped closer. "A red light."

"It's disabled. It should be green."

"How did this happen?"

"In some instances, weather or system upgrades can knock a camera or two offline. But all eight of yours went off within minutes of each other, suggesting to us that they have been manually disabled."

Manually disabled. Somebody had shut off all the cameras. "When was this?"

"We were alerted just now. Our overnight employee had an emergency of his own so we can't give you the exact time they went offline. The good news is—if you have a ladder I can tell you how to switch them back on."

"Thank you." Tara listened to the instructions and hung up. Turning them back on was not her main concern. The fact that someone had deliberately turned every camera off was stealing her focus.

Danny O'Donnell.

The question boomeranged to her once again. Was it him? He seemed genuine when he said he wanted the security cameras installed in the salvage mill. Had it all been an act? Could she trust him? Or was Johnny Meehan's right-hand man the killer they'd all been searching for?

Danny didn't show up for his shift. Tara had tried calling several times. She still had no idea where the man lived. At the very least she wanted to tell him about the cameras and gauge his reaction. She also didn't want to be on a twenty-foot ladder in the rain trying to turn security cameras back on.

She tried calling Alanna and got her voicemail as well. It had to have been either Alanna or Danny who messed with the cameras. Unless someone else out there had a key to the mill. Tara supposed that was possible, maybe even likely, given that Johnny had been here his entire life, and until the murders, this was a place where some folks still didn't even lock their doors and visitors were known to pop in at any time of the day or night, and when they did they would be welcomed in with tea and digestives.

She was on her way out the door when Alanna burst in. "There you are," she said, as if she had been looking for Tara all night.

"Don't you have school?"

Alanna narrowed her eyes. "We're all working out of our own kitchens today."

"Were you looking for me?"

Alanna nodded. "Danny wanted me to give you this." She dug into her pocket and handed Tara a note:

Heard from our friend George
Gone to see him

Alanna watched as Tara read it. "Who's George?"

"Nobody." Tara shoved the note in her pocket. Why was Danny going to see O'Malley? Why not bring her? Or call her? He was the one who had given her a cell phone. It was no mistake that he'd given the note to Alanna. He wanted to be long gone by the time she read it. What was he up to? What if the killer was circling in on him—setting him up? Or what if Danny was the killer and he was circling her, setting her up?

Alanna brushed past Tara and headed upstairs. "What are you going to cook?"

Alanna stopped. "Sorry?"

"You said you were cooking from home today."

"Right."

Tara wondered if there was much of a kitchen up-stairs. "May I see your place?"

"Excuse me?"

"I've never seen your flat. I'd love to have a tour."

"Not today." Alanna plodded up the rest of the steps.

"I suppose the smells will start wafting down soon."

"Smells?"

"Cooking."

"Oh. Right."

"Unless you're doing your homework somewhere else?"

"I haven't decided yet." Alanna stomped up the rest of the stairs. A few seconds later, her door slammed shut. Tara stood, taking deep breaths. She'd purposely not mentioned the cameras. If Alanna had been the one to disable them, Tara didn't want her to know she was on to her. If she had nothing to do with it, Tara didn't want her to know they were off. She had already turned the one in the office back on, climbing on top of the desk as a way of reaching the camera. If there was a ladder hanging around, Tara couldn't find it. She was more interested now in why Danny was going back to the Aran Islands. But there was one more thing she wanted to do first.

Tara called a taxi. It was time she paid a visit to a certain cookery class.

Chapter 24

Tara stood in front of the Galway Cookery School, surprised to find an adorable cottage/café situated on a busy street, open for both classes and the public. The students worked back in the kitchen, and as Tara entered she was greeted by no less than three young, smiling faces, welcoming her to the café. Trays sailed by filled with mini-quiches and fruit, and the smell of baking bread wafted out from the kitchen. There was a garden in the back visible through French doors, and it was thriving with herbs and flowers. This was her kind of cooking school.

She let herself be seated, which hadn't been her plan at all, but now that she was here, she simply had to try the food.

A young girl waited on her, and Tara waited until after she was served a cappuccino and had ordered wheat pancakes with berries and fresh cream, to ask if the girl was a student.

"I'm a graduate," she said, smiling. "I was offered a permanent position here."

"Congratulations."

"Thank you." She started to walk away.

"I was wondering if I could speak with the instructor."

The girl turned, her face slightly aghast. "Is there something wrong?"

"Not at all. I wanted to talk to her about the program."

The beaming smile was back. "I'll let her know."

A tall woman with blonde hair pulled into a tight bun and big glasses rimmed in neon pink delivered the pancakes. They were heaped with blueberries, strawberries, and, as promised, fresh cream. Tara allowed herself a moment of hedonism.

"I'm Lady Bea," the woman said. "This is my café and cookery school." Tara didn't want to tear her eyes away from her plate, but had no choice. The woman laughed, putting Tara at ease. "How about we have a chat when you're finished."

"Thank you," Tara said, loving the woman already.

The sun was out, so they sat in the back garden. Lady Bea insisted on tea service and Tara wasn't about to complain. "Were you interested in catering services?"

"Actually, I wanted to check a reference."

"You could have just called."

"I'm so glad I didn't. That was delicious."

A smile came and went as quickly as the Irish weather. "I'm not sure I can help. I get a lot of students."

"Alanna Kelly."

Her eyebrow arched up. "Lovely girl."

"Yes." *No.*

"She did receive a certificate of completion." Lady Bea didn't offer more, although Tara could see a lot swimming behind her brown eyes.

"Completion?" Tara said, trying not to sound too alarmed.

"Yes. Her attendance was a bit spotty during the twelve weeks—"

"Twelve weeks?"

"Yes." Suspicion had landed, Lady Bea was on alert.

"I'm sorry. I thought the program was several years."

"No."

"When did Alanna attend?"

"I'd have to check to be sure, but I believe she was with the late January group."

"So that would have ended in April?"

"Correct." Lady Bea set down her tea. "You're Johnny Meehan's niece."

Tara sighed. That darn Irish grapevine. "Yes."

"Why in the world would you be interested in Alanna's attendance last winter?"

"She's a tenant. I'm currently filling in for my uncle."

"I see." Lady Bea continued to stare. "She's a *decent* cook. But I don't think that's where her true passion lies."

"I heard she wants to box," Tara said.

"Yes. I think she took the classes to appease her father."

Tara was sure Alanna's father thought the cooking course was much longer than twelve weeks. Was he still paying for classes she wasn't taking? And if he was—was this any of Tara's business?

She lied about her alibi. But she'd lied to Tara. Not necessarily the guards. Had the guards even questioned her? Or were they only trying to find Johnny, still convinced that *he* was the killer?

"She's a lovely girl, if that helps," Lady Bea said. "I'm sure she'll be a wonderful tenant."

"Thank you."

"Come back for supper some night."

"I will."

Lady Bea walked her back inside the café and then to the front door. "I don't want to step out of place." She hesitated.

"Go on."

"Have you met Alanna's father?"

"Yes."

"He's a bit old-fashioned. He's the only reason Alanna took classes with me. It was obvious from day one that it was his idea, not hers. I wasn't as strict with her as some of my other students who truly want to become chefs. You're probably not used to the ways of the older generations here. I just thought you should know. In case you were thinking of stirring things up—I think she could use a break."

They held eye contact. Tara suddenly felt guilty. She had been dropped in the middle of all these lives, each brimming with drama, and she *was* stirring things up. Wasn't it worth it to find a killer? One that had already struck twice?

Tara thanked her and headed out. Another warning about Ben Kelly. Alanna's lies were most likely a lifelong habit, to avoid the wrath of a father who had different ideas about how his daughter should live her life.

Tara began to walk. It helped her think. Alanna also had access to the key at the inn. The key with drops of blood on it. Had she killed Emmet, then raced to the inn? Had she been unaware there was blood on her? Was she the hooded figure in the car?

It just didn't make sense. Why kill Emmet? Perhaps there was a case to be made if she had killed Johnny. But Emmet? And then Carrig Murray? Alanna wasn't involved in theatre.

Motive was the thing to look at. Who wanted Emmet Walsh dead? Who gained the most if he was gone?

Tara wished she could access everything the guards could. Did the wife and kids get everything in Emmet's will? Had the wife snuck into Ireland to kill her husband?

That was probably far-fetched, and assuming Carrig Murray was killed by the same person, then the entire theory was shot.

Johnny was connected to both victims.

Johnny was hiding.

Tara had to admit, it was possible the guards had it right. That Johnny Meehan was their man. A murderer.

She needed to see Johnny again. He had to turn himself in. She would get him the best lawyer. She would keep investigating. And she would accept the truth, even if it meant her last living relative would spend the rest of his life behind bars.

Chapter 25

Tara wondered if the guards were still processing Carrig's room at the Bay Inn. She also hadn't had a chance to speak with Grace about the key, or about the harp, and Rose. She didn't relish running into the guards at the inn, especially Gable, but she had to see what was transpiring before she did anything else. After the inn, she would find Ben Kelly and confront him about his secret meetings with city planners. There had to be some amicable way to sort this out. She left yet another message with Danny, and tried not to overanalyze when he didn't pick up. She needed to speak with him about the security cameras and the lease on the retail shop. At this point she was starting to wish she'd never started investigating Johnny's disappearance. She had a spotlight on her now, and the killer seemed to be several steps ahead of all of them.

Tara almost expected to see guard cars parked

near the inn, and waited to see yellow crime-scene tape, but there was no one standing in front of the inn, nor were there any guard cars to be seen. Tara stepped into a lobby so quiet she could hear the clock behind the counter ticking. Grace was just ending a phone call, and looked startled when Tara approached. She quickly covered it with a smile.

Tara glanced at the parlor doors. They were shut. "Is Alanna here?"

"No. She has exams today."

No she doesn't. "Have the guards already left?"

"The guards?"

"To process room 301."

Astonishment lit up Grace's face. "What on earth are you talking on about now?"

"Oh my God," Tara said. "She didn't tell you."

"Tell me what?"

"Carrig Murray stayed here the same night that Emmet was killed."

Grace straightened up. "He most certainly did not."

"He did," Tara said. "Alanna found the body of the cast-iron pig in the dresser. That's why she wanted me to switch rooms—and that's why there was blood on the key."

Grace slid a glance toward the cubbyholes, but didn't reach for a key. "You've lost your mind."

"Alanna told me she was calling the guards. They have to process the room."

Grace swiped the key for room 301 from the cubbyhole and started up the stairs. Tara hurried after her. "I don't know what you're up to, but I want you to stop it."

"I don't think you should go in there. It's a crime scene."

"This is my hotel. Do not tell me what to do."

She was fast for an old lady. "At least put on gloves," Tara said.

"Don't be ridiculous." Grace forged ahead.

"Stop!"

"I'll do no such thing. In me own inn, you have some nerve, so you have."

Tara took out her mobile and called 999. "Detective Gable please. It's an emergency." Grace stopped in the middle of the stairwell. "What are you doing?"

"I saw the room," Tara said. "The police need to go through it."

Breanna tried to take a message. Detective Sergeant Gable wasn't taking Tara's call. "I need guards over at the Bay Inn right away." Tara hung up, then met Grace's eyes, filled with rage.

"You're nothing but trouble. I knew it the moment I realized who you were." She whirled and headed back down the stairs, her hands shaking with rage.

Tara followed. "What's that supposed to mean?"

"Don't make me say it. Don't make me speak ill of the dead."

"You'd better be talking about Emmet or Carrig," Tara said.

"I most certainly am not." Grace reached the desk, and Tara could hear her wheeze as she tried to breathe.

"Do you need an inhaler?"

"The only thing I need is for you to get out and stay out."

Tara went to the stand across from the check-in

desk and poured Grace a glass of water. She was surprised when she took it, half expecting Grace to pour it over her head. She waited until Grace had taken a few sips and her breathing had calmed down, before continuing. "Everyone here is hiding something," Tara said. "Including you." Grace guzzled her glass of water like it was her last. "You think you're helping, but you're actually hindering the investigation."

"Whose investigation? You are not a detective."

"I'm trying to protect my uncle, and our business."

"Your business?"

"My mother had a legal right to half of the business. That's between me and my uncle."

Grace slammed the empty cup down on her counter. "What about my business?"

"What about it?"

"You're going to ruin my reputation, spreading your lies."

"I'm not lying. I saw the room. Ask Alanna."

"Carrig Murray did not stay in this hotel. Not recently. Not *ever*."

"You'll see. When the guards get here, you'll see." Tara stopped. This probably was not the right time, but it was now or never. "Rose has your cast-iron harp."

Grace gasped. "She stole it?"

"She said you gave it to her."

"More lies! Why would I do that?"

"There was a note with it. On the inn's stationery. It said: 'An old harp for an old harpy.' "

Grace shook her head. "I would never."

Was she lying? If she was, she was a very good actress. Then again, you had to be good at a lot of things to get away with murder. "You're saying you did not give Rose the harp."

"I did *not*. Why would I do that?"

"Well, someone did. And she assumed it was you."

"Where is it?"

"In her caravan."

"Have you told the guards? She's a thief and a liar. Why aren't you over there accusing her of being a killer?"

"Please stay with me for a moment. Why would Rose steal your harp and then type a nasty note to herself, on the stationery from your inn?"

"Why would I give Rose me own harp and then pretend it's missing?"

Funny. I was wondering exactly the same thing. The door opened, startling both of them. The guards had arrived.

They stood in room 301, four guards, staring at Tara as she and Grace entered. It was sparkling clean. There was nothing in the dresser. No pig. No blood. No mess.

"I was here right before discovering Carrig's body. I saw the pig. Alanna told me Carrig came here the same night—morning—Emmet was killed. Presumably after the murder. With part of the murder weapon. As if he was cleaning up, hiding his tracks."

"And why would he leave the room a mess if he went to such trouble to hide his tracks?" Gable asked.

That was a good question. "I'm just telling you what I saw. What Alanna said."

Detective Gable sighed.

"She also said that Rose Byrne has my stolen harp," Grace said. She nudged Tara. "Tell them about *that*."

"It's true. She has the harp and a note—"

Gable held up his hand. "Enough. You'll have plenty of time to tell us at the station."

"At the station?" Fear tickled Tara's throat.

"Yes. You're coming with us."

"I can tell you everything right here. Call Alanna." *She was going to lie. She had already lied. Or had Grace lied? Did Alanna tell Grace about room 301 first? Had she immediately cleaned out the room, wiped out the evidence? Why would she do that?*

Was Alanna running scared? Had the killer somehow threatened her after Tara left? Or had Alanna played Tara like a harp? Maybe it wasn't Carrig who stayed in that room.

Her father . . .

Or maybe the room was simply used to hide evidence of a murder.

Lady Bea from the cooking school was right. Tara was stirring things up. It wasn't worth it if it put an innocent person in danger. She had to make sure Alanna was okay. "Unless you're arresting me, I can't go to the station right now."

"Why is that?" Gable walked to within a few inches of her face.

"I have an important meeting with the city planners." Now she was doing it. Lying. It was awful. But she didn't have time to sit around a station. She wanted to find Danny. And see what Ben Kelly was up to at this very moment.

"Either you come to the station voluntarily, or I will arrest you," Gable said. "Your choice."

Tara sighed. "Just let me make a phone call." She turned to Grace. "At least show them the key to 301."

Grace sighed, then grabbed the key. She stared at it. Tara stared at it. Gable stared at it. It was sparkling clean.

"Tell them," Tara said to Grace. "Tell them there used to be blood on it."

Gable shook his head. "I don't have time for games."

"There was something on it," Grace said. "I thought it could be nail polish."

Tara turned to Grace. "Alanna said she wasn't going to give me room 301 because of a leak. Was there really a leak?"

Grace bit her lip. "I haven't gone through the records."

Tara was confident there were no records. "Surely if a plumber came in to fix a leak, you would remember."

"You're not a detective," Gable said. "Let's go."

Grace remained silent, but Tara could tell the wheels in her mind were spinning. The only question was—was it the wheels of a murderer trying to juggle all the lies, or was it an elderly lady frightened for her life?

"Outside," Gable said. "Make your phone call and make it quick."

Chapter 26

Tara stood on the sidewalk, wishing she felt as cheerful on the inside as the streets of Galway were on the outside. She wished she was just a tourist and that her biggest problem was whether to go into this pub or that pub. Right now, she'd take any of them. Danny answered on the third ring. "Are you alright?" he said. "Did you get my message?"

"Yes," Tara said. "And I want to hear all about your second visit with George."

"We also have that meeting with the solicitor. Do you want to meet at the mill?"

"I'm on my way to the Garda station," Tara said.

"Oh, no," Danny said. "What happened?"

"Apparently they have a lot of questions for me."

"For you?"

Tara sighed. Gable was glaring at her. "I'll tell you later. But before I go—Dawson Security called me. The security cameras at the mill are disabled."

"What?"

"Did you have anything to do with that?"

"'Course not. When?"

"Yesterday." At least she thought it was yesterday. Was it the day before? So much was happening, Tara was losing her grip on time. "The day before yesterday. A few days ago. I don't know."

Danny's low laugh eased her mood a bit. "I'll take care of it. Why didn't you call straightaway?"

"I was waiting to see you in person."

"Let's go," Gable said.

"Are you going to need a solicitor?" Danny asked.

"No." *Am I?* "I know about the retail shop too," she said. She was sick of secrets. "I'm not mad. I just don't understand why you didn't tell me."

"What retail shop?"

"Now." Gable wasn't joking around.

"I've got to go." Tara hung up. Now Danny was upset with her. *What retail shop . . .* Was he playing her? Or had he spoken with the real estate agent so long ago that he forgot? Maybe Heather had weaseled her into signing the lease by pretending someone from Irish Revivals had been interested in renting it. Now that she thought about it, Heather had consistently referred to "her employee." Everyone in town knew about Tara and Johnny Meehan by now. Had she been played?

Even if that were the case—she *loved* the retail shop. As soon as she was finished at the station she might head over there, just to start planning, to distract herself—make herself feel better. She didn't need this. She didn't want it.

She supposed she was lucky that when Gable opened the back door to the guard car she wasn't in

handcuffs. But people were watching anyway. The
Irish grapevine. She was starting to hate grapes.

Breanna was behind the counter and offered a
weak smile when Tara entered, flanked by Detective
Sergeant Gable and the other guards. Tara tried to
smile back, but she couldn't make her lips move in
the direction she wanted, and feared it came out as
more of a snarl. She felt nervous, and could see how
bad this looked from their perspective. She had been
the one to discover both murder victims. They might
easily think she was lying about room 301 and the
blood on the key. They might think she was lying about
her phone being stolen and that's why she didn't tell
them about discovering Johnny right away. And she
was going around and talking to all the suspects. What
if they sent her home? *Could* they? She didn't know
her rights. She did know that Ireland offered citizen-
ship to anyone whose grandparents were born here,
and given her parents—according to her mother, her
father was Irish too—had been born here, then Tara
could become a citizen. She'd never considered it before. But the more people wanted her gone, the more
she wanted to stay. If that kind of obstinance wasn't an
Irish trait, she didn't know what was.

They led her to a room empty of everything but a
long table and several chairs. Then they left her
there. They were treating her like a suspect. She still
had her phone, but she had a feeling they wouldn't
be happy to see her using it. She didn't know who
she would call anyway.

Detective Gable returned, and to her surprise set a
cup of coffee in front of her.

"Thank you."

"What else haven't you told us?"

Tara chewed on her lip. Was this a good sign, or was he circling in for a kill? "Alanna lied about her alibi."

Gable stared at her, his face turning red. He crossed his arms. "Go on."

"I visited the Galway Cookery School. She only took their twelve-week program, and that was last spring. When I asked where she was the morning Emmet was killed, she insisted she was in class. She's been pretending to go every day. Ask Grace." *Or her father.*

"Alanna Kelly is playing you for a fool," Gable said. He took a seat but his arms remained crossed. "She may be a liar. But that doesn't make her a killer."

"I'm just telling you what I know."

"What else?"

"I think Carrig Murray was taking money from his theatrical production."

"And you know this . . . ?"

Tara sighed. She filled him in on their meeting with George.

Gable glared. "Is that it?"

"Why would he sell George a light then turn around and insist on getting it back?"

Gable tapped his pen. "I suppose you have a theory."

Tara shook her head. "It's still an open question."

"Let's focus on the matters that pertain to Emmet's murder, and by all means if we have time we'll move on to open questions."

The sarcasm wasn't lost on Tara, but she was happy to move on. "Johnny was going to propose to Rose, and for some reason he didn't. I found the stem of a rose left outside his cottage. He had a tattoo done recently of a rose with an engagement ring. So why didn't he propose?"

"You didn't think to ask him when you discovered his hiding place?"

"I was so stunned I forgot all about it. I didn't even remember to ask Rose when I saw her."

"Once more Ms. Meehan . . . what does this have to do with the murders?"

"I don't know. You asked me to tell you everything. I'm telling you everything."

Gable jotted a few notes down, stared at his pad. "Don't stop now."

Tara held out her hands. "You get the significance of how Carrig was killed, don't you?"

Gable's head popped up. "In what sense? *Stabbed in the back* or *Shakespeare*?"

Danny was right. Most Irishman *did* know their Shakespeare. Yay them. "Both," Tara admitted.

"Leave those threads to me." Gable shut his notebook.

"I thought you wanted it all," Tara said.

Gable arched an eyebrow, opened his notebook again with a sigh, and waved for Tara to continue.

"The security cameras around the mill were disabled by someone the other day. And the paint used to write 'Go Home Yankee' was taken from in front of Rose's caravan. I confronted Alanna and she admitted to leaving the message." She swallowed. This next one was a betrayal, but she had to come clean. "Remember the cast-iron pig that Emmet Walsh hired Johnny to find?"

"How could I forget? That was the tipping point to their feud."

Tara didn't want to tell him. It didn't bode well for Johnny. But she was in way over her head and she wasn't going to keep any more secrets. "I found out that the cast-iron pig—the one that was used to kill Emmet—was a copy of the original."

Gable stopped writing. "What?"

It was too late to turn back now. This wasn't her fault. She should never have been in this position in the first place. "I think Johnny was fed up with Emmet hounding him about it so he . . . he cheated. I got a phone call from a man who did the work— asking if the client believed it—bragging about how good his workmanship was."

Gable crossed his arms. "Why am I just hearing about this now?"

Tara pretended it was a rhetorical question and kept going. "And it might not be the first time. I had planned on checking the authenticity of a granite slab, a cast-iron harp, and an old theatre light. These items involved Carrig as well."

"Involved Carrig how?"

"He asked Johnny to find him a granite slab so that he could trade it for his old theatre light that he sold to George O'Malley in the Aran Islands." Gable's right eye appeared to be twitching. *Not such a ridiculous question now, is it?* Tara felt sorry for him. "Do you need a cup of tea?"

"No. I do not need a cup of tea. Keep talking."

"Johnny told Rose that he was fed up with Ben Kelly trying to get his shop—and he thought they were all plotting against him. Everyone thinks my uncle was paranoid—but I think he was being targeted."

"He's fabricating items and you're calling *him* the victim?"

"No. That's the problem with our case—"

"*My* case."

"Of course. Semantics. That's the problem with your case. Most of the suspects are guilty of *something.* But there's quite a span between lying, or fabricating items—or even spray-painting a threat—and murder. Fabricating items was wrong. Johnny will have to answer for it. But that doesn't make him a murderer."

Gable took a moment to think this over. "And who is framing him for murder?"

"Either Johnny is the killer, or he's not. If he's not, the killer counted on him being fingered for it. And you've played right into his or her hands."

"It's my fault now, is it?"

"Of course not. I'm just saying, this killer we're dealing with—you're dealing with—is very, very smart."

"And what do you think of us?"

"Us?"

"The guards. Are we very, very stupid?"

"No. I'm not saying that at all."

"I've heard enough." Gable stood.

Tara shot up from her chair. She needed him to believe her. She needed him to take charge so she could go back to being a tourist. She could be on a tour bus to the Cliffs of Moher. Or headed to Dublin for a change of scenery. Or anywhere else for the *craic.* She hadn't asked for this. "I don't know why the theatre light was so important to Carrig—what if it was fake too? What if he was squeezing Johnny?"

"Even more reason to believe that I had our killer

pegged from day one." He pointed at her. "Johnny Meehan is our killer."

"He didn't run me off the road. Or disable the cameras. Or steal company money—"

"Please get out of my station. I'm going to be needing headache tablets."

"I didn't lie about the room at the inn. Maybe Alanna spun this story just to make me look crazy."

"I think you're doing a good job of making yourself look crazy. I want you to buy a plane ticket home within the next twenty-four hours. I want proof of your reservation."

Could he do that? "You can't make me go home."

"It's either that or I will arrest you."

"You don't have the grounds to arrest me."

"You're interfering with not one but two murder probes."

"You're the one who told me not to leave town."

"This is for your own safety."

"That's for me to decide."

There was a knock on the door. Gable called for them to come in. Breanna poked her head in. "Danny O'Donnell is here with a solicitor. He's insisting you let them in."

Gable turned back to Tara and studied her. "Interesting."

"He's an employee," Tara said. "He's looking out for me."

"Not much of an investigator if that's the conclusion you're drawing," he said. He pointed. "I want you on a plane, or a train, or a bus twenty-four hours from now. I don't care where you go. As long it's a long way from Galway."

Chapter 27

"Thank you." Danny had been surprisingly quiet on their way back to the mill. It was obvious he wasn't happy with her. She almost had to run to keep up with him. Apparently, nothing much had come from his visit with George other than the old musician trying to get dirt on Carrig's murder and complaining that his theatre light was on the blitz.

"He summoned you all the way out there for that? Do you think he knows anything about Carrig's murder?"

Danny put his hand up. "You swore to me you'd stay out of this."

"I tried. It keeps dragging me back in."

He stopped. She almost barreled into him. "I don't want to see you get hurt. I hate that Johnny is messed up in this." His concern for her uncle was genuine.

"You seem to be the only one in town who cares about him."

"Are the guards still convinced he's our killer?"

Tara sighed. "I don't know. I've told them absolutely everything. If it doesn't stir up some curiosity for someone other than my uncle, then they aren't interested in finding out the truth."

Tara didn't take the normal path to the mill. She cut right and headed for the retail shop. "Where are you going?" Danny called out.

"To the retail shop," Tara said. "Are you coming or not?"

They stood in the middle of the shop, Danny open-mouthed, staring at the granite slab. "It wasn't me," he said again. "I've never been in here in my life."

"But you're the one who told me you had this idea."

"Yes. I had this idea. And if I had gone scouting for shops—this is perfect. But I *didn't.*"

Tara was going to have to speak with Heather Milton. "And you have no idea where that came from?" She pointed to the granite slab.

"That's the one Carrig was after," Danny said. "No. If Johnny got ahold of it, he didn't mention it to me."

"I don't know what any of this has to do with our murders," Tara said. "But there must be some connection."

Tara's cell rang. It was Victoria, in New York. Tara had missed the deadline for the vision board. "I have to take this."

"I have a few errands myself. I will see you later." Danny gave her a nod and a wink, and exited the shop. Tara had an urge to run after him, in case he was about to go investigating after warning her not to—but instead she went out to the garden and took the call.

"Hey." Tara was relieved for the distraction. Anyone else would have chitchatted about Ireland, asked how she was doing. Victoria had one speed and it was always set to Go.

"I need your vision boards shipped by the end of today, and send digital photographs ASAP."

That was a tight turnaround. She had been distracted by the investigation. "I don't know if I can."

"You can. Or you won't work for me again."

"Got it."

Victoria clicked off, her favorite form of goodbye.

Tara stood in the middle of the retail shop, filled with a sense of renewal. Danny had given her the names and numbers of two lads who had agreed to bring a simple wooden table, two red leather chairs, and a Buddha statue over to the retail shop from the mill. She placed Buddha in the garden, hoping his calming presence and big stone belly would bring her good luck. For a moment she empathized with how Emmet Walsh must have felt about his prized pig.

His *phony* prized pig. She'd been so wrapped up in other business, she'd forgotten to mention that bit to Danny.

Or had she deliberately left it out of their conversation, still unsure whether she could trust him? She glanced at the granite slab standing in the corner. She took out her cell phone and scrolled through the call history until she found George O'Malley's number. On a whim she dialed. His voicemail picked up.

"George. It's Tara Meehan. I have your granite slab. I don't know who will get possession of the one Carrig had, but I thought you'd like to know. Call me if you're still interested." Maybe it was a long shot, but she wanted to examine the light fixture Carrig had been so desperate to get back. George O'Malley was in a wheelchair and all the way out on the Aran Islands. Unless he was faking his condition, he was not a viable suspect. He was still a piece of this puzzle—or the ornate theatre light he was coveting might be. She would like to gauge his reaction to Carrig's murder. If he was mixed up in this, the murder should frighten him. Maybe he would be willing to open up this time.

Ben Kelly was another one she had to confront. The eviction and violation notices were also looming. She would have to tackle the easiest things first. She left a message with Heather Milton to call her back. She was going to find out just who had rented this retail space if it wasn't Danny. It was going to be difficult to concentrate on work, but she had to give it a try. Someday this would all be over, and she couldn't afford to burn her bridges in New York.

She centered the table in the room and set up the two easels and canvases she'd purchased at a local art shop. She opened her computer and brought up the wish list from Victoria's eccentric client.

Rustic
Industrial
Flair
Unleashed

In parentheses Victoria had added (He's one of *those*). She meant he had provided very little detail, leaving the designer freedom, but that also included the freedom to fail. Tara asked her to send photographs of the vision boards he'd already rejected.

The first one was all modern and neon colors. The only rustic bit she could make out was a pair of antlers hanging above a fireplace. The second was way too rustic without any modern—all log furniture and flannel. What was the designer thinking? The third and last looked like Jackson Pollock had decorated stark white furniture with slops of paint.

Tara would start with the furniture—the foundation upon which to build. She opened the layout of his penthouse in Manhattan.

It had bamboo floors and a wall of windows overlooking Manhattan from some thirty floors in the sky. She saw why the designers were having a hard time with the rustic element. The furniture would look funny if it was darker than the wood floors. She set up four canvases:

> Foundation
> Accessories/Accents
> Timeline
> Color Schemes

She would check out the mill for furniture, but also look through online catalogues. She would find a fabric shop in town and hopefully collect samples. Excitement thrummed through her as she fell back into what she loved doing. This was fun. Creative. Fulfilling. If only there was a way to create a vision board to catch a killer . . .

The thought caught in her throat. She stared at the categories. Couldn't she at least try? What sorts of things would she put under Foundation?

Everything she knew to be true. She changed Foundation to Facts.

She glanced at the next category: Accessories/Accents. This category could be changed to Suspects.

Timeline. This category could stay as is. She needed to establish a timeline before, during, and after the murder—for both Johnny and Carrig Murray.

Color Scheme would change to Motives. She would go back and buy more canvasses for her work project. She wouldn't force any connections—just like designing a home, you had to let all of your ideas exist until one by one they dropped off, leaving the true intent.

What is the killer's true intent? Was it over? Or did the murderer have more victims in his or her sight?

She started with Facts:

Emmet Walsh was supposed to meet Johnny the morning he was killed. He showed up to the mill just before sunrise.

Johnny wasn't there.

Someone left a threatening note—typed—on the door to the mill.

Emmet decided to go to Johnny's cottage.

Someone lobs the cast-iron pig at Emmet's head. Emmet dies in the doorway of Johnny's cottage.

On the back wall of the cottage, in Emmet's blood, someone scrawls the name TARA.

Ben Kelly wants the salvage mill.

Rose has been hiding Johnny.

Someone dumped the murder weapon in the Galway Bay.

The murder weapon—i.e., cast-iron pig—was not an original.

Johnny's boat is missing.

Tara stopped. And looked over the list. Shoot. She should have asked Johnny about his boat when she met him. She was going to have to make a list of questions in case she saw him again. Her eyes scanned over the list of facts.

Why hadn't Johnny showed up for the meeting with Emmet? If only she had thought to ask him this as well.

She added to the list of facts: *Johnny arrives, sees Emmet's dead body—writes* Tara *on the back wall.*

Tara stopped. Had Johnny confirmed this? No. He had emphatically denied it. Was he a liar or a truth-teller? Until she knew for sure, she could not put this down as a fact. She drew a line through it.

She wrote: *Johnny didn't know Tara Meehan was in town.*

Now that was a fact. So he *couldn't* have written her name on the wall. She placed a square of red fabric next to that one, signaling it was something to pay attention to.

She decided to put George O'Malley's name under Motives. She couldn't see him as a suspect. Then added a few more:

THEATRE LIGHT
CAST-IRON PIG—FAKE
GRANITE SLAB—HIDDEN IN SHOP

SHOP—NOT RENTED BY DANNY
SECURITY CAMERAS
CLOAKED HOOD
SHAKESPEARE
HARP
STEM OF A ROSE
PROPOSAL . . .

Johnny hadn't mentioned the proposal and neither had Rose. Had the murders thrown him off course? She supposed love was all in the timing. Something Johnny said came hurtling back to her. *So sorry about the mess. I'm ashamed.*

She thought he'd been referring to Emmet's murder. But what if he'd meant something else? What if he was being literal?

The warehouse had been organized. Spotless. Danny showed some surprise. Johnny's office was a complete mess. Ben Kelly referred to the mill as a jungle. Either Johnny had suddenly cleaned up his act after all these years—

Or someone else had.

Was someone else cleaning up after Johnny? Was it Rose?

Tara drew a red rose under her Suspects board. Rose was taking care of Johnny, literally making herself an accessory to murder. What if she was more than that? What if she was the mastermind?

She had seen Tara in town within hours of Tara arriving. What if she wrote TARA on the wall in blood?

But why?

Was she trying to frame her for murder to take the heat off Johnny? Was that why Tara registered shock in Johnny's eyes when she mentioned her name on the wall? A flash of the inside of Rose's caravan came to mind. Spotless. And then there was the thorny stem left by her door—

Death is all around you. Tara shivered. That would make sense too. Rose, intent on killing, would have known, because *she* was all around Tara. Had she killed Emmet to protect Johnny? Was that enough of a motive? Had Carrig somehow figured out it was her?

Rose was not hanging around the caravan, she was in hiding with Johnny. Was she pretending to love him? Was he in trouble? Perhaps she knew death was coming because she was the one delivering it.

Just a quick visit. Tara could just have a look. She thought of the keys hanging in Johnny's office. Did one belong to his girlfriend's caravan?

Chapter 28

As Tara stood in Johnny's office, clutching the clump of keys, the question wasn't going to be whether or not he had a key to Rose's caravan, but instead, which one was it? She could hardly stand outside Rose's caravan trying key after key without being spotted.

Danny was coming in just as she'd given up. "What's going on?"

Tara jiggled the keys. "Rose wanted me to look in on her caravan. She said Johnny had the key. I have no idea which one it is." Danny went to the desk, opened the drawer and pulled out a single key. Relief and guilt swept over Tara. "Thank you."

"Now tell me why you really want to get in there."

"There were too many things I forgot to ask my uncle when I met him. She knows where he is."

"And you're hoping—what? She's left a map open on her dining room table?"

"I have to eliminate her. What if she's the murderer? What if she's the one who ran me off the road? She was the only one who knew for sure where I was that morning."

"You followed her on a bicycle," Danny said. "Rose doesn't even drive a car."

"Rose doesn't own a car. Do you know for sure she doesn't *drive* a car?"

Danny blinked. "No."

"What are you doing back here?"

"I met with the attorney. He's given me a list of documents to find that might help. Thought I'd get started." His eyes traveled around the messy office.

"Have you spoken to Ben Kelly?"

"My lawyer warned me not to contact him. Makes it less personal."

Making it *less personal* was getting impossible for Tara to do. Everything about this case was getting personal.

"On a better note," Danny said, "the cameras are back on. All of them except for the one in Alanna's flat."

Alanna's flat. Tara glanced at the keys in her hand once more. She couldn't have stood in front of the caravan trying key after key. But she could do it in the mill. Was this really her plan? Break into all the suspects' homes and do a search? If she could just force people into telling the truth and nothing but the truth . . . "Were you able to tell how they were disabled in the first place?"

"I'm afraid it's a simple setting. If you know what you're doing."

"I didn't do it. You didn't do it. Who did?"

"I'm ahead of you on that one. There's one camera that never shut off."

"What? Where?"

Danny pointed to the corner of Johnny's office where bits of straw were poking out. She moved closer until she could make out the curved shape. "A bird's nest," Tara said. "It's a bird's nest."

"It's a decoy," Danny said. "That's where the camera is hiding."

"Have you accessed it?"

"I was waiting for you." He pointed to the laptop that was set up on Johnny's desk.

Tara glanced at the bird's nest. "Why did you disguise the camera in the first place?" Danny's face reddened and he glanced away.

"Me," Tara said. "You were spying on me."

Danny shoved his hands in his pockets. "You're a stranger. This is Johnny's livelihood."

"I understand."

"I hated being sneaky."

"I had to consider you a suspect too."

Danny nodded. A sad smile played across his face. "I've decided to trust you. Do you trust me?"

"I want to."

"That'll have to do." He walked to the laptop and brought up their account for the security system. "The camera is rewound to just before they were disabled. Soon we'll have our culprit." Tara's finger tingled. He pushed play. The screen came alive with a shot of Johnny's office from behind the bird's nest. The other camera was in the opposite corner. They would have a clear shot of the guilty party.

There were a few seconds of silence and then Johnny's door opened and a man slipped in, dragging a ladder. He was wearing a navy tracksuit with a hood, and he had it pulled up and over his head. He made sure never to look directly at the camera—the one he knew about in the far corner of the room. He was short but muscular and sturdy.

"That looks like Ben Kelly," Danny said. "Breaking and entering."

He glided straight over to the camera and leaned the ladder against the wall. He kept his face averted until he had the camera shut off. He descended the ladder and folded it up. He turned, clueless he was still on camera, his face visible. It was Ben Kelly alright. He hovered near Johnny's desk, eyeing it.

"What is he looking for?" Tara asked.

"Whatever it is—he's breaking several laws already."

Ben Kelly slid open the middle desk drawer and began to root around.

"Do you think Alanna knows?"

Danny bit his lip. "I doubt it. The two don't exactly see eye to eye." Ben Kelly knelt and opened the bottom drawer.

"She's been lying to him about going to cooking school." Tara hadn't been sure if she was going to spill the beans on that one until it was already out of her mouth.

"What?" Danny said.

"It's no surprise she didn't notice a shard of glass in my salmon. She only took a twelve-week class last spring, and even then she wasn't a stellar student."

"And you know this how?"

"I visited the school." Ben Kelly moved on to the next drawer. Tara didn't take her eyes off him. "I wonder if he's after the same papers the lawyer asked for."

Ben Kelly stood, holding a folder. He tucked it underneath his arm and grabbed the ladder with the other hand. "And looks like he got it," Danny said.

"Did Johnny keep copies anywhere?"

Danny shrugged. "Not that I'm aware."

"We can confront Ben Kelly with this tape—or the guards."

"We can. But he's never going to give us the correct documents back."

"Then we don't go to the guards first. We threaten to go to the guards unless he gives the folder back."

"You stay here. I'll handle this." Danny headed for the door.

"You're not doing this on your own."

"Says the woman whose been doing this all on her own."

"That's because you're a suspect too."

"You're not keeping me away from Ben Kelly."

"You're right. But I am going with you."

They found him in the Ring of Kelly just as one of his coaching sessions was ending. Sweaty lads bounced out as Tara and Danny entered. Tara had the footage from the camera on a USB stick and it was tucked safely in the pocket of her jeans.

Ben Kelly looked at the pair of them and shook his head. "Look what the wind blew in."

"We need to talk," Danny said.

"If it's about the violations, talk to the city planners." Ben Kelly held his arms up as if surrendering.

"We plan on it," Danny said.

"And the guards too," Tara said. "Unless you give us back our folder."

Danny looked at her. "I thought we'd ease into that."

"Does he look like a man who is capable of easing into things?" She pointed at Ben, who was bouncing around one of his punching bags.

"What are ye on about?" Ben said.

"We have you on camera breaking into the mill, disabling cameras, and rooting through Johnny's desk. You left with a folder. I'm assuming it's the same folder the city planners have asked us to produce. Even if the folder is empty—which I'm guessing it's not—you could still be in a lot of trouble."

"I have no idea what you're talking about. I'd think twice about spreading lies."

"She's telling the truth," Danny said. "We've got the proof. What you didn't know was there was another camera in the opposite corner of Johnny's office."

Ben's mouth dropped open. "I knew there was something funny about that bird's nest."

"What were you looking for?"

Ben Kelly headed for his office without glancing back. Danny and Tara exchanged a look and then followed. Ben opened a drawer in his desk, removed a folder, and then threw it on top.

"This is what I took." He handed it to Danny. Tara tried not to take it personally and looked over his shoulder. The folder contained a report from a private investigator. Ben Kelly's name and photo were on the front page.

"Johnny had an investigator on you?"

Ben's face was already red with fury. "He thought he could dig up dirt on me. Blackmail me, or shame me into giving up my quest for the mill." His hands started to shake. He turned to pour himself a glass of water. He opened a bottle of pills, hands trembling through every step. "He was convinced I had something to do with his missing pig. Why on earth would I be taking such a hideous thing?"

"To ruin his reputation?" Danny suggested.

Ben scoffed. "He'd have been doing a good job of that on his own, like."

"What's in this report you don't want anyone finding out?" Tara asked. She didn't expect a direct answer, but it couldn't hurt to rile him up and gauge his reaction.

Ben Kelly glared. "I simply wanted to find out what was in it. As it turns out, there's *nothing*. See for yourself. If you can stay awake. Johnny found nothing." He slammed his hands on the desk. "Because I've done nothing wrong."

It seemed to Tara that a person who had done nothing wrong wouldn't go to such lengths to assure them that he had done nothing wrong. She continued applying pressure. "How did you know Johnny had hired an investigator?"

Ben sunk into his desk chair and began to fidget. His nervous energy would drive Tara crazy. Just watching him was exhausting. "Emmet told me."

Tara perked up at this. "Emmet?"

Ben nodded. He'd been at the mill a lot, on this journey for that blasted pig. He thought he saw a folder with my name on it. When he asked Johnny about it, Johnny got defensive—said it was best to know your enemy. Then I caught the guy. Not very smart to tail a man on a bicycle when you're in a car."

"You don't drive?"

"Haven't in years," Ben said. "I'm prone to seizures."

He nodded to the bottle. "Medicine helps, but there's no guarantee. Gave me license up long ago."

So he couldn't have been in the car that ran me off the road . . . "We're never giving up the mill," Tara said.

Ben Kelly nodded again. "I filed those violation complaints before Emmet was killed and Johnny went missing. Now with Carrig's murder . . . I don't *want* the mill anymore. It's nothing but bad luck!"

That was at least one problem Johnny wouldn't have to worry about when or if he ever returned. "Was Johnny having anyone else tailed—or just you?" Tara asked.

"I stopped when I found my folder. I didn't see any others."

They guards hadn't been as thorough going through his desk as Tara would have liked. It didn't appear as if they'd removed anything from it. If Johnny was digging up dirt on the residents, who knows what he uncovered. And if this private investigator wasn't doing such a good job of being private—then Johnny could have thoroughly ticked off the wrong person.

She scanned the report. "I don't see the name of the investigator."

"I do," Danny said, pointing to a name in the corner.

"Paul Elliot," Tara said.

"You'd have met him," Danny said.

Tara was startled. "Me?"

"He's also the publican at O'Doole's. He's a re-tired copper."

"Oh, right. He makes lovely napkin-maps." The two of them just stared at her. "I'm thinking I could use a pint," Tara said to Danny. "You?"

Chapter 29

They found Paul behind the bar with a foot up on the ice bin, toothpick in his mouth, watching a rugby match. The only thing Tara knew about the game was that men didn't do much talking when a match was on, although there was often a fair bit of hollering. She and Danny sat and sipped pints while they waited. When there was a break in the game, Danny waved Paul over. He slid Ben Kelly's folder over to him.

Paul glanced at the folder, then gave a curt nod. "Are you looking to hire me or is this an inquisition?"

"Did my uncle ask you to investigate anyone other than Ben Kelly?"

"That's between me and Johnny Meehan."

"Because if he did," Danny said, "and you dug up something about someone that they didn't want anyone else knowing . . ."

"That's the one who could be our killer?" Paul

filled in. Tara nodded. "You're saying something in my reports caused someone to kill Emmet or Carrig?"

Danny stepped in. "We're simply saying we won't know what the possibilities are until we see what the investigations unearthed. We have to follow every breadcrumb."

"Yes," Tara said. "I'm pretty sure Johnny would be fine with you sharing your results with us."

"Why don't you just go through his papers?"

"We did," Tara said. "We didn't find anything else. I didn't even find this when I looked and that was before—" She stopped herself, not wanting to give away the bit about catching Ben Kelly breaking in.

"Before?" Paul asked, eyebrow raised.

"Before I found Ben's report."

"Wait," Danny said. "What do you mean?"

He sounded defensive. "I've been going through his papers since I first came to the mill," Tara said. "Trying to understand the business."

"Do you think you just hadn't gotten to this folder, or it wasn't there?"

That was a good question. "I can't say for sure. But if it wasn't there—and then it was—that could only mean that someone removed it and then put it back."

"Either they wanted us to find it—or they rifled through it and removed incriminating evidence." Paul removed his foot from the ice bin and frowned. Tara leaned in eagerly. "Do you have a copy of your original report?"

He squinted. "I might."

He did. "You can at least give us that. Can't you?"

"Why don't you leave this folder with me and I'll

compare it to my original. If anything is missing I'll let you know."

Tara wanted to argue, insist that he hand over the original to them, but New York stubbornness, as strong as it was, was no match for Old Stock Irish Stubborn.

"Deal," Danny said. He stuck out his hand and the two men shook on it. Tara rolled her eyes and drank the rest of her pint.

"Now what?" Danny said as they exited O'Doole's.

"I'm going to see the real estate agent to find out who checked out the retail shop," Tara said. "Then I have to work on a few vision boards."

"Vision boards?"

"It's for a client in New York. I create poster boards where I play around with design ideas."

"Will you show me sometime?"

"Sure." She hesitated. "I've also created one to help solve these murders." Danny came to an abrupt stop and Tara plowed into him.

"That's a fantastic idea," he said.

Tara sighed. "It's not really getting me anywhere."

"Keep at it. You never know what will break loose."

"What are you doing with the rest of the day?"

"Our solicitor is going to ask for an extension on the violation and evictions—with Johnny missing, he feels it could qualify."

"The longer we keep them at bay the better."

"Agreed."

"We also need to visit George O'Malley again. Use the granite slab as an excuse."

"Okay. But what's the real reason?"

"He was holding something back. With Carrig murdered, maybe he'll be ready to talk. And I want to have another look at that theatre light Carrig wanted back so badly."

"Why don't we go tomorrow?"

"Perfect."

Danny grinned. "It's a date."

"It's not a date."

He winked. "Whatever you say." She watched his broad shoulders flex as he strolled away.

"Not a date," she called after him.

Heather Milton was not in her office. It was locked tight. Tara had left three messages and the woman wasn't calling her back. Was she purposely avoiding her, or was Tara just being paranoid? The retail space was a great location, so whoever had rented it was doing Irish Revivals a favor. Maybe it was time to open the shop. With Johnny gone, none of the usual mill customers were calling. Business was at a standstill. And if they did get shut down, there would be nothing to fall back on. Tara would start bringing over pieces to the shop and officially open. She was tired of all this murder business. She was itching to do something creative and fun. But today she had to finish the vision boards for Victoria's client in New York, or she would no longer have that to fall back on either.

She settled into the shop, opened the garden doors, and began to immerse herself in the boards. By the time she was done, she had what she felt was a fantastic living room. There was a suede sofa the color of burnt orange, with a bamboo coffee table. Silver sculptures helped modernize the look. She found old industrial lights in the mill, large dome-shades the color of emeralds. She took photographs of them, had them printed at a local shop, and added them to the vision board. Time no longer held any meaning as she worked—a throw rug, the color for the walls, art work, additional seating. Before she knew it, the board was complete.

She hurried to the post office to mail the boards to New York, then picked up fish and chips from the seafood restaurant by the bay, and ate them on a bench in Eyre Square. It made her think of her time here with Breanna. They'd had fun. Tara needed fun and friendship. She sent her a text.

Let's get together soon!

She finished her lunch, hoping to hear back from Breanna, then strolled back to the retail shop, taking in the sights and sounds of Galway in the summer. Street performers were out again, including the unicycling knife-juggler.

She thought of Carrig, the knife in his back. Were the guards getting anywhere? Were there any clues? Cameras? Did the knife yield anything?

She went back to the retail shop and stared at her vision boards for the murders. She added RETAIL SHOP to the list, as well as INVESTIGATIVE REPORT ON BEN KELLY. FILES MISSING?

She added items to the timeline:

BEN KELLY DISABLED THE CAMERAS AND STOLE HIS FILE.
PAUL AKA PRIVATE INVESTIGATOR

CHECKING ORIGINAL FILE AGAINST ONE
RETURNED BY BEN.
    HEATHER MILTON NOT RETURNING
MY CALLS.

She glanced at the granite slab in the corner and
hoped their second visit to George O'Malley would
give her something a little more substantial to add to
the boards.

George agreed to meet with them again on Thurs-
day after his trad session. Two days from now. Tara
made a note of it and tacked it to her vision board of
the murders. There was something about what Paul
said about his investigations for Johnny that was
bothering her. She just couldn't figure out what exactly, but her mind kept circling around it. On a napkin, to associate the note with Paul, she wrote: *Paul's
investigations for Johnny.* She tacked it to the vision
board and then added more:
    Which pieces were the most puzzling?
    Tattoo/proposal
    Paul's investigations
    Forgery of the pig
    Carrig inflating theatre budget
    The theatre light
    Had Sergeant Gable looked into Carrig's bank ac-
counts? If he was skimming from the theatre, what
had he planned on doing with the money? Was that
even important? She headed over to see Rose. She
would get the answer to the proposal once and for
all. The note on the caravan door read: IN SESSION.
    Tara opened the door anyway. Rose was sitting at

her table in front of a spread of cards. Hamlet was sitting across from her, tears streaming down her face.

"Get out," Rose said.

Tara ignored her and turned to Hamlet. "Why are you crying?" The young woman's eyes widened. Tara moved closer. "Why are you still here?"

"Carrig's blood is on my hands," she wailed. "It's all my fault."

Chapter 30

Tara escorted the actress to the Garda station. "I'm not normally a gossip. I never knew the information would be used to blackmail him," Magda said. She sounded sincere. Then again, she was an actress.

Apparently, there was a reason Carrig had decided to do an all-female production of *Hamlet*, and it had nothing to do with supporting women. In his last production he'd had a hard time keeping his hands to himself around some of the male actors. These were the rumors Magda/Hamlet had referred to when Tara was trying to convince her to break into his phone. She should have followed up then but she'd been too distracted.

"Was he accused of forcing any of them?" Tara asked.

"Nobody filed any official complaints," Hamlet said. "But his reputation was starting to get out. Every male actor he had offered the part of Hamlet to had turned him down."

"If there were no legal ramifications—why pay a blackmailer?"

"His reputation. He thought this production would revive his reputation. He had been bragging about the bold idea of having an all-female cast."

"And if reviewers and theatre bigwigs found out it was all tied to his past scandals . . ."

"The show would have been panned."

"How did you find out he was being blackmailed?"

"He flew into a rage at rehearsal the day he was killed. Hinted that one of us was a traitor. Sharing vicious gossip. Costing *him*, costing the theatre. I didn't realize he meant literally."

A woman was hurrying out of the guard station when Tara and Hamlet approached. She looked so familiar. When her head turned their way, Tara saw that it was Lady Bea. What was she doing here? She made eye contact with Tara, then bowed her head and hurried away. Breanna was at the reception desk.

"Is Lady Bea okay?" Tara asked.

Breanna leaned forward. "She's a bit shocked."

"About what?"

Breanna glanced at Hamlet. "I can't say."

"You're right. I'm sorry." Tara should know better than to pry in anyone else's business.

"I'm sure you'll hear soon enough," Breanna said. Tara explained that Hamlet had information on Carrig's case.

"That's two," Breanna said. "I wonder what the third will be."

"Two?"

Breanna looked stunned. "Just an expression. You know. Things come in threes."

"Right." *Lady Bea had come to the station with information on Carrig's case.*

Tara left Hamlet at the station. One more piece of the puzzle was in place. Carrig was being blackmailed, so he inflated the theatre budget to pay the person off.

If he was paying—why was he killed?

Tara had just left the station when Rose appeared in front of her, concern stamped on her face. "Is she going to be okay?"

"She'll feel better when she tells them everything." Tara stared at Rose. "So will you." Rose stared back, then nodded. "Walk with me," Tara said. "I have to head to the shop."

"What do you want to know?"

"Did you attack me in the fun house?"

"*Attack* is the wrong word," Rose said. "I was just trying to scare you away from prying any further. Johnny was worried about you. You're the one who bit me."

"Did you leave the stem of a rose on the porch of the cottage?"

"Yes. You're terrible at heeding warnings."

"Did Johnny show you his tattoo?"

Rose stopped. "Tattoo?" She shook her head. "Johnny doesn't have a tattoo."

"I think you'd better double check," Tara said. *So he never went through with the proposal. Why not?*

"I don't know where he is," Rose said.

"Did you try and run me off the road?"

"Of course not."

"Were you blackmailing anyone?"

"Blackmail? Don't be absurd."

"Did you steal Grace's harp?"

"No. She gave it to me."

"You saw her?"

Rose looked away.

"Please. It could be important."

Rose seemed to shrink. "She left it at the door to my caravan with that nasty note." Tears came to her eyes and she clamped her lips shut.

"Thank you," Tara said. She hurried away, eager to get to the new shop, stand in front of her boards, and fill in some blanks.

Tara stared at her timeline. Her eyes landed on the banker from Manchester. Then the artist from Donegal. Had the police called either of them yet? Most likely they'd been too busy with murder probes to get to the forgery case. Besides, with the client deceased, who was there to press charges?

She checked the dates of Paul's investigation. Paul wasn't just hired to dig up dirt on Ben. Apparently, he was also tasked with finding the missing pig. That was *before* the forgery was arranged. Why didn't she see it before? There was only one reason to hire someone to find a missing item. Johnny had had the original pig. So where was it now? And who took it?

Whoever that person was—he or she would have

heard about the second pig. He or she would have known it was a forgery. A secret that could have taken Irish Revivals down. Johnny was right. This was all about taking him down.

Tara hurried back to the salvage mill and stared at the vision boards. She'd brought them from the shop to the mill, hoping that having them close would break something open. Carrig's light . . . George said the light was malfunctioning.

She was starting to see the light herself. Carrig, so desperate to get an item back despite not having a theatre or even permanent home to hang it . . .

And no matter how many times she revolved through the suspects, one kept coming back . . . only one was really at the center of it all, deftly weaving out of the way, causing trouble behind the scenes.

From the beginning, the writing had indeed been on the wall.

But before she could go accusing someone of murder there were two more people Tara desperately needed to speak with. Stephen Kane at the tattoo shop, and Heather Milton. As soon as she had the last two pieces to the puzzle from them, she would be able to unmask a murderer. She grabbed her purse and headed for the tattoo shop.

Tara was headed for the Garda station, armed with her accusation, when her mobile rang.

"Hello?"

"I'm on the ferry. Where are you?" It was Danny and he sounded as if he was shouting through the wind.

She stopped. The wind whipped through her. "The ferry?"

"You said to meet you."

Oh, God. "It wasn't me."

"What?"

"I didn't leave you that message." Static spiked through the phone.

"I'll catch the next ferry," Tara said. "Stay with people. Go to the pub. Stay with large groups of people. Do anything you can to stall . . ."

"No," Danny said, sounding a continent away. "I have a bad feeling about this."

"Listen to me—" There was a high-pitched screech and the phone went dead. Tara's hands were shaking as she called the guards. Breanna answered and listened, but explained there was insufficient reason to alert the authorities on the islands. Someone lying about a message wouldn't be seen as any cause for alarm. Tara texted Danny a warning just in case it went through. Then she jumped in a taxi and told him to drive like he stole it.

It was impossible to make a ferry move faster than a ferry wanted to move. She'd tried Danny a dozen times. No answer. She stared out at the endless waves, and went over it in her mind. Everyone was right about one thing: It did all start with the pig owned by a princess.

Emmet paid a good amount for the pig, and Johnny finally purchased it for him from the man in Manchester. Upon Johnny's return, it was stolen, thus forcing Johnny into hiring someone to forge a copy. In the meantime, Ben Kelly was working hard behind the scenes to take the mill, and Carrig Murray was skimming from his theatre to pay a blackmailer. Carrig then sells a light to George way out in the Aran Islands, only to want it back almost immediately . . .

The killer was cozy with all of them, directing the takedown of Irish Revivals from behind the scenes. At the same time the killer needed money so that once the mill belonged to him or her, the killer had the funds to do what they wished. That's when the blackmail started. *Before* the cast-iron pig was stolen. Perhaps it was never supposed to go this far. If Johnny hadn't forged the pig, then maybe Emmet would have turned on Johnny, ruining his reputation and business. There was only one question Tara still had. Since Johnny was the intended target, why kill Emmet? Was he simply at the wrong place at the wrong time?

No.

The killer had upped the game. Instead of merely bringing down a man's business, why not bring down the man? Was Emmet killed to frame Johnny Meehan for murder? Or was Emmet about to point fingers at the killer for something else?

For stealing . . .

Hardly a reason to kill someone. No. Emmet was interfering in the killer's larger plan. The plan to take over the mill. The plan to live happily ever after. *The proposal* . . .

Why not kill Johnny himself?

Because Danny loved Johnny. He was the only one in town who did.

Tara thought through it all, once more, slowly.

Emmet is killed. The forged pig breaks. The killer manages to pick up the cast-iron body, stashes it in the inn. In haste, the killer leaves the head of the pig behind.

Hours later, the killer must return to the crime scene to retrieve the head.

That is when the killer wrote TARA on the wall—not before. Because by now the killer had met Tara, knew who she was and why she was in town.

But that doesn't mean there wasn't a name written on the wall. There had been. The name of the true killer.

Emmet tried, while dying, to name is his killer. That explained the carpet of blood from the wall to the front door. Emmet crawled to the wall to name his killer. But he didn't get to complete the job before he died. The killer returned, and saw what had transpired. It would have been impossible to wash off the name painted in blood, so the killer wrote *over* the name, and changed it to TARA.

That's why the letters were so bizarre.

The killer then dragged the body back into the doorway. The guards had to have figured out that the body had been dragged around—but never made it public. Had they figured out why?

The killer hadn't wanted anyone to come into the cottage until they were long gone, and placing the body directly in the doorway would accomplish just that.

Which meant the killer returned *after* meeting Tara that morning, but before Tara discovered the body.

The killer also did the dishes. It sounded ludicrous, yet those were the facts. Was there a particular reason for it, or was it some kind of psychological tic? Either while waiting for Emmet to show up, or after the killer returned for the rest of the murder weapon. Had the killer touched one of the dishes and thought washing them would wipe away fingerprints?

Had Johnny Meehan been on some errand that morning? The killer had to have known that Johnny wouldn't be home until after Emmet was killed. Perhaps Johnny was in the mill after all. The killer typed the letter, diverting Emmet away from the mill and to Johnny's cottage.

It was all part of the larger scheme. The killer's own Shakespearean drama. A new shop. A marriage proposal. The killer was in love.

Carrig, in the meantime, most likely through Hamlet, had orchestrated a theft of his own. The cast-iron pig. Carrig, sick of being blackmailed and led to believe Johnny was the blackmailer, stole the cast-iron pig. Hamlet admitted she'd spied before. That she would do anything for Carrig. She must have been in the mill with Alanna when the cast-iron pig arrived. Either she stole it for Carrig, or he stole it himself, but either way, he had a very good reason for stealing it. *Leverage.* To end the blackmail. Playing Emmet and Johnny against each other in a very dramatic fashion. The killer had already struck twice. Tara could only pray she wasn't too late to stop the third. In this case, three times would not be a charm. On her way to the ferry she had made her last phone call, to Paul at the old men's bar.

Chapter 31

✦

Tara was so relieved to see George O'Malley in his chair outside the pub that she almost wept. She asked if he'd seen Danny, her heart in her throat as she awaited his answer.

"Aye. You just missed him. Stayed for a bite to eat and some music, then got some kind of message and headed up to the cliff."

Terror zipped through her. "The cliff?"

"Aye. Dun Aengus. The fort, like."

"Yes. I know." Hovering at the edge of a three-hundred-foot cliff. "What's the fastest way there?"

"The tour vans have all just pulled out. I guess it depends how fast your feet or your cycle will take you."

Tara glanced at the bicycles lined up, taunting her. "Great," she said. "Oh—you haven't broken your light, have you?"

"My light?"

"Your theatre light. Is it still intact?"

"Why wouldn't it be?"

"I'll let you know later. If you see any guards at all, will you send them up to the cliff?"

George raised his eyebrow. "You wouldn't be thinking of jumping off, now would you?"

Tara was relieved she'd decided to message Sergeant Gable while on the ferry. Whether or not he responded was another matter. She wouldn't be able to wait.

"Can you call the local guard?" she asked George.

"What's going on?" George wheeled closer to her, worry stamped on his face.

"I have to get up to the cliff. I'm pretty sure there's someone up there who wouldn't hesitate to push people over the edge."

There were two options to cycle to the cliff. Either take the route with an incline, or the flat roads along the seal coast. Both routes were known to take around thirty minutes, but the seal route was known to be more leisurely, as people stopped to take in the cute little creatures. Tara took the incline route, grateful that a sense of urgency fueled by adrenaline took a lot of the sting out of the trip. She was breathing heavily and drenched in sweat, but her ordeal wasn't over yet. From the bike park to the top of the cliff it was a fifteen-minute walk. Tara would take it as fast as she could without drawing unwanted attention. She didn't want Danny to see her coming.

The site of the semicircular prehistoric stone fort perched over the Atlantic Ocean took Tara's breath away. For a second she forgot she was here to confront a killer. The jagged stone walls were originally built to keep out attackers. This time, Tara was certain one was waiting inside the structure. If the answer to the proposal was no—was there going to be another death? Not if Tara could help it. She tried to blend in with the other tourists, keeping her sunglasses on and hood up. Just like they'd used the costumes from *Hamlet* as a disguise during their reign of terror.

Tara was out of breath by the time she reached Dun Aengus. Ahead, the ancient fort rose out of the ground, three massive dry-stone walls from 1100 B.C. She took in the wooden spikes of the cheviot-de-fries, a medieval anti-cavalry device. Beyond the remains of the fort, the cliff rose three hundred feet above the thrashing ocean. Tara's heart began to tap dance at the thought of being so high, and she prayed she wouldn't have to get close to the edge.

What exactly was her plan here? Just get Danny out in the open? Hope for a confession? The island had eighty percent cell service, but up here her phone had only a couple of bars.

She hurried over and entered the fort. She scanned the tourists, moving quickly among them, drawing closer to the edge. And there he was. Out at the very end. Danny, staring off at the ocean. At first Tara didn't see anyone else with him and her heart lifted with hope, but as she drew closer she saw blonde hair blowing in the wind. Standing slightly behind him, rolling up her sleeve, was Alanna Kelly.

Stephen at the tattoo shop had confirmed her suspicion—Alanna was the one with the rose tattoo. Heather had confirmed it was Alanna who had rented the retail space. Which meant it was Alanna who had stolen the items to bring down Johnny. All but one. The cast-iron pig. The one that really mattered.

But it didn't quite start with the pig being stolen. Alanna had set the deadly chain of events in motion by blackmailing Carrig. Hamlet had confided in her about the rumors that Carrig had been in appropriate with his male actors. Alanna would need money to take over the mill once it was hers. The blackmail plot was hatched. Paul had enlightened Tara about the line-item missing from the report on Ben Kelly— the fact that his daughter was no longer in cookery school. Alanna was the one who had deleted all mention of it from the report. Her father was controlling. He would have been enraged that she was no longer in school, and would have demanded to know what happened to her tuition. Once her father started digging he may have uncovered this entire plot.

Alanna was going to propose to Danny. The only real question left was—what was she going to do if he said no?

When he said no. Tara couldn't give them time to find out. She picked up her pace. "Hey," she called, trying to sound chipper, wondering how to disguise her voice so it didn't seem as if she were approaching a woman who had already murdered two men just for this moment. Neither Danny nor Alanna looked up; the wind was swallowing her words. Alanna took a step back. She got down on one knee. Danny looked in Tara's direction, most likely trying to make sense out of what was happening. He didn't see Tara. She began to run toward them.

Alanna wanted the salvage mill. And she wanted Danny. In order to have them both she needed Johnny Meehan gone. But Danny loved Johnny. Was that why she decided to spare his life and instead frame him for murder?

Perhaps all she had originally planned was running Johnny out of business, scooping up the mill, and working day-by-day with her imagined lover. Renting the retail shop that he'd mentioned he'd always wanted. Running it all with money from Carrig.

She had just assumed Johnny got the rose tattoo with the ring. It was Alanna.

Danny was staring at Alanna's arm. He took a step back. In the direction of the cliff. "Hey," Tara shouted again, louder this time. "Danny!"

He finally heard her, looked up, saw her. Alanna's hands were holding on to Danny's arm. Danny was off-balance, not expecting either the proposal or to see Tara headed for him.

"Let go of him," Tara shouted.

Alanna's head jerked her way, her eyes filled with tears. Danny had already said no. Alanna let go of Danny and charged Tara. She lunged for her, grabbing both Tara's hands and dragging her closer to the edge of the cliff. Danny jumped in front of them.

"Move back," Tara said. "She'll push us over."

"What are you doing?" Danny yelled. Tara didn't know which one of them he was talking to.

"She killed Emmet," Tara yelled. "And Carrig." A crowd was forming around them. "She wanted to frame Johnny for murder so she could have you and the mill."

"She's lying," Alanna said. "You're a liar."

Alanna lunged forward and shoved Tara. Tara stumbled, then fell. Her face hovered over the cliff. Time stopped. The jagged rocks, the height, the ocean ready to receive her. Maybe she should just let go. See Thomas again. Her mother.

"Stop," Danny yelled from above. Tara began to inch away from the cliff. She felt a shoe on the back of her neck. "Stop," Danny pleaded with Alanna. "What are you doing?"

"I didn't mean for anyone to die," Alanna said. "Emmet was crazed."

"Tell us what happened," Danny said. He knew he had to keep Alanna distracted. Keep her talking. If she was going to confess to anyone, it would be Danny.

"I'm sorry," she said.

"Tell me what happened," he repeated.

It was odd to lie on the ground with a foot pressed to her neck, listening to Alanna's pleas to Danny. But it was working. She had let up some of the pressure. Tara concentrated on staying calm. "Emmet put it together that I was stealing from Johnny."

"How did he put it together?" Danny pressed.

"I suspect he snooped in my room at the mill or he saw me bringing items into the retail shop. That was careless of me."

"Why didn't he just tell Johnny you were stealing from him?" Danny asked. "Or me?"

"He saw the cast-iron pig wasn't in the shop. I told him I was doing Johnny's bidding. That I didn't know what happened to his pig but I promised him I'd find out. He was so obsessed with getting it he was willing to wait. He didn't know who to trust. But then I couldn't find it fast enough! He wouldn't stop hounding me. I don't know what happened to his pig. But he wouldn't stop. He wouldn't stop, Danny."

Alanna was making herself sound like the victim. She didn't feel the same pity when Johnny was framed for Emmet's murder. Or when she wrote Tara's name on the wall in the blood of the man she'd murdered. Framing other people was a game to her. Alanna was still counting on Danny believing her sad stories.

"Carrig stole the pig," Tara said. It was difficult to speak, but Tara managed to get the words out. Alanna's foot twitched.

"What?" Alanna's voice wavered above her.

Danny picked up the thread. "Carrig thought it was Johnny blackmailing him."

"I didn't know any of that was going to happen," Alanna said. "How could I know?"

"How did you manage to collect the payments?" Danny asked Alanna. "Make Carrig think it was Johnny blackmailing him and not you?"

"I sent typed letters. The drop-off point was at the mill. I made sure Johnny was never in for the drop-offs. He paid in cash."

"Clever," Tara said. Alanna must have told Carrig she had his granite slab to keep him happy. That's why Carrig was so squirrely about the granite slab. He didn't want to admit to being caught up in Alanna's web of deceit.

"But why?" Danny's voice was laced with horror.

So she could be with you—run the mill and have the man of her dreams. "For you," was all Tara could say.

"Shut your gob," Alanna yelled. Her foot pressed harder into Tara's neck.

"Let her go," Danny said. He took a step forward.

"Stop, or I'll crush her neck," Alanna said.

Tara believed her. Danny must have too, for he

came to a halt. "Called . . . guards," Tara uttered. "It's over."

"Why don't you want to be with me?" Apparently, Alanna was still stuck in the past.

"Carrig?" Danny said. His mind was still on the murders. "You killed him too?"

"He had the pig. All this time. He's the one who turned me into a killer. Johnny was supposed to be accused of stealing the other items and arrested. That's it. Nobody had to die. But Carrig couldn't keep his nose out of it. Carrig thought he could turn it all around but all he did was turn Emmet into a raging lunatic. Over a pig! A stupid, cast-iron pig! I still don't even know where it is!"

You didn't give Carrig a chance to tell you, Tara thought. *You stabbed him in the back.* Carrig never spent the night at the inn. Alanna is the one who had stashed the murder weapon in room 301. But Tara entered soon after. She noticed blood on the key. She could attest that Alanna wouldn't allow Grace to let her stay in room 301. Because room 301 was a bloody mess. It's where Alanna had stashed the murder weapon, most likely showered and changed her clothes after the murder. Then returned to the scene of the crime to fetch the head of the pig. Murdered Carrig to frame him as the killer. The only witness who could have refuted her story. *Poor Carrig. Poor Emmet.* "You switched the prop knives with a real one," Tara said. She was getting more confident at speaking with the foot on her neck. If Alanna wanted to crush her, she was going to do it whether Tara talked or not.

"How did you know that?" Tara could hear the rage in Alanna's voice.

Truthfully, it was a shot in the dark. Even though

the chef's training wasn't her idea, she would still have a set of sharp knives. And framing Magda/Hamlet for the murder fit into Alanna's devious pattern. "You just confirmed my suspicion."

"Think you're so smart, do you?"

Or maybe she should have kept her mouth shut.

"Was Hamlet aware of what you were doing?" Danny cut in, sensing that Tara had just wound Alanna up again.

"I thought she didn't have a clue. But she must have betrayed me too. Helped Carrig steal the pig."

"We can talk about this later," Danny said. The shoe pressed harder. Tara kicked as hard as she could and wiggled, trying to move away from the edge. Danny grabbed Alanna around the waist and pulled her back. She clawed and kicked. Tara scrambled to her feet.

"It's over," Tara said. Alanna leaned down and bit Danny. He let go with a yell. Alanna rushed toward the edge and turned around. She glared at Tara.

"This is your fault. And your uncle's." She spit on the ground, pure fury stamped on her face. "I'm going to jump," she screamed. "But not alone."

She grabbed Tara's arm and pulled. Tara stumbled and tried to pull back, but Alanna succeeded in yanking Tara too close to the edge for comfort. *Don't look down. Whatever you do, don't look down.* "Thomas," she whispered.

"Alanna, don't do this," Danny said. He lunged and grabbed Tara's other arm. The crowd moved in closer.

"Stay back!" Alanna's voice carried through the wind. "Or the three of us go over together." The crowd stopped. Cameras around her clicked.

"I was so close," she said. "I can't go to prison."

"Nobody is going to prison," Danny said. "Whatever this is, we'll work it out."

A tug of war began, with Tara in the middle.

"I'm sorry," Alanna said. "I would take it all back if I could. I love you, Danny. I did it for you!"

"Stop talking," Danny said. "We'll go get a cup of tea, sit down, take a few breaths."

"I just wanted to run Johnny out of business! I didn't mean for any of this to happen. Danny, you have to believe me."

"Where is the original pig now?" Danny asked. Tara knew he didn't really care, he was grasping at anything to keep Alanna's focus.

Hamlet . . .

"The light," Tara said.

"What?" Poor Danny, he alone was in the dark.

"I think Carrig hid the pig in the theatre light," Tara said. "First he wanted to get it out of the way. But when he learned a replica pig was the murder weapon, he knew the original was now precious evidence. That's why he was so desperate to get the light back."

"He didn't suffer," Alanna said. "He never even knew it was coming." She glanced behind her, taking in the same dramatic view of the drop, the ocean below.

Danny stepped closer to Tara and the three inched that much closer to the edge. This time Tara did look. The jagged rocks, the steep drop, the ocean thrashing below.

"Be careful," Tara whispered.

Alanna eyed Danny's hand. A pair of security

guards were making their way toward them, keeping the crowd behind them.

Alanna took another step toward the edge. One more and they would plummet three hundred feet.

The guards stopped.

"You've always had to fight for your place," Tara said. She wasn't going to tell her that it was all going to be okay, or that she wouldn't spend the rest of her life in jail. "You have to face this," she said instead. "You have to face it."

"What do you know?" Alanna said.

"I know how it feels to lose the most important thing in your life."

"What?" Alanna shouted. "What have you ever lost?"

"My son," Tara said. "My three-year-old son. His name was Thomas."

Alanna faltered. Tara caught Danny's eye, and together they stepped away from the cliff. One step, two steps. At three, they flanked Alanna and took her to the ground.

Chapter 32

Sergeant Gable met the Aran Island guards at the ferry. Danny and Tara remained behind to fill George in on what had happened. They stood in his kitchen near the theatre light.

O'Malley crossed his arms. "I don't want to break it just to see if there's a pig inside."

"The pig could fetch up a ton of money at auction," Danny said.

Now that the pig was part of a murder mystery, it's worth had probably skyrocketed. Human beings never failed to perplex Tara.

George grabbed a broom and wheeled over to the light, as if he was going to knock it down.

"You could end up breaking both," Danny said. He approached the light. "If you have some tools I can take it apart properly. Would you like that now?"

"Ah, sure, look it." George wheeled over to the cupboard beneath his sink and came out with a toolbox. Danny used the tools to open the light, stick his hand in, and remove the item. It was a cast-iron pig, once owned by a princess.

On the ferry ride back, Tara filled Danny in on how she put the pieces of the puzzle together. "Once I stood back and looked at the timeline and my vision boards, I could see the common denominator was Alanna. The place used to be a mess—a junk heap. You even mentioned how Johnny's dishes were piled in the sink."

"And?"

"Alanna was cleaning the counters at the inn when I first met her. Her cooking instructor remarked how organized and clean she always was, and everyone said the mill used to be a junk heap."

"Alanna organized it."

"Yes. Alanna cleans compulsively. It sounds ludicrous she would do the dishes after a murder but that's the power of a compulsion."

Danny stared out at the churning water. "What did Alanna have over Carrig?"

"Apparently he had a reputation of being handsy with male actors. None of them would work with him. Alanna threatened to expose this to reviewers and ruin his all-female production of *Hamlet*."

"I can't believe you pieced all this together." Danny sounded impressed.

"There were other clues."

"Go on."

"Alanna was the one with access to the stationery— she wrote a nasty note to Rose, pretending it was from

Grace. She typed the letter that was left on the mill door, luring Emmet to Johnny's cottage. I bet the guards will find a typewriter in Alanna's apartment."

Danny nodded. "We often had antique typewriters in stock."

"Johnny must have had an appointment that morning and Alanna knew he wouldn't be around. Or maybe he was in his office at the mill and never knew that Emmet was reading a note sending him to the cottage. It was Alanna who got a tattoo of a rose and an engagement ring—"

Danny flushed scarlet. "I thought it was just a harmless crush." He bowed his head. "I kissed her once. I had no idea she would become obsessed."

Tara thought as much. She put her hand on his arm. "It's not your fault. Alanna isn't well. If not you, she would have obsessed over someone else. This is not on you."

"You saw it right away. You mentioned it so many times. I just thought you were jealous."

"My name on the wall was the one clue that couldn't have been done by anyone else."

"I don't understand."

"Emmet used his last moments to try and write the name of his killer on the wall." She removed a brochure from the Aran Islands and a pen from her purse. She started to write: *Alan*.

"Alan?"

"He didn't have time to finish." Tara began to scribble over it, replicating the look of Tara on the wall.

Danny gave a low whistle. "She turned *Alan* into *Tara*."

Tara nodded. "That's why the letters are so weird. Capital T—a giant one—then a capital A to change the L, and on down the line."

"My God." He stopped. "She was trying to frame you next."

"I do believe that's where she was headed. And I'm sure folks around here would have preferred it was the awful American."

Danny stepped closer. "Not all of us," he said. And then he kissed her.

The next ten days passed in a blur of reunions and police interviews. When Grace Quinn summoned Tara for a cup of tea, she accepted. Now that justice had been delivered, Tara decided to forgive the imperfections of those around her, including Grace and her uncle. She had even opened the letter from her mother, the announcement of the birth of her grandchild, Thomas Meehan. Tara could now look at the picture without breaking down. He had been here. It was only a short time, but Thomas Meehan had been here, on this earth. And he would live in Tara's heart—and now in the tattoo on her back— the rest of her days.

Grace rocked, and knitted, and seemed eager to talk. "Johnny was a shy boy. Your mother always protected him."

"Protected him from what?"

"From whom. Your grandfather. He wasn't the nicest man when he drank. And he drank a lot."

"Is that why my mother left?"

Grace kept knitting, and rocking. "Your grandfather is buried behind the cottage, did you know that?"

"No. I didn't know that." *There's no headstone, no marker.*

"They said it was an accident."

"They?"

"Johnny and your mother. They said Thomas was cleaning his gun and it went off."

"Maybe it did."

"I guess we'll never know. After that your mother left for the States and Johnny took over the business."

She was also pregnant when she left. Tara was pretty sure Grace knew that too. Her mother hadn't looked back because there were too many secrets, too much pain. Instead of working through it, Johnny and her mother just stopped talking altogether. It hadn't been out of anger. It had been out of sadness. Shame. Sibling dynamics were complicated even without factoring in past trauma. Perhaps they each secretly blamed themselves for their past and harbored resentments at the same time. Maybe, over time, Johnny could shed more light on it. They had time. Precious, precious time. Tara stood. "I'd better get to the retail shop. We're having an official opening today."

"When will you be going home?"

Tara stopped at the parlor doors, turned, and smiled. "I am home," she said.

Johnny Meehan popped the cork on the champagne and poured glasses for the four of them. They stood in the garden of the retail shop, Johnny and Rose, Danny and Tara, and toasted. Between the current inventory and Emmet's widow selling them back everything her husband had purchased, they were well stocked for both the mill and the shop.

"*Sláinte.*"

"*Sláinte*," they all repeated as they clinked glasses and drank.

Tara handed out the long-stem roses. They would set off for the bay and say a proper goodbye to her mam.

The sun was rising as they made their way toward the water, causing droplets to dance on top of the Galway Bay like diamonds. A boat horn sounded in the distance. Danny took her hand. A sense of belonging wound around her like a protective shawl. Somewhere along the way, Hound had slipped in behind them, and joined the procession. "I feel love all around," Rose said. Tara smiled; so could she. She could feel her mother walking beside her, hand in hand with her grandson, all proceeding to the edge of the bay, the ever-changing, wild, unpredictable, Galway Bay.